BAGGAGE CHECK

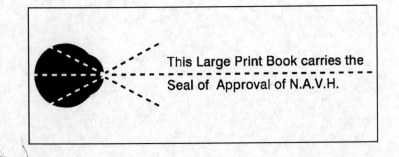

This Large Print Book carries the
Seal of Approval of N.A.V.H.

BAGGAGE CHECK

M. J. PULLEN

THORNDIKE PRESS
A part of Gale, Cengage Learning

GALE
CENGAGE Learning·

Farmington Hills, Mich • San Francisco • New York • Waterville, Maine
Meriden, Conn • Mason, Ohio • Chicago

GALE
CENGAGE Learning·

Copyright © 2016 by Amanda Pullen Turetsky.
Thorndike Press, a part of Gale, Cengage Learning.

Thorndike Press® Large Print Women's Fiction.
The text of this Large Print edition is unabridged.
Other aspects of the book may vary from the original edition.
Set in 16 pt. Plantin.

LIBRARY OF CONGRESS CATALOGING-IN-PUBLICATION DATA

Names: Pullen, M. J. (Manda J.), author.
Title: Baggage check / by M. J. Pullen.
Description: Large print edition. | Waterville, Maine : Thorndike Press, 2016. | Series: Thorndike Press large print women's fiction
Identifiers: LCCN 2016024684 | ISBN 9781410493750 (hardcover) | ISBN 141049375X (hardcover)
Subjects: LCSH: Single women—Fiction. | Middle-aged women—Fiction. | Large type books. | GSAFD: Love stories.
Classification: LCC PS3616.U465 B34 2016b | DDC 813/.6—dc23
LC record available at https://lccn.loc.gov/2016024684

Published in 2016 by arrangement with St. Martin's Press, LLC

Printed in Mexico
1 2 3 4 5 6 7 20 19 18 17 16

For my boys — my heroes always

Love must be learned, and learned again;
there is no end to it.

— *Katherine Anne Porter*

1

June 17, 2016

Rebecca Williamson picked up a smooth, rust-colored clay bowl for the fifth time in as many minutes. She ran her hand along the sloping curve from the base to the rim, and then bounced it lightly in her arms for heft. It was two pounds, she decided. Maybe two and a half once they wrapped it for the plane. She put it down again and stepped back to look at the rest of the artist's display, dusting her hands together.

"Oh, just buy it already!" Valerie said from a few feet away. "I've gotten married after shorter courtships than you're having with that bowl."

"I don't need it," Rebecca said.

"It would look nice on your kitchen table. You never buy anything, Becky." Valerie had been calling her "Becky" since she joined the airline three years before. For the first several months, Rebecca had corrected her.

Now she just accepted it.

"What would I do with it?" Rebecca said. "I mean, you can't serve food in it, not that I ever cook anyway. I don't have anything to store in it. And I'm never home to look at how my apartment is decorated. How is a red clay bowl necessary?"

Valerie rolled her eyes and patted Rebecca's shoulder with a veined hand. "Life needs beauty, doll. Every girl should have something beautiful and useless in her life. Like my first husband, for example. That man was pure eye candy; the poor idiot couldn't change a lightbulb."

Rebecca laughed. She had never asked outright how many husbands Valerie had been through, but her current guess was four, and at least two of them had been pilots. Valerie was in her late sixties, ancient by flight attendant standards, and a legend among all the younger women they worked with. Rebecca had been paired with her during the first week of training and they had flown together more often than not since then. At first, Rebecca had resisted becoming Valerie's protégé, but through sheer force of will and nonstop chatter, Valerie had become Rebecca's only real friend at work. Tonight, they were in an artists' co-op in New Mexico, killing time during an overnight layover.

"Are you ready to go to the bar?" Rebecca asked her.

"What's your hurry?" Valerie said. "You never take anything home from there, either."

"Don't start with that."

"What? Come on, you know I'm right. And don't use me for an excuse, either. I may be an old lady but I know how to make myself scarce when I see a brassiere on the doorknob."

An aproned woman behind the counter looked up, smirking.

"Shh . . . ," Rebecca hushed. But even she could not help but smile at the way Valerie said "brassiere on the doorknob" in her New York accent. Rebecca herself had never used this signal, but it had been a frequent sight in her sorority house at the University of Georgia. She tried to imagine finding one of Valerie's big beige contraptions hanging on their hotel room door.

"Ready to go?" she asked again.

"Oh, all right," Valerie said. "Just let me add this to my collection." She held up a blue-glazed mug that had been formed to look like the squished-down face of an old man.

Several of Rebecca's coworkers kept little

collections from places they visited — postcards, spoons, shot glasses, snow globes, you name it. There was a sort of unspoken code that it was only acceptable to collect items from cities you had truly visited, meaning you had to leave the airport for more than a couple of hours. Even so, Rebecca could not understand this tradition. Yes, it was cute in the moment, but they went so many places. What did you *do* with all that crap? Put it in a box so you could relive your glory days of passing out peanuts? Have it gather dust on the shelves while other people pretended to be interested at parties?

Once or twice, something had caught Rebecca's eye, particularly when they flew to exotic locations. A tiny but exquisite crystal vase from Waterford in Ireland. Hand-carved candlesticks painted black and inlaid with gold in Toledo, Spain. A set of Russian dolls in Moscow. Each time, she had stood paralyzed in the gift shop, debating why she needed this thing and where she would put it and how often she would really look at it. Then she would sigh, and, to the dismay of each patient shop owner, return the item to the shelf, and walk out. Except for an irresistible silk scarf from Milan and an emergency T-shirt she'd been forced to buy in New York, Rebecca had not bought souvenirs anywhere. Once in a while she regretted this, but never for long. She would deposit the amount of the foregone purchase into her savings account with satisfaction and move on. Always move on.

A short cab ride later, they found the rest of the flight crew exactly where they expected: gathered in the small bar off the hotel lobby, all in their civilian clothing. The two pilots, both middle-aged family men, sat nursing beers at the bar, watching the broadcast of a local rodeo on the TV overhead and chatting with the bartender. Shanna and Lizzie, the other two attendants, were playing darts in a corner with some guys still wearing name tags from a convention. They waved when Valerie and Rebecca walked in. A couple of the conventioneers smiled hopefully at Rebecca.

"I think I'm just going to go up to bed," she said.

"What?" Valerie said. "No. If I can stay for a pint of beer and some darts, so can you. Maybe we can even hustle them for a few bucks."

"I'm terrible at darts," Rebecca complained.

"Perfect," said Valerie, hoisting up the support hose she still wore from the flight, beneath her elastic-waist jeans and bright-white tennis shoes. "That will make it more believable. Then I swoop in and kick their asses."

It was hard not to smile at Valerie, and even harder to argue with her. Rebecca followed her to the booth by the dartboard. She pulled a packet of wipes from her purse and wiped the table and vinyl seat before sliding in. She managed a tired smile as the perplexed-looking convention guys introduced themselves. *I should try to learn their names,* she thought. But even that was more effort than she wanted to invest tonight.

Two hours later, Shanna and Lizzie had allowed themselves to be led away by a pair of the more attractive conventioneers, and Valerie grinned as she collected more than fifty dollars from three sheepish others, tucking it victoriously in her "brassiere." Rebecca leaned her head back against the wall of the booth and stirred a watery rum and Coke, wondering at exactly what point it would be okay to insist that Val come up to the room with her so they could sleep for a few hours before tomorrow's flight to San Francisco.

One of the dart players sat down next to her. He had dark skin, neatly trimmed black hair, and wore a light-blue Oxford shirt

14

open at the collar. Rebecca was not good at identifying ethnicity: Indian, maybe? Or Hispanic? His speech was smooth and without accent. "So, you're leaving tomorrow, too?"

"Yes."

"That's too bad. I would have liked to have seen more of you," he purred. He placed a hand on her arm.

Rebecca sighed. She was too tired to be flattered. "Um, that would be a 'no thank you.' "

His grin slowly faded. "Hey, I was just trying to be nice, sweetheart."

"I'm not your sweetheart, sweetheart."

Something flashed across his eyes and he slid out of the booth. "Okay, then, goodnight."

"Goodnight," she said, with a flick of the wrist and her best airline smile.

He muttered something to his companions and they looked at her appraisingly. Then one of them shrugged, and they nodded at Valerie as they made their way back to the bar.

"What the hell was that?" Valerie asked, sliding in across from her. "He was a nice-looking kid. You don't like foreign guys?"

"That's not it," Rebecca said.

"Well, I had that one primed for you. Such

a waste."

"Thanks, Val, but I don't need you to find guys for me. And I'm sure he won't go to waste. Look, he's talking to that girl at the bar already."

"I didn't mean him," Val said. "I meant you. You're such a beautiful girl: educated, nice nose, and that pretty brown hair is your real color as far as I can tell. We've flown together three years and I never hear about you dating anyone."

"Well, maybe I —"

Valerie leaned across the table with a loud whisper. "Are you a lesbian?"

"What? No!"

"Because I'm okay with it, really. I'm very hip about this stuff. I even have a lesbian niece. Very attractive, if she would just let her hair grow out. Of course, she's younger than you, but —"

"Valerie!" Rebecca said too loudly. Then softer, "I am not a lesbian. I used to date men all the time. I just haven't lately."

"Why not?"

"I don't know. The hours?"

"Bullshit."

"Come on, Val. Why the sudden interest in my love life? Can we talk about something else?"

"No."

Rebecca knew from experience Valerie had no intention of letting up. She took a sip of her drink, which was not terribly helpful since it was mostly melted ice. A long sigh under Valerie's unwavering stare. "I guess you could say I got my heart broken a few years ago, and I just haven't gotten over it yet."

"Really? Who was this? How come I haven't heard about him?"

Rebecca sighed. *In for a penny . . .* "You have heard of him. It was my friend Jake."

"Jake?" Valerie furrowed her brow. "You mean . . . your friend, the girl with the blog, what's her name — Marci? *That* Jake?"

"Yes. That Jake."

Valerie whistled. "So how long ago was this?"

"How long ago was what? They got married four years ago. And they have Bonnie now."

"Yeah, but when did you stop . . ." Valerie trailed off.

Rebecca shook her head. "I don't think I have stopped. I know that's ridiculous, but I — I loved him for so long. It's like I don't know any other way to be."

Val looked down at the table for a minute, and slid the rest of her neat Scotch across to Rebecca. "Here, kid. I think you need this a hell of a lot more than I do."

2

The next night, another layover — this one in San Francisco after a full day going up and down the West Coast. By the time their shift ended, and they were once more on a shuttle to an airport hotel, Rebecca was exhausted. There were times when she enjoyed the many locations to which her job carried her, and times when the city didn't matter at all. This could be San Francisco or Boise; tonight she didn't care. Maybe because tomorrow she would finish up on the South Carolina coast, where a beach weekend with her girlfriends awaited her.

Here in San Francisco, however, it was still light out, and the rest of the flight attendants were intent on going out again. There was some "bead shop" they had been talking about all day, and Rebecca had gathered that "bead shop" was a euphemism. Apparently what the shop mainly sold was adult novelties and drug paraphernalia.

"Coming to the Purple Feather with us, Rebecca?" asked Shanna. She had been smug all day because her overnight experience with the guy from the convention had proved far more satisfactory than Lizzie's. Rebecca did not know or need the details.

"I don't think so, thanks."

"Oh, come on . . . you of all people should take advantage while we're here. It's a classy place. Very clean."

Rebecca wrinkled her nose. "I'm sure it is." No matter how many women or solicitous boyfriends tried to convince her to go to sex toy shops, Rebecca found the idea repulsive. She could only imagine low lighting and oily surfaces, with nasty booths along the wall for men to watch porn behind curtains.

"Well, I think you ought to go, doll," Valerie said.

"Are you coming, Val?" Shanna asked. "Because that would be awesome!"

"Sure, why not?" Valerie said. "I don't get embarrassed."

Rebecca had to admit, she did feel more like a fuddy-duddy now that she was the only one not going. But she'd already said no, and she was tired. "I'll go next time, okay?" she said.

"I'm going to get the Tickler 2000 this time," Shanna said. "I got the petite version last time, but it's sort of lost its appeal."

"Oh, I don't like those big bulky things," Lizzie said. "I'm getting the little portable one that goes in your panties. You know, with the remote control?"

"Who are you going to give the remote to?" Shanna asked.

"Just me," Lizzie said. "It's tiny. You can hold it in your hand, and get a little, er, *pick me up* in the middle of the day and no one would be the wiser."

"Next time you seem a little too happy to be at work, we'll all know why," Rebecca said.

"Yeah, that could make turbulence a lot more enjoyable," Shanna said.

Valerie smiled and shook her head. "You girls have no idea how lucky you are. It's so nice people *talk* about these things now. When I was young, sex was so taboo. People just didn't talk about it, except for all the free-love people. You know, I think one of those vibrator machines might have saved my first marriage."

"I thought your first husband couldn't change a lightbulb?" Rebecca asked.

"That's right. But maybe I could have

looked past that if he knew where to find my cookies!" She said this loudly enough that some businessmen turned to look, and they all four dissolved in laughter.

At the hotel, Rebecca wasted no time showering and getting into her pajamas, hoping to avoid more invitations to the Purple Feather. She had to leave earlier than everyone else — she was splitting off from the group to work the flight to Cincinnati tomorrow, while they were heading for New York. She had traded routes with another girl so she could end up working the evening flight from Atlanta to Charleston. It meant having to do gate duties in South Carolina after the flight instead of getting to go straight to the beach house, but she got paid for the trip and didn't have to do standby. A good trade.

Rebecca watched, bemused, as Valerie put back on her grandma jeans — over the stockings, naturally — white tennis shoes, and a shade too much red lipstick. She resprayed her large helmet of sandy-gray hair, buttoned her white blouse, and was out the door. Rebecca smiled to think of the reception Valerie would get at the sex shop, and whether Shanna and Lizzie would stay with her or leave her to her own devices. *Is this even Valerie's first time going?* She certainly never seemed shy about new experiences when Rebecca was around. *How did I end up with these people for friends?*

When the door had clicked closed behind Val, Rebecca called her friend Suzanne to confirm the plans for the weekend and to make sure someone could come pick her up at the airport in Charleston tomorrow night.

"Yes, darling, someone will pick you up. The four of us are all driving out in the morning. Are you *completely* sure you can't join us?"

"Completely. I'm in San Francisco and they need me tomorrow." She saw no need to mention that she had chosen to fly in with work, rather than endure a five-hour car ride with four women, all of whom were rather disgustingly happy.

"All right, sweetie. It's going to be super-casual, okay? Just girls hanging out at the beach."

"You got it."

"For heaven's sake, don't let them put some kind of hideous fake veil on me."

"I won't."

"I'm counting on you. I know you hate that tacky stuff as much as I do."

Rebecca smiled. At one point in her life, she would have given her right arm for Suzanne to include her in this sisterly confidence, to see them as being the same. Rebecca had since given up, at least partially, on this idea. You couldn't replicate Suzanne. She simply had a charmed life. "Don't worry, Suze. I've got your back."

Next, Rebecca called to check in with Kendall Brighton-Higsby at the Junior League, to review the minutes from last week's gala committee meeting. After years of trying to break out of provisional status and move past duty at the league's thrift store, Rebecca was finally on the committee to plan the Christmas Gala. It was the year's biggest fund-raiser and supported about twenty children's charities. Rebecca suspected Suzanne had pulled some strings to get her on the committee, and it was a bit of a challenge with her flight schedule, but she was too happy to care.

With her calls made, Rebecca pressed her uniform and left it hanging in the bathroom so she could dress and leave in the morning without waking Valerie. She packed and repacked everything else three times: spare uniform, bathing suit, towel, flat sandals, and a sundress that would work for the beach and dinners out over the long weekend. Two tank tops, one pair of wrinkle-resistant white shorts, one pair of jeans, makeup kit, cotton robe, and underwear.

Everything perfectly organized, and four pounds under the carry-on weight limit in case she brought something home from the beach.

She left her suitcase half-zipped on the little closet trestle so she could put in her pajamas and toiletries without needing the light. Settled on the bed, she flipped through the channels on the hotel TV twice, and then snapped it off. Her phone was resting on the nightstand, on top of a dog-eared book she'd picked up in an airport bookstore: *Calm Your Mind, Live Your Life.* She knew she should read some affirmations and get a good night's sleep, but she picked up her phone instead.

Rebecca had just signed up for Instagram a few weeks earlier, and already she was coming to the conclusion that it was just another way for the universe to remind her that life was passing her by. Just like Facebook, the feed was full of babies, kids, and wedding photos. Artisan cupcakes for a two-year-old's birthday party. Pregnancy photos. Happy glowing girls, mostly sorority sisters from her class and younger, turned sideways with a hand draped across each of their bellies (a variation on this included the hands of an equally ecstatic partner). Some grinned at the camera, others contemplated

25

the miracle of life in subdued, artsy black-and-white. All positively swelled with happiness and potential.

These torture sessions were something of a necessary evil. Because of her travel schedule, she sometimes needed social media to keep up with even her closer friends — like the girls going to the beach this weekend. Beth was a Facebook junkie — posting everything from her deepest religious beliefs to what she ate for breakfast. Beth and Rebecca had never been particularly close — they had only hung out regularly during their senior year of high school — but since the advent of Facebook, Rebecca knew more about her than ever. Marci posted on both platforms: frequent pictures of Bonnie, shots from nice dinners out with Jake (*delightful*), and a blog about her happy life. It was called "The Care and Feeding of a Suburban Husband," and was so popular Marci had been offered a book deal based on it.

Suzanne was less active on Facebook these days. She favored the simplicity of Instagram, and having a superfamous fiancé like Dylan Burke meant taking more care with her privacy (and his). But she had not given up her own personal spotlight yet, and she was constantly being tagged in photos from charity events she planned or attended, especially those related to her foundation for the children of slain law-enforcement officers.

Rebecca was also Facebook friends with Dylan's little sister, Kate, who seemed almost as shy in the virtual world as she was in the real world. Her older sisters were pseudo-Kardashians, and their ridiculous behavior had earned them not only constant coverage in the tabloids, but the dubious honor that they would soon be filming their own reality show. Soft-spoken little Kate seemed to be doing her best to keep herself and her baby boy as far from that limelight as possible.

Tonight, Rebecca scrolled through the streams of pictures quickly, too tired to take a strong interest in anything. Baby, kid, baby, cat, kid, anniversary, shoe ad, political rant, sonogram, and finally, a picture of someone's steak dinner and glass of wine. *Really?* she thought. *Can we do nothing alone?*

In a heartbeat, a quiet voice answered her own question. *You should know. You do almost everything alone.* She turned on the small lamp over Valerie's bed and the light in the bathroom, and then put on her satin eyeshade and earplugs.

Her head had scarcely hit the pillow when the alarm went off at three thirty and it was time for her to go. Valerie's snores were still loud and regular as she let herself into the hallway, pulling her reliable wheeled case.

BY MARCI THOMPSON STILLWELL

BLOG: THE CARE AND FEEDING OF A SUBURBAN HUSBAND
{Entry #174: Dirty Diapers and Fairy-Tale Endings}

Thursday, June 16, 2016
Morning, everyone! Just a reminder that the blog will be on hiatus for a few days while I'm on vacation with my girlfriends. I am adding several other great blogs to the list at the left to keep you occupied while I'm gone. Just promise you'll come back, okay?

So. Last time we got a little history lesson about how my sweet Suburban Husband (or SubHub, as longtime readers know him) and I met, became friends, and ended up together . . . eventually. (You can read the whole story *here*.) Like the stories of Brothers Grimm, our fairy tale

---

was not always smooth sailing. There were problems and dark forests and even a couple of characters who wanted our story to end differently.

SubHub was certainly my knight in shining armor, but there was a dark knight on the scene, too. And another princess, who obviously was not SubHub's true love, but wanted to be rescued from her own tower all the same. After many battles, things worked out, in the end, and we got our happily ever after. Was that because Sub-Hub rescued me? Not exactly. I think what he did was give me a chance to rescue myself.

No one ever explains that part when you're a little girl watching princess movies or listening to fairy tales. We hear about the damsel in distress and the handsome prince. So we spend our lives assuming we're her, and looking for him. But what no one says is that your knight in shining armor might look a lot like an old friend who forgets to take the trash out.

They don't mention, either, that before your knight can rescue you, you must first be able to rescue yourself. And that the process doesn't end at the happy ending, or even "I do." It's an ongoing thing: you will both be in distress sometimes, sometimes at the same time, and you must find a way to rescue one another. Every day. Once you have kids, if you have kids, the definition of "happy ending" becomes far more loose. Sometimes it's just being the one to get up in the middle of the night to change a dirty diaper. Or, for true gallantry, to clean a sudden projectile poop out of the crib (and off the walls and rug, too). Sometimes it's coming home from work early so your princess can take a shower, or not rolling your eyes when the prince wants a Saturday for golf.

I will admit I'm still working on that last one. But SubHub and I have managed, so far.

I do wonder, sometimes, how the other characters in the fairy tale are doing. In the storybooks, they never talk about what happens to the trolls, the wolves, or the wicked kings after they are "never seen again." But in real life, the villains don't fall off the face of the earth, and it's not always so clear who the wicked ones really are.

The other princess, for example, is a friend of mine, and I have to admit that even though I was angry when she tried to lure my Prince Charming to her side, I'd still like to see her with her own happily ever after. And what about the dark knight? Did he learn anything from our little adventure? I may never know.

So for us, the happy ending means Cheerios, projectile poop, and compromising on personal hygiene. Each day feels like we are trying to save one another again. For others, the end of one story is just the beginning of their own adventure. So maybe the term "happy ending" is the problem. Because there are no endings. Just moments. And you have to savor every one.

3

The things most people hated about being a flight attendant were all the things Rebecca loved most. The crisp, standardized uniforms were feminine and professional — and though she had originally turned up her nose at the polyester blend, she had come to appreciate its versatility. The personal body weight requirements (framed as suggestions but expected by the airlines nonetheless) gave her a sense of self-discipline and control each time she stepped on the scale, as did pulling her hair back into a tight, neat bun each morning.

Airplane galleys were a Mecca of orderliness — there was a place for everything and absolutely no room for clutter. Most people would never appreciate how every inch of space was utilized to the fullest, and the airplane always left the runway with everything necessary for a comfortable flight and not a single thing more. And while the pay was low and the schedule was what most people would consider incomprehensible, Rebecca found that rising at 3 A.M. and returning home days later made her tiny apartment feel less lonely somehow. It gave an explanation for her solitude.

As she boarded the DC-9-50 from Atlanta to Charleston, however, she felt a little less in control than usual. It had been a fairly smooth day: no major delays or angry passengers, and only three short flights before this one. A bit of turbulence on the last leg, but nothing that would provoke her anxiety these days. She did a mental inventory, and everything seemed right: bag, schedule, outfit. All that was left was to finish the last flight and enjoy her time at the beach. She twisted the ring on her right hand, three times clockwise, three times counterclockwise.

Suzanne, Marci, Beth, and Kate would all be at Kiawah Island already — drinking, probably. They would select whoever was willing to be the designated driver to pick her up at the airport. Probably Beth or Kate, she guessed.

She helped shove carry-on bags into bins, fetched a couple of blankets, and went through the flight checks automatically. It was Thursday evening, and the flight seemed split between business travelers returning bleary-eyed from Atlanta and vacationers heading to the coast for a long weekend. Everyone seemed calm and reasonably content, which made Rebecca's job easier and the already short flight go by faster. Takeoff, pause, cruising, beverages, questions, blankets, more ice, questions, seat belts on for the descent. The captain predicted a warm, clear weekend for those staying in the Charleston, South Carolina area — perfect for catching up with old friends.

It turned out to be Marci waiting in her behemoth SUV when Rebecca had finished all her duties and wheeled her suitcase out into the humid air of the South Carolina coast. Rebecca's heart sank a little at this. She and Marci had been part of the same circle of friends for more than fifteen years, ever since Rebecca had escaped to Georgia her senior year in high school, but they could never seem to get comfortable being alone together. Rebecca supposed the fact that she was in love with Marci's husband didn't help.

"Hi!" Rebecca called too loudly, too cheerily.

"Hey," said Marci, as Rebecca put her suitcase on the floorboard in the back. She tried to ignore the distinct crunch of Cheerios or Goldfish or some other kids' snack as she rolled it in. *It will wipe clean.* She slid into the passenger's seat, pushing away the visions of crumbs wedged into the black fabric of her bag.

"So you drew the short straw, eh?" Rebecca said.

"Of course not," Marci said, sounding tired. "I was happy to come pick you up."

"I really appreciate it."

"No problem. I'm just sorry you weren't able to drive out with us. We missed you," Marci lied.

"Oh, I wish I could have, too," Rebecca returned. Also a lie. A five-hour drive trapped in this car with everyone? *No, thank you.* "I just couldn't get the extra time off."

"Oh, no, of course. We all understood. Suzanne understands."

"How is she doing? Getting excited?"

Now Marci smiled for real. "You know Suzanne, she hates weddings. It's been kind of funny watching her try to weasel out of her own."

"She's still fighting it?"

"Yes. Dylan says the best way to get rid of the tabloids and the press is just to face them head-on. He says if you just give them what they want on your own terms, they'll go away. But she's, well . . . obviously she doesn't have the best relationship with the press."

They both smiled. Last year, Suzanne had been plastered all over several major national publications, nearly naked in front of the High Museum and jeopardizing her career and reputation. It hadn't been her fault, exactly, but the papers had been far less interested in printing the explanation afterward than in the explosive pictures. Now that Suzanne was marrying the man who was arguably the most famous person in country music, the press had become even more of a challenge.

The car got quiet; the darkness outside made it hard to focus on anything but the awkward silence. "So how far is it to the house?" Rebecca asked. She'd never been to Kiawah Island.

"About forty minutes, I guess," Marci said. They both sighed.

"How's Bonnie?"

"Great, she's really great. Getting so big — she's almost nine months old now."

"Wow," Rebecca said, realizing she had no idea what questions to ask. Nine months was too early to walk and talk, right? "So she's . . . crawling?"

"Uh, yeah, she's been crawling for a few

months now," Marci said.

Rebecca tried to ignore the "any idiot would know that" tone in Marci's voice. "It must be hard keeping up with her then."

"Yes," Marci said. "She's everywhere. Jake and I are constantly chasing her around the house."

Rebecca nodded. She knew there was something appropriate to say in response but had not the faintest idea what it was.

"Jake is really great with her, of course," Marci said. She was looking intently at the road in front of them. "He's a wonderful daddy."

"I'm sure," Rebecca said, proud that the crack in her throat did not make it to her voice. Outside, the city lights of Charleston receded and the mercury-yellow pattern of streetlights blurred along beside the car.

It was nearly eleven by the time they made it to the luxurious rental house on exclusive Kiawah Island. This weekend was technically supposed to be a bachelorette party for Suzanne, but Rebecca was happy to see that the four-bedroom house was not bedecked in pink streamers and plastic penises. The only sign of the party atmosphere was a blender half-full of margaritas on the kitchen counter and a single discarded pink feather boa draped across the back of a chair. Otherwise, the house was tastefully appointed with soft-green walls and sedate rattan furniture, and a few subtle pieces of decor on the built-in bookshelves. Only a tiny driftwood sculpture showed any sign of being from the sea: no whimsical beach signs or framed starfish. *Only Suzanne could find a beach house that didn't look beachy,* Rebecca thought.

They found Suzanne, Beth, and Kate on the back porch, talking by the light of a few citronella candles and a waning moon over the Atlantic. Rebecca inhaled deeply of the thick sea air as she exited the screen door, hearing the ocean's soft roar in the background, and feeling instantly calmer than she had in weeks. She made her way to an empty chair and sank into it, returning the smiles and blown kisses from the other girls, who all seemed a few margaritas in the bag.

"I don't understand, Suze. I just don't," Beth was saying, waving a plastic cup emphatically in the air. "I'm sorry but it makes no sense."

"What about it doesn't make sense?" Suzanne's Southern drawl countered a little slurrily. "It's simple, really. I just don't want a big wedding."

"But you're an event planner," Beth said.

"Who hates planning weddings!" Suzanne

said. "Present company excluded, of course, girls," she added and raised her cup in the direction of first Kate and then Marci. "Your weddings were a delight to coordinate, obviously."

"Obviously," Marci and Kate answered simultaneously, giving one another a little grin as Marci pulled up a chair. The two of them seemed to have become fast friends since Suzanne had introduced them. They both had babies the same age, which Rebecca supposed brought them together.

"Anyway," Suzanne went on, "I hate planning weddings for other people, and I sure as hell never wanted to plan my own, especially not under these circumstances."

"I have an idea," Marci said, leaning forward with mock inspiration. "Why don't you let your amazingly rich, famous, and adoring husband-to-be get a wedding planner for you, as he has offered to do about ten thousand times in the last two months?"

"Because no one else would do it right," Suzanne said bitterly. Even though it was too dark to be sure, Rebecca thought there was a collective eye roll around the table.

"Look," Suzanne said, standing and wobbling just slightly as she swept her cup around the table before finishing it. "It's not just the planning. I mean, yes, it's a pain in the ass and all the extra security and stuff makes it even harder. But the main thing is, I just hate that it all feels like a show for someone else. For the world. Every decision I make, from my dress to the flowers, I have to think about how it's going to hold up under scrutiny on E! News or Giuliana Rancic, or whether there's a Kardashian getting married this year. Other brides just have to worry about what they want, and maybe their parents. I have to think about the whole damn world."

Beth sniggered. "Poor little famous bride. I don't know how you do it, waking up every day to the unlimited budget and superhot fiancé. Is there anything we can do for you?"

Everyone laughed, even Rebecca. Lately, her relationship with Suzanne had been growing closer, and she'd been more inclined to take Suzanne's side on this issue. But hearing it now, she supposed Suzanne's problems did sound a little absurd.

"I get it," Kate said softly. Dylan's younger sister had spent her life under the glaring spotlight of her family's exploits and her brother's rise to fame. "They follow you everywhere. A nurse or someone managed to get a picture of my face with her phone while I was giving birth to Adrian and sold

40

it to the tabloids. They don't care that it's like the most private moment possible or that I was in horrible pain. They printed it anyway."

"See? Fucking vultures," Suzanne said loudly, heading for the kitchen to refill her cup. "Kate gets it. That's why I love you, Kate."

This would have been a graceful enough exit for the tall, lithe, platinum-blond Suzanne, except that in her inebriated state, she fumbled quite a bit with the screen door, nearly pulling it off the track in frustration. Rebecca stood to help her while the other three giggled.

"May I present your future sister-in-law," Marci said to Kate when Suzanne had finally cleared the door. "I'm sure she'll do you proud."

Kate laughed. "She can't be any more embarrassing than my real sisters." The table was silent as the other women tried to think of some polite but truthful way to counter this, but there was no way. With the exception of Kate, whose worst offense was being three months pregnant with her baby son when she'd married Dylan's promotions manager last summer, Dylan's sisters were a train wreck made for the tabloids.

In the kitchen, they could hear Suzanne

fumbling with the blender, letting out a stream of profanity in her lilting Southern accent as she did so. "Why don't I help her?" Kate said, standing. "I need to call Jeff to check on Adrian anyway."

"Oh, that reminds me, I should make sure Jake gave Bonnie her tummy medicine before he put her to bed," Marci said and trailed behind Kate into the house.

"So, Rebecca, how was work?" Beth said.

"Fine, thanks."

"Marci and Suzanne are in the huge master and Kate is in the back bedroom. I put my stuff in the other queen room. I thought we could share, unless you're a fan of bunk beds."

"Sure," Rebecca said. She and Beth had known one another for a long time, but at moments like this their relationship had the awkward feel of acquaintances rather than old friends. With little in common other than the friends in the other room, they sat in silence as the other women all talked on their phones in the kitchen. Apparently Suzanne had either called Dylan or gotten a late-night call from her assistant, Chad. After a professional disaster last year, Suzanne had more than rebounded. She ran a thriving nonprofit in addition to planning events for an ever-expanding roster of

Atlanta's elite, and it seemed that she and Chad never went off duty.

"It's great, isn't it?" Beth said, as though she could read Rebecca's thoughts. "How well she's bounced back from everything that happened last year?"

"Yes, it is," Rebecca said. Even though she had always envied Suzanne's poise and social status, she had not enjoyed watching her friend suffer the year before. Still, a famous, young, hot-as-hell fiancé was probably a pretty good consolation. "It really is."

"What about you then?" Beth said suddenly.

"Sorry?"

"When are we going to see you settled with your Prince Charming? Like in Marci's blog?"

"Uh, I don't know," Rebecca fumbled. "I'm not even really seeing anyone right now." *And haven't for the last two years.*

"I've always heard that love finds you when you quit looking for it," Beth said.

Rebecca held back the withering retort that occurred to her — how easy it was to give sage grown-up dating advice when you'd been with the same guy since you were fifteen. She just nodded. What could she say? *I found love my sophomore year in college, and he's married to our friend who's ten feet away?*

"I know this must be hard on you," Beth said gently.

Stop, Rebecca thought, tears brimming unexpectedly in her eyes. *Just stop.* For some reason, the sympathetic tone in Beth's voice was more cruel than any coldness she'd experienced from her friends over the past few years. Sometimes she thought she hid her feelings for Jake well, and other times it felt as though they were just below the surface — a fact that everyone knew but no one mentioned. "I'm fine," she said.

"I know," Beth said. "But is fine enough?"

Rebecca said nothing. She willed someone in the other room to please, for the love of God, come out and end this horrible conversation. She knew Beth was trying to be caring, but Rebecca didn't need this kind of caring. Mothering was what Beth did best, and it was the absolute last thing Rebecca needed.

Mercifully, Beth seemed to sense that her nurturing superpowers were not well received, and she turned her attention back to the bride-to-be. "I think I get what Suzanne is saying, you know? About how it feels like her wedding is for the whole world instead of for her and Dylan?"

Rebecca shrugged. "I guess that's part of

marrying someone famous. You have to learn to live with the idea that the world is watching you."

"Maybe," Beth agreed. "But I can see how it's hard. The reporters have been all over her for months. She had to get Chad to leak a fake wedding date for September just to get them to back off for a while."

Rebecca thought about this for a moment. *Invest yourself,* she thought, as the authors of her book might say. *You cannot create meaningful friendships if you are sitting on the sidelines.*

"You know what? You're right, Beth."

"I am?"

"Yes. Suzanne is our friend and I think we should try to help her."

"What? We can make Dylan Burke somehow not an international superstar?"

"No," Rebecca said slowly. "The public will have their expectations, but maybe we can give Suze what she wants, too."

"I'm confused," Beth said.

Rebecca's head was spinning. Maybe she could be the good guy for once. "Can you get Suze's phone away from her and get it to me for a few minutes?"

There was a clatter as the plastic margarita pitcher hit the kitchen floor on the other side of the wall, and Suzanne's voice: "Oh, shhhhugarcakes!"

Beth and Rebecca both smiled. "I think that's doable," Beth said. "What do you have in mind?"

4

When she finally stumbled to the bedroom she would share with Beth during the weekend, Rebecca felt quite tipsy. She was intoxicated both by the brutal margaritas Suzanne had concocted and the excitement of the plan the rest of them had created in snatches each time Suzanne left the room. Beth was already out cold, still wearing her clothes and draped diagonally across the bed.

Rebecca hoisted her suitcase carefully onto the bed, trying not to think about what Beth had said about looking for her own Prince Charming. Such an absurd, outdated cliché. And still painful.

She also wrestled with the idea that had planted itself in her brain lately and seemed to be taking hold despite her attempts to ignore it. It had been on the tip of her tongue tonight, and it had been hard not to say it to Beth. She was afraid that saying it out loud would make it true.

Maybe, she thought in these moments, *everyone is capable of truly loving just one person. And if you waste that love on someone who is unavailable, you simply don't get another chance.*

After some fumbling with the zipper, and opening the door a little to let in light from the hallway, she was able to get her bag open. The contents swam in her vision; something was not right. Something had been moved, she saw right away. The clothes around the edges of the case were still rolled up neatly, but in the middle, underneath the pajamas she had slid in herself this morning, they were sloppier. She pulled out the pajamas and saw her sundress had been moved to cover something foreign.

Rebecca opened the bedroom door another few inches to cast more light, and Beth snuffled and rolled over in her sleep. When she crept back to the bed and reached for the new item in her bag, her fingers touched something velvety and soft. When she picked it up, it was solid underneath and heavy.

Her first thought was that there had been a mistake at security. Several of those guys had seemed extra shifty and weird today. But these were her pajamas, just as she'd worn them the night before. *What the hell?* It was some kind of velvet bag with drawstrings at the top and something bulky inside. She took the bag out of her suitcase and down the hall to the bathroom, where she could look at it in the light.

The bag was deep-purple velvet, with a lavender feather embroidered across the front. *Oh, shit. Valerie.* For a moment, she hoped that it had simply been a late-night mistake on Valerie's part, but when she reached into the bag, the note she found dispelled all confusion. Under the note, her fingers brushed something rubbery and firm, and she cringed. She was able to open the bag wide enough to see without taking it out: it was a full-sized, hot-pink, penis-shaped vibrator.

Rebecca sat down on the toilet, dazed. *What am I going to do with this? I'm sharing a room with Beth. What if she finds it and thinks I'm a pervert? I could just kill Valerie.* She thought about just throwing it in the bathroom trash next to her, but the bag had THE PURPLE FEATHER, SAN FRANCISCO stitched in bold letters under the feather logo. Kate and Beth shared this bathroom with her, and everyone knew she'd been in San Francisco the night before.

It would have to go back to her suitcase,

she decided, and she would bury it under everything else, along with the note. It was in Valerie's neat cursive, on hotel stationery, with an insipid smiley face at the bottom. "Kid, you need this more than anyone I've ever met. Enjoy your vacation. 'Come' back rested. Ha, ha. — V"

Everyone in the house slept in the following morning, except Marci, who emerged from her room fully showered and dressed, while the other girls were still lounging in their pajamas and nursing the coffeepot. Even though she hadn't drunk much, and had clearly risen early, Marci looked almost as tired as everyone else. Suzanne was the worst off, and wore dark glasses even on the living-room couch, clinging to her coffee cup like a life preserver. *We should get her a nap,* Rebecca thought.

Kate and Beth were at the kitchen table, where they had cleared the empty cups and bottles from the previous night and were now idly flipping through magazines and tourist brochures. Rebecca filled a coffee cup and joined them. She watched as Marci plopped down beside Suzanne on the couch, and they both stared straight at the television, which no one had yet bothered to turn on.

"What's your excuse?" Suzanne muttered eventually.

"What?" Marci said.

"You look like shit," Suzanne said.

"Uh, thanks? I can always count on you for a lift."

"No, really. You look tired. But you barely touched a drink last night."

A smile flitted across Marci's lips, but she contained it. By now the other two girls had tuned in to the conversation. "I think you drank enough for both of us, my friend."

"So. What's. Your. Excuse?" Suzanne repeated. Rebecca wondered why she was grilling Marci this way, and why Marci's feathers weren't more ruffled by the rude line of questioning. Maybe it was Rebecca's inability to understand this strange, adversarial interaction that had kept her from having close girlfriends.

Marci glared at Suzanne momentarily and then burst into laughter. "I think you are wasting your talents as an event planner. We need you interrogating terrorists or something."

"Are you serious?" Suzanne said, ignoring Marci's attempt to deflect. "Really? Already?"

Marci nodded. From across the room, Beth stood up. "Wait, are you saying what I think you're saying?"

Rebecca was completely lost. Only when she heard Marci say something about "ten weeks, so we're not really telling anyone" did she realize. Marci was pregnant, again. *Jesus*. Little Bonnie was not even a year old yet. Soon they were all crowded around Marci in the living room, everyone asking questions and laughing, and calculating how old Bonnie would be when her new baby brother or sister arrived.

This didn't technically impact her, but Rebecca felt overwhelmed nonetheless. Life was moving too fast. People seemed in such a hurry to get married, settle down, and have babies. What was the rush? They were still in their midthirties. There was plenty of time for all this, wasn't there? Of course she knew that her feelings for Jake played a role: Marci being pregnant reminded her that Marci and Jake were having sex. *Duh, Bec, of course they're having sex. They are married, after all.* But somehow this indisputable evidence brought the idea to the forefront of her mind, and it was opening the same old wound from her quiet battle for Jake's heart four years ago.

Rebecca shook her head to banish the images from her mind. She tuned in to the conversation to find that Marci was talking about Jake's reaction to the pregnancy.

"He's thrilled, of course," she said. "I mean, we both wanted a big family."

"But?" Suzanne said.

"Well, I guess he thinks it's a little soon after Bonnie. And he's . . . well, he's sort of ticked with me for letting it happen."

"Letting it happen?" Beth said. "Like he had no part in it?"

"Well," Marci said, her voice rising to a squeak. "I might have told a teensy white lie about birth control. . . ."

"Marcella Beatrice!" Suzanne said. "You didn't!"

Beth shook her head, tut-tutting. Kate giggled.

"Look," Marci said, "it's not the end of the world. It happened, and I know Jake will be thrilled when he gets used to the idea. He thought we should put more space between the kids, but I'm thirty-five. . . ."

There was a collective groan from the other women. Except for Kate, who was nearly ten years younger, they were all the same age. Rebecca wondered if Marci had any idea of her impact on Suzanne and Rebecca, who did not yet have children, when she judged herself essentially too old to reproduce.

"Well, you know what I mean!" Marci

protested. "I know it's fine to have babies for a few more years now, but why wait? Once you're married and ready for kids, I mean." This last seemed to be directed at Rebecca herself. She could have slapped Marci in that moment. She reminded herself that assaulting a pregnant woman was a felony.

"One reason to wait would be that your husband isn't ready for another baby," Rebecca said, gritting her teeth in a painful attempt at a smile. "For example."

Marci glared at her, and Rebecca felt exhilaration: half-scared to have challenged Marci so openly, half-proud of herself for standing up for Jake.

"Okay, okay," Suzanne said gently, "ease up, everyone. The most important thing is that you and the baby stay healthy. And of course we're all thrilled for both of you."

"Of course," Rebecca said, plastering on a smile. Damn. She was trying so hard to be a good person, but sometimes . . . Marci just brought out the worst in her.

"Hey, Rebecca," Beth intervened. "Didn't you say you were going to the grocery store? Can I come with you?"

"Um, sure," Rebecca said slowly.

When they pulled out of the gravel driveway

in Marci's SUV, Beth turned to her. "What the hell is going on with you and Marci?"

"What?" Rebecca said. "Nothing."

"Right, nothing," Beth said.

"I don't know," Rebecca said. She sighed. She was so tired of holding it all in, and this most recent conversation with Marci made her feel as though she was not doing such a great job with that anyway. "It's just that Jake is my friend, too, and sometimes I think Marci takes him for granted."

"What do you mean?" Beth said. Her tone was neutral, but something told Rebecca to tread lightly.

"I don't know; it's hard to say. Maybe I'm just tired from work. Don't listen to me."

"Maybe you need to listen to yourself," Beth said. "Because an observer who didn't know better might think you're still in love with your friend's husband. And that, my dear, is a recipe for disaster."

Rebecca sat in stunned silence as Beth navigated to the neighborhood market. By the time they had unglued themselves from the sticky leather seats and the screen door banged behind them on the way in, Beth seemed to have dropped the subject. Rebecca was relieved that she didn't press the point any further, but she also couldn't get Beth's words out of her mind as they scoured the shelves, looking for supplies.

She felt nervous — a nagging sense that nothing was quite right. Last night on the porch, her little scheme had felt thrilling and noble. Even talking to Dylan at almost midnight had felt only slightly daring. He had still been up, of course — even though he had kept his word to Suzanne and was not doing a formal tour this summer, he and a few of his bandmates were still out several times a week, listening to other bands.

But the whole plan felt a little ridiculous by morning light, and Rebecca was almost embarrassed by her own gall in suggesting it. If she could have taken it back now, she would have done so in a split second, but the wheels were in motion already. The girls were excited. Dylan was on his way. It was sink or swim now.

Rebecca could say none of this to Beth, who was strolling happily along the tiny store's aisles, picking things up and putting them into the rickety old shopping buggy. "Beth, how on earth are we going to make this work?"

"Don't worry," Beth said, with a glint in her eye that led Rebecca to suspect she was tackling this challenge with the same fervor with which she would construct a baking soda volcano for her kid's class project. "We just have to think outside the box."

They left the tiny grocery half an hour later with the frenzied owner helping them out to their car. They loaded up four dusty boxes of mason jars in various sizes, some leftover holiday votive candles that smelled like cinnamon, the two least expensive fishing poles they could find, a couple of wind socks with fluttery ends, underwater disposable cameras, and a large pack of industrial-strength toilet paper. Rebecca also held a grocery bag with some snacks and skim milk, so they would have something to walk in with upon returning to the beach house.

Beth whistled happily on the drive home, and Rebecca marveled at her confidence. As soon as Rebecca had proposed this plan the evening before, Beth had embraced it with certainty and excitement. It was as though they were planning a Cub Scout meeting and Beth had perfected the recipe for gummy-worm cupcakes. Rebecca, on the other hand, checked her phone every six minutes, chewed her nails, and had to resist the urge to steal Marci's SUV to drive all the way to Charleston. Maybe for better supplies. Maybe to catch a plane and be gone. What if Suzanne didn't like this? What if she was offended? Suzanne was the most sophisticated event planner, most stylish person, Rebecca had ever known. Was toilet paper strung between fishing poles really going to cut it?

5

By Friday afternoon, Rebecca and Marci had reached a sort of silent truce. Rebecca regretted her snide comments from that morning, but Marci no longer looked venomously angry. In fact, she didn't seem to be registering much emotion at all. Tiredness had overcome her features and beaten down everything else. Rebecca wondered how the human race continued at all, given the sheer awfulness of pregnancy and childbirth. She had never particularly wanted children; not that she had to give it much thought since she had never been in a serious relationship. But even if she had, Marci's whitewashed face and ill temper made her second-guess the whole enterprise.

Eventually, Marci retired to the big master bedroom she'd been sharing with Suzanne to nap. Kate sat outside on the porch, reading. She'd left the door open so the other three could hear the sound of the waves and gulls as they played cards at the kitchen table. It was idyllic. Rebecca tried not to appear too nervous about the plans for the next day.

The general idea was that sometime Saturday evening, Marci was going to drag Suzanne out to satisfy a pregnancy craving for something that, of course, would be impossible to obtain easily on the island. That would keep Suze busy for a couple of hours while the rest of them set everything up and hopefully, Dylan would appear with Jake and Kate's husband, Jeff. Rebecca had offered to call in favors at the airline to get them last-minute tickets, but she sort of hoped they wouldn't take her up on this. She wasn't entirely sure how much clout her three years of service had earned her in this regard.

She, Beth, and Suzanne were on their third game of rummy when her phone vibrated in her pocket. Rebecca jumped, startled, and Suzanne looked puzzled. She pulled the phone from her pocket and checked the number. Her heart skipped a beat. Jake.

"Hey," she said, getting up from the table and mouthing "work" to Suzanne and Beth.

Then she realized she probably wouldn't

answer a work call with "hey," so she added, "Hello, Mr. Roberson," in a fumbling voice. Judging by Suzanne's confused expression, this was even worse. In her panic, Rebecca bumped into a table, cursing loudly, as she headed out the front door and closed it behind her so they could speak freely.

"Hey, slick," Jake said. "Remind me not to hire you as a spy or anything."

"Yes," Rebecca said. Her knee throbbed from the collision with the table, and her heart pounded with the same intensity.

"I called you since my darling wife is probably napping," he said.

"Yes," she repeated, stupidly. "She is." Was Rebecca imagining things, or was there a hint of sarcasm on *my darling wife*?

"I guess she told you girls, then, about the baby?" His tone was unreadable, awkward.

"Um, yes. Congratulations, Jake, of course."

"Not Jacob, huh?"

"What?"

"You never call me Jacob anymore. I always thought it was kind of endearing, how only you did that. Well, you and my grandmother."

It was as though Rebecca had hit her head instead of her knee. Everything was spinning in the glaring sunlight, so she shaded her eyes, wishing she had thought to grab her sunglasses on the way out the door.

"Well, it's been — different," she managed. *You know, I haven't felt as affectionate and playful since you broke my heart and married the other girl.* Where was he going with this?

And then, it was as though he had never said any of it. "Okay, so anyway, Dylan's got a charter booked for tomorrow afternoon and we should be there by five. We're bringing a bunch of fishing stuff in case the paparazzi are lurking around. Do me a favor and text me when Suze and Marci leave, so we don't cross paths with them on our way to the beach house."

"Sure," Rebecca said. "Will do."

"Thanks," he said. "You're wonderful as always, Bec." The phone had disconnected before she could think what to say next.

Saturday morning was leisurely at the beach house, and Rebecca had finally managed to quell some of her nervous excitement. It was overcast until almost noon, and the girls sat in their pajamas drinking coffee and scarfing down pastries Marci had obtained from a bakery in Charleston while the rest of them slept in. They got sub sandwiches for lunch, and spent a couple of hours on the beach before Marci retired for her daily nap at three, with strict instructions for them to wake her by four thirty.

Rebecca had stepped out the front door to take a walk when her phone rang. Hoping for Jake, she made out her mother's number through the glare and her stomach sank. She twisted the ring on her right hand, breathing deeply, and answered.

"Becky! You have to come home!" Her mother's voice, high and strained. "Come tell them I'm not leaving!"

"Mama, what is it?"

"They're saying I have to leave."

"Who is?"

"I don't know. There's a note on the door. On my door! They had to walk on my private property to put the note here. It's an outrage. I pay my taxes!"

Rebecca inhaled deeply, twisting her ring again. "I know you do, Mama," she said, using the calm voice she normally reserved for white-knuckle passengers during turbulence. "I'm sure there is some kind of mistake. Did you call Daddy? Did you remember to pay the bills?"

"Your *father*" — Lorena Williamson spit out the word — "hasn't returned my call. He's probably with that whore!"

"Okay, calm down. I'll call Daddy, okay?

Just try not to panic. We'll get it straightened out." She said this, as she always did, with far more conviction than she felt. But it worked.

"You'll get me a lawyer, won't you, Rebecca?" Her mother's voice was thin, but at least calmer as she pleaded. "You know people over there in Atlanta; you'll find someone who can help?"

"Of course I would, Mama, but I'm sure you don't need a lawyer. This is probably just a mistake, and we'll get it straightened out. Why don't you take a walk and get a little fresh air?"

As soon as it was out of her mouth, Rebecca knew it was the wrong thing to say. "I don't need to take a walk. I need people to leave me alone and stop putting papers on my damn house, Rebecca!"

"Okay, Mother, I'm sorry," Rebecca said. "I'll try to find out what's going on."

"And you'll come home?"

"I'm on a trip with some girlfriends, Mama," Rebecca said gently. "I'm supposed to go back to work on Tuesday."

"Oh," Lorena said. Then she made the statement that was the signal of motherly guilt worldwide. "Well, don't worry about me, then."

"Tell you what, I'll call you back today if I

find anything out, and then I'll look at the schedule when I get back and find out when I can get over there. Okay?"

"Okay," her mother said. Now her voice had a thin, faraway quality, and Rebecca knew just as surely as if she were standing next to her that her mother was in Cory's room, holding his worn baseball glove to her chest and staring out the window at the backyard. Rebecca hung up without saying anything else, knowing that she wouldn't have been heard if she did.

Her father answered after two rings. "Rebecca Rockstar!" he said gleefully. He had given her this nickname at age eleven, toward the end of a two-week period during which she enjoyed singing into her hairbrush and pretending to be Joan Jett, until Tanya Boozer informed her that she couldn't sing. Joan Jett and the Blackhearts were long gone, but despite her best efforts, Rebecca Rockstar would never go away.

"Hi, Dad." She decided to get straight to the point, glancing at the house behind her. "Do you know what's going on with Mama?"

There was quiet on the other end of the line, and Rebecca was pretty sure she heard whispering. "No, darlin'," he said at last. "She tried to call me a little bit ago, but

I . . . well, I'm kind of busy."

"But you answered when I called," she said.

"I'll always answer for you, Rebecca. But the truth is I'm down at Playa del Carmen with some friends and —"

"Wait a minute. You're in Mexico?" She tried to picture her dad in his full beard and postal service uniform, hanging out on a beach, sucking down margaritas. It didn't compute. "Who with?"

He hesitated. "Just some friends."

"Friends?"

"Yes, George and Annette Brown — you remember them — and a couple of others from church —"

"And Sonia?" Rebecca hated the accusatory tone in her voice.

"Yes, Rebecca, and Sonia." His voice was impatient.

"You didn't even tell me you were going," she said. It sounded even more ridiculous spoken aloud than it had in her head, especially since she had not mentioned to him that she would be at the beach this weekend, either. "I could have gotten you a flight."

"Oh, that's okay, darlin'," her dad said. "The group all flew down together and I didn't really have much to do with the ar-

66

rangements. Annette sort of led the charge on that. Anyway, we're heading out to do some — what is it? — parasailing. Hopefully I won't break my neck and drown. So, what can I do for you?"

"Well, Mom called and she's really upset — something about a note on the door. You've paid the mortgage and everything, right?"

"Of course. I always pay it way ahead." There was high-pitched giggling in the background. Rebecca gritted her teeth and twisted her ring, counting — seven, eight, nine. . . .

"What about the bills? Like the utilities and stuff. Do you think she lost them again?"

"I don't think so sweetheart — I'll be right there! See if they have an extralarge life jacket! — Rebecca, I pretty much stay on top of all that, for her house and mine. But I'll check into it when I get home. If it's the power company, I'm sure she has a few days before anything will happen. They put those notices up to scare people into paying the bills."

"So what should I do?"

"Nothing you can do, darlin' — just go have a good time. Live your life. It will be fine. Now I need to run." Before the call disconnected, she heard more talking and laughing and some kind of horns playing in the background. Mexico? Parasailing? Her parents' small-town-Alabama Sunday school group partying like college kids? It was some kind of alternate universe.

She debated about calling her mother back, and decided against it. What could she say? *"Daddy doesn't know anything and he's busy partying on the beach with his new girlfriend and all your old friends"?* Rebecca sighed and began walking along the asphalt driveway they shared with neighboring beach houses. Two doors down, a man was being pulled to a minivan by three children chanting, "Ice cream! Ice cream! Ice cream!"

Rebecca and her father were both at different beaches today, and at least one of them was doing a bang-up job of getting on with his life. He'd suggested that she do the same, and she knew he was right. If Rebecca really knew what was good for her, she'd keep walking right now, leaving her former life and her friends, and even Jake, behind. She should jump on a plane to Madrid or Paris and never look back. Marry some exotic guy with a sexy accent and a powerful job. Get a cottage in the European countryside. Raise goats. Make cheese.

She'd had this fantasy before but had only gone so far as to get a job that put her on planes every day. Now it called to her again — the desire to be somewhere, someone, else. To get as far away from Oreville, Alabama, as possible and never go back.

Rebecca had been one foot out the door since her freshman year in high school, but even when she left to live with Aunt Louise before college, Rebecca knew she could never *really* leave. Almost two decades later, even though she had no obligations to hold her back, she could never bring herself to stay where the planes brought her. Something stopped her. Maybe the same thing that stopped her dad from filing for divorce, even though he'd been out of the house for years. They were both inextricably tied to that small house in Alabama, where Rebecca's mother lived with her cats and collections and the lingering memory of a boy long dead.

6

Rebecca made her way down to the water and walked for a while, letting the Atlantic froth against her ankles. It was late in the afternoon and still hot; the beach was mostly populated by older children and their tired, sunburnt parents, with a few young-adult sunbathers here and there. She tried, without success, to make her mind as clear as the blazing blue sky.

I am fine. Most problems are temporary. It's not my job to fix everyone else.

When she returned, she took the railroad tie path up to the house and overheard Marci trying to get Suzanne out of a lounge chair on the back deck. "Please, Suze, we never get to do anything just the two of us!"

"We get pedicures every other week. And we have dinner just the two of us at least that often."

"I know, but this is different. No one else understands my cravings like you do."

70

"I don't understand them, Marci. I indulge them. There's a difference."

Marci caught Rebecca's eye and shrugged slightly. Suzanne seemed firmly planted where she was, her giant sunglasses glinting in the late-afternoon sun and a stack of six or seven magazines next to her, beneath a bottle of ice water.

"What are you craving?" Rebecca asked, not sure how to help Marci but needing to make her presence known.

"You know, something greasy but not too greasy, and salty and a little bit sweet," Marci said.

"Hmmm . . . I could always come with you," Rebecca said. "When we figure out what you want, we can just pick up dinner for everyone."

Suzanne sat up straight. She hated it when other people ordered her food — she was so picky about how things were prepared. "That's okay," she said, "thanks, Rebecca, but I'll go with her. You should stay here and relax — you have to wait on people all the time at work. I was just going in anyway."

When Suzanne had hurried in through the door to change, Marci gave Rebecca a smile. "Nice work," she said. "Thanks."

Rebecca shrugged. "No problem."

They stood awkwardly there for a minute, each one apparently waiting for the other to go into the house first. They did this: traded niceties, traded occasional barbs, and then stood outside doorways, trying to decide who should go first into a room. It was exhausting.

"Please, go ahead," Rebecca said.

So Marci did, brushing past with a forced smile and a hand at her lower belly.

Once Marci and Suzanne were gone, Rebecca texted Jake, and the guys arrived within moments. In his characteristic style, Dylan had managed to secure a shiny white Jeep from somewhere, so the three guys all looked ruddy and windblown as though they'd been on the island for days instead of hours. Dylan grinned at the girls as he signaled for the other two to get out. Jeff was out of the passenger's seat and sweeping little Kate into his arms in a flash.

"I missed you, baby," he said.

"Jeff, it's only been a couple of days," Kate said. "What's it going to be like when you guys are on tour?"

"You'll just have to come with us. You and Adrian." Before she could answer, he was planting a kiss on her mouth that made Beth and Rebecca look first at one another, and then quickly back to the Jeep in embarrassment.

The horn sounded and Dylan yelled from the car, "Dude! You might be my best man, but that is still my baby sister!"

Behind her, Rebecca heard Kate whisper, "I missed you, too, babe."

She stepped forward toward the Jeep to help unload. Climbing out of the backseat, Jake looked to Rebecca the same way he had in college, wearing a faded UGA T-shirt, worn khaki cargo shorts, and flip-flops. He even had a baseball hat on backward the way he always had when he had driven his own battered old Jeep around Athens. He was the kind of guy who was more at home eating hot dogs at a football game than a steak dinner at the country club. Even Marci, who was far from a slave to fashion herself, complained that she could never convince him to get rid of his ratty old clothes and buy anything new. You would never know he was in line to inherit a fortune of old textile money.

He pulled a battered black duffel and his camera equipment out of the car with practiced ease and kissed Beth and Rebecca each on the cheek on his way into the house. He lingered, or Rebecca imagined he lingered, for a split second with his lips against her cheek. He smelled like deodorant and soap, with a faint hint of beer on his breath, presumably from the plane.

She avoided Beth's gaze as Jake went inside and Dylan backed out of the driveway to park the car farther away, so Suzanne would not see it when she returned. If Beth had noticed anything in Jake's behavior or Rebecca's face, she said nothing.

The sun was already sinking in the sky, so the six of them worked quickly to get everything set up. Kate and Jeff giggled and kissed like teenagers in the kitchen while they set up food and drinks. These consisted mostly of microwave appetizers with bottles of champagne and beer in ice buckets. Each time she passed the two of them during the setup, Rebecca wondered whether this was the first time they had been away from Adrian since he was born six months before. It must have been hard to enjoy being newlyweds, Rebecca guessed, when you were three months pregnant walking down the aisle.

Outside, Jake and Dylan helped Rebecca set up the fishing poles in the sand and create a makeshift garland out of toilet paper. It took some practice because it ripped so easily, but soon they had a passable bough between the two poles and what looked like crepe paper streamers hanging down from each one. Beth had managed to find some wildflowers to tie up on each with dental floss, and Rebecca used the mason jars and cinnamon candles to create a path from the railroad ties to the spot on the beach. She lit them and hoped they would burn long enough to be visible when Suzanne and Marci got back. As the sun began to set, they all changed quickly into their nicest beach clothes, and waited on the back porch.

"You ready for this?" Jeff asked Dylan.

"Yep," Dylan said simply. He wore pressed khaki shorts and a tan-and-white Hawaiian shirt. It was one of the few times Rebecca had seen him — in the media or in person — without his trademark camouflage hat. She noticed that he had a bit of a receding hairline, surprising for someone who was just twenty-seven. Normally larger than life, tonight Dylan Burke looked like an average guy.

They heard the car pull up out front, just as the sun began to dip below the horizon. It was perfect timing — the little scene they had created on the beach was bathed in orange light, with the mason jar candles flickering cheerfully along the path in the sand. Dylan, Jeff, and Jake hurried down the stairs and took their places beneath the streamers, while Kate, Beth, and Rebecca gathered up the extra wildflowers and listened at the door.

"Where is everyone?" Suzanne was saying irritably. "I told you we didn't need to get all this stuff — they obviously went out."

"How would they go out? We had the car," Marci said. Then she called loudly, "We're back!"

Beth, Rebecca, and Kate, huddled on the back porch, suppressed giggles and squeals, as though they were waiting outside the eighth-grade dance. Beth motioned for them to take a deep breath and calm down.

"I'm going to put this shirt in the washer before the ketchup sets, you klutz," Suzanne said. "I still don't know how my sundress ended up in your car."

"You're just that lucky," Marci said, with just the right amount of sarcasm. She was the only person who could get away with talking to Suzanne like that. "Let's go out back."

"What?"

"Let's go for a walk or something. Maybe the other girls are outside."

"Go ahead, I'll catch up," Suzanne said.

"Come with me!" Marci whined.

"What is with you?" Suzanne said. "You're

so needy today, even for you. Even pregnant you."

She could not hear what passed between them next, but Rebecca guessed Marci was running out of artifice, because Suzanne's next question was in a completely different tone. "Marci, what is going on?"

And then the doorknob turned. Suzanne stepped out of the beach house with a perplexed expression. Marci followed, and Beth handed each of them a loose bunch of flowers. "What?" Suzanne said. Then again. "What?"

Marci answered with a hug. "We love you." And then, surprisingly, "It was Rebecca's idea."

"But . . . ," Suzanne started, and then her eyes lit on Dylan, standing patiently on the beach next to a local judge whose teenage daughter would be getting ten front-row tickets to Dylan's next concert in Charleston. "But —"

"Just follow us," Beth said, and began a slow stride down the wooden path.

As they filed into place opposite the guys, Marci leading a shocked Suzanne by the hand, the bride stopped a few feet back. She gaped at Dylan. "You're here," she said softly.

"Yes, ma'am," Dylan said, giving her a soft

salute with two fingers.

"But . . ."

It was strange to see Suzanne in this state. Normally, she was the most polished and professional person any of them knew. She prepared for every contingency. Nothing surprised her. Ever.

Finally, Dylan took a step forward and took her hands in his. He extracted the bouquet of wildflowers from Suzanne and handed them to Marci.

"Listen, Scarlett, I'm going to be honest. We are probably going to have to do something that includes a bunch of other people — including our families and the press and everyone.

"But that will be for them, and to some extent for my job, and I know you will be gracious and go along with it. But tonight is for you. For us. No press, no chaos, just us. This will be what's real. This is the anniversary we will celebrate for the rest of our lives together. What do you think?"

Suzanne stood silent, staring.

"I mean, unless you've changed your mind?" Dylan said. "Afraid to take the plunge?"

The challenge seemed to bring her back to herself. "Dylan Burke, you know damn well I am not afraid of anything. You least of all."

"That's my girl," he said, and scooped an arm around her waist.

Marci sniffed loudly and tore a piece of the toilet paper garland with one hand. She passed pieces to the other three women, and they all dabbed at their eyes.

Dylan Burke and Suzanne Hamilton exchanged vows simply as the sun sank over the Atlantic. The groom and his groomsmen wore Hawaiian shirts, shorts, and flip-flops. The bride and her attendants wore various cotton sundresses and skirts they'd packed in case of a sporadic night out at a local Italian restaurant, which was as fancy as they'd expected the weekend to get. None of them had anticipated a wedding.

Suzanne had planned nearly every must-attend upscale event in Atlanta for the last five years, and had dedicated her life to making sure everything was perfect for her clients. Dylan had spent every waking moment since his teenage years in front of cameras, stage lights, and flashbulbs. And yet, here they were, at the wedding that would break the hearts of women everywhere, beneath toilet paper streamers strung between fishing poles. The portly judge gave the rites, after fast-tracking their marriage license. Rebecca snapped a few photos on a disposable underwater camera. It was perfect.

As Dylan reached for his new wife and gave her a soft kiss, Rebecca felt a thrill of pride that she had set this in motion. For once, her contribution to the group seemed to be more than just filling out a seat at happy hour. Though they hadn't always seen eye to eye, Rebecca had come to appreciate that Suzanne's quirkiness and snobbery hid a kind of sweet vulnerability. And while it had never been said by either of them, Rebecca thought maybe Suzanne was learning this same truth about her.

7

After sunset, they built a bonfire. Kate and Jeff brought out the buckets of beer and champagne, and paper plates overflowing with appetizers. The group sat on folding chairs and towels and chatted loosely, as though people got married on the spur of the moment every day. As though the groom weren't one of the most recognizable people in all of country music. Jake had brought out speakers, so they listened to music on his phone and stared out at the blackness of the ocean.

"Sorry to ruin your girls' weekend," Dylan said to Suzanne, who looked more relaxed in the firelight than Rebecca even thought it possible for Suzanne to be.

"Sorry to ruin your big wedding," she said, kicking his bare foot with hers.

"Do you want to hear your song?"

"What?"

"I've been writing a song for our wedding.

It's not finished, but . . ."

Dylan picked up his guitar and began picking out a few chords. His voice was melodic and perfect, even without rehearsal. "Baby put your hair up, or wear it down, or shave your head . . ."

Suzanne shook her head and chuckled.

"We can go out dancing, to a ball game, or just stay home and rock the bed."

Jeff whistled loudly, and then yelled, "Ow!" as Kate elbowed him in the ribs, nearly knocking him off a tiny fabric camp stool.

Dylan was unfazed. "Honey, I don't care, what you do or what you wear. You don't have to be perfect, because you're perfect for me. . . ."

Marci stood abruptly, glancing apologetically at Dylan. She clamped a hand over her mouth, turned, and sped toward the house. She only made it as far as the bushes, however, where she stopped to vomit loudly.

"Well, like I said, the song's not done yet," Dylan said, smiling. "That's not exactly the reaction I was going for."

Suzanne pulled him toward her by the sleeve. "I love it. I love you."

The group broke into separate conversations as everyone began discussing the song and Marci's morning sickness that was apparently also midnight sickness.

Rebecca stood, stretched, and walked back down to the water, enjoying the sand under her feet. It had grown more overcast as evening came, and there was no moon. The night was inky black over the water. Except for the tiny waves at her feet lighted by the blaze, there was nothing to see but a few dim stars visible between the clouds. It felt like standing on the edge of nothing.

She felt him behind her before she saw him.

"Quite a night," Jake said.

"Yes," Rebecca said. A chill ran up her spine. She could not bring herself to turn around.

"I heard this was your idea," he said.

"Well, sort of. I mean, I guess it was my idea but Beth did most of the planning."

His hand on her bare shoulder was warm and strong. Rebecca sometimes forgot how little real human contact she had these days, aside from the bustling and jostling of the airport. For years, she had measured her life in increments of Jake: a smile, a phone call, a brush with his hand, a peck on the cheek. And for a few moments, four years ago . . . But that had been between his engagements to Marci — the disastrous first one, and the real one that stuck. Now, he belonged irrevocably to Marci, no matter what Rebecca's feelings were.

The hand on her shoulder seemed to radiate warmth. She knew she should turn and walk back to the safety of the fire and the gaze of other people. But her feet were glued to the sand. "Congratulations again on the new pregnancy," she said. She wasn't sure if she was building a bridge between them or trying to tear one down.

"Yes. It's . . . it's such a blessing. Of course."

The thing was, and Rebecca didn't think she was imagining this, he didn't *sound* blessed. She hesitated. "I'm sure you're thrilled to have another baby. Bonnie is so beautiful."

"She's the light of my life," he said. This much was genuine. "And, yeah, I'm thrilled, it's just —"

"Hey guys," Suzanne said suddenly. Rebecca jumped. She hadn't heard anyone approaching over the sound of the waves. And the blood pumping in her ears.

"Hey there, Mrs. Dylan Burke." Jake did not remove his hand, but simply put his other arm around Suzanne so that he was draped between the two of them. It was an affectionate gesture. Brotherly.

"Ugh, don't say that," Suzanne said.

Without looking, Rebecca knew Suzanne was wrinkling her nose. "It makes me feel old."

"You'd better get used to it," Jake said. He kissed Suzanne on the cheek. "Congratulations, Suze. Really. He's a good guy, especially for a famous person."

"Thanks, Jakie," Suzanne said, using the nickname she'd had for him in college. How was it possible that had been almost fifteen years ago? "Now we just need to find the right guy for Rebecca. Don't you know anyone? Maybe one of those pro football players from your film? Just think, she could be on the *Real Housewives of Atlanta* in a couple of years."

Jake mumbled something to the ocean. Rebecca felt humiliation rising in her chest. "Actually," she said impulsively, "Rebecca is already seeing someone."

Suzanne's shock was visible even in the dim light from the fire behind them. "What? Who? Why didn't you mention this?"

"You didn't ask," Rebecca said. "He's a pilot."

"Really?" Suzanne said. "How wonderful. Anyone I've met?"

Rebecca was already regretting the lie. "No, he flies the international routes. His name is . . ." She searched her database of pilots for someone who was real and single. Better to keep a lie as close to the truth as possible. "Sandy."

"Sandy. What's he like? Why have you been keeping him secret?"

Rebecca thought about the real-life Sandy, a pilot she flew with once every couple of months back and forth to London. *Because he's twenty years older than me and kind of a dick, actually. He has a mustache that looks like a dead mouse and he's always telling gross, racist stories about venereal diseases he picked up when he flew the Asian routes. Oh God, why did I do this?*

"Well, he is recently divorced." In truth, she thought Sandy had been divorced for about a decade, but he still referred to his ex-wife in such bitter terms it felt recent. "And obviously since we work together . . ."

She trailed off, hoping that the vague implication would be enough to placate Suzanne. It wasn't. "So, is it serious?"

Jake looked at her now, too. "Well, sort of," Rebecca stammered. "I mean, it's still early in the relationship. So, no. I guess not serious yet."

They waited for her to expand on what she'd said. Rebecca, however, had no earthly idea what to say next. Why had she lied? She was lonely, yes. She could admit that.

But was she really so bad off that she had to make up fake relationships?

Fortunately, Marci emerged from the beach house and called to Jake, who waved at her and walked up toward the house. "I am glad you're seeing someone," Suzanne said when they were alone. "We've all been a little worried about you. Especially Jake and Marci. Jake is really fond of you, you know. I mean, we all are."

The tone in Suzanne's voice was unreadable, and her eyes were fixed on the bonfire twenty feet away. "Mmm . . . ," Rebecca said, noncommittal. At least tonight, there was one topic she knew was safe. "Congratulations again, Suzanne. I know you and Dylan will be really happy together."

Suzanne bit her lip. "I'm afraid so," she said, admiring her new husband, who was arguing animatedly with Jeff about something while Kate shook her head and laughed. "I don't really know how to be a wife, though. Long-term relationships aren't exactly my specialty."

"You'll be great," Rebecca said. "It's one of those things you can only do well when the time is right." *As though I know a damn thing about it.*

"Thanks, Rebecca," Suzanne said. "I can't believe you did all this. It's wonderful."

"You weren't disappointed? I mean, it wasn't fancy."

"Are you kidding? It couldn't have been more perfect." Suzanne kissed her on the cheek and Rebecca flushed. They waded arm in arm through the powdery sand and rejoined the others at the fire.

8

Everyone stayed up until long after midnight, drinking beer and dancing in the sand
by the fire. Rebecca spent the evening
deflecting curious questions about her
imaginary relationship with the nonexistent
Sandy, and fighting off pangs of envy as the
three couples nuzzled and slow danced in
the sand around the fire. Beth, who was also
alone, disappeared for a while to talk to Ray
and check on the kids. When she was satisfied that they were surviving without her,
she set about to make herself very drunk.

Rebecca didn't like to drink heavily — she
was never happy feeling out of control,
especially in big groups — so she watched
with bemusement as Beth got sillier and sillier, saying over and over how she never got
to do this anymore.

The beach house had four bedrooms: a
large master on one end with its own huge
bathroom, where Suzanne and Dylan spent

their first night as a married couple, and three smaller bedrooms in a row on the other side. One of these had a queen-sized bed, and doors to the living room and the back deck. This had originally been where Rebecca and Beth were sleeping, but was now designated for Marci and Jake. Another had a double bed and large windows facing the front of the house, across from a sizable shared bathroom. Kate had already been in this room and now Jeff was with her.

Wedged in between those two cozy rooms was a narrow space Rebecca suspected had been squeezed in somehow to make the house more appealing for rentals to families. It had none of the understated elegance of the rest of the house, and was dusty from disuse. Apparently the housekeeping service often skipped over it. It had a single fluorescent light, and exactly enough space for a set of cheap wooden bunk beds with dated fish-themed comforters, Rebecca and Beth's suitcases, and a tall corner bookshelf with baskets for clothes and a tiny TV on the top shelf. There was no closet, and no other furniture, just a worn rag rug on the linoleum floor. Of course, Suzanne never would have booked this house if she had known the guys would be joining them, and she and Dylan both offered to either go to a hotel themselves or to pay for Beth and Rebecca to stay elsewhere.

That, Rebecca and Beth had both insisted, was ridiculous. The hassle alone of moving themselves and their stuff late in the evening would have been enough of an obstacle, even if Beth had not been three sheets to the wind by the end of the night. Now that the clock had struck one in the morning and Beth was passed out on the couch with her cell phone in her hand, Rebecca was beginning to wish she had taken Dylan and Suzanne up on their offer.

The dingy linoleum floor seemed even dirtier by the light of the greenish bulb overhead than it had during the day. Rebecca could not help but notice the dead fly on the tiny windowsill and a fine layer of sand on the bedspreads when she touched them. She heard muffled giggles coming from Kate and Jeff's room as she pulled back the covers to inspect the sheets. She decided to try some affirmations from the book. *These sheets are clean, they are just a little dusty, and beach houses have sand everywhere. Sand won't hurt me. Dust won't hurt me. Facing my discomfort will only make me stronger.*

She slipped into her pajamas, trying to focus on how tired she was. How quickly she would fall asleep. "Facing my discomfort will only make me stronger," she said softly. She turned off the light and promptly hit her head on the top bunk as she climbed into bed. The sheets were clean, but they still had the faint musty odor of neglect in a humid place. Rebecca closed her eyes and inhaled deeply. "In a few minutes, I won't even notice the smell. Facing my discomfort will make me stronger."

Through the wall next to her, Rebecca heard Kate and Jeff murmuring to one another, with occasional laughter interspersed. "I am alone, but I am not lonely," she said. Soon, the talking died down and in its place she heard the telltale rhythmic groan of bedsprings. *Oh, no. Please don't let this go on for long.* Soon, she heard panting and soft moaning accompanying the sounds of the bed. She held the pillow over her ears, but the sounds grew louder and higher pitched. She could not help but notice that Kate seemed to really be enjoying herself, which struck Rebecca as funny.

During the day, Kate seemed demure almost to the point of mousiness, but there was nothing demure about the noises she was making now. In spite of herself, Rebecca smiled, wondering what kind of lover Jeff really was. Gentle? Passionate? She had only ever seen Jeff laughing and joking and being a bit crass. It was hard to imagine him with the serious face of someone consumed by passion. Despite trying her best to tune them out, and feeling slightly repulsed that she was overhearing something so intimate, Rebecca began to feel a familiar tightening in her lower belly. Desire. But for whom? Her hand traveled beneath her pajamas and skimmed the top of her panties.

Ugh. What was she doing? She got up from the bed and turned on the light, searching for the earplugs she kept in her bag at all times. She spent half her life at airport hotels, and the earplugs were indispensable. She found them, her hand grazing the purple velvet bag as she retrieved them.

She turned back toward the bed and flicked off the light. As if on cue, she now heard talking from the room on the other side. Jake and Marci were louder, though thankfully it sounded more like arguing than anything else. Were they arguing? She stood and removed the earplugs. A little ashamed of eavesdropping, she listened anyway, trying to catch what was said. She could only make out tone, and thought maybe Jake was reprimanding Marci for something. Marci sounded defiant at first, and then softened.

Meanwhile, Kate squealed rather loudly and Jeff moaned audibly. There was a rhythmic banging sound that must be their headboard hitting the wall. This was unbearable.

She put the earplugs in and got back into bed. Now she could only hear the banging sound, and she shuddered at the thought that children might stay in this room on family vacations while their parents were getting it on next door. *What I Learned on My Summer Vacation.*

Rebecca tried to sleep, but to no avail. Kate and Jeff quieted for a few minutes, during which Rebecca took the earplugs out again and strained to hear what was going on in Jake and Marci's room. Just as she began picking up a stray word here and there — "baby," "our life," and something she was fairly sure was "manipulated" — Kate began to giggle in the other room, and the sounds of passion started anew on the right side. Rebecca put the earplugs back in, this time adding the pillow over her head for good measure, and tried to think about the travel schedule to and from Cincinnati. And then San Diego, New York–LaGuardia, and Seattle. She forced herself to visualize the schedules in front of her, numbers swimming in and out of her mind's eye as she tossed and turned and squeezed the pillow over her head.

Nothing helped. The high-pitched breathy sounds found their way to her ears no matter how she tried to drown them out. And despite her best efforts to think of anything else, her body began to ache and throb without her permission. *Are they making a porno in there or something?* Rebecca knew she would never look at little Kate the same way again, and she was glad for Jeff's sake that his brother-in-law's room was all the way across the house, or he might be out of a job for what he was doing to Dylan's little sister.

Rebecca could not remember the last time anyone had made her feel the way Kate sounded right now. Maybe it had never happened at all. She had dated men, of course, and even had a few relationships that lasted several months. And like nearly everyone in the airline industry, she had to own up to a couple of careless nights with charming pilots and men she'd met in bars. But no one had ever inspired that kind of *abandon*. She had never been a wild girl, and always preferred what she assumed was pretty standard sex. She liked the feel of a man on top of her, in a dark, quiet room. She liked the lights off and the covers up, and soft, hot breath in her ear. Even *that* had been months ago at this point, the last time anyone had touched her at all. Her pulsing ache deepened, grew more insistent.

She stood up, breathless. The purple velvet bag burned out of her suitcase in the corner as though it were on fire. "No," she said softly, feeling giddy just at the thought of it. "Not here."

But why not?

As she paced in the tiny room, she could now hear that Jake and Marci had lowered their voices, and while the sound was muffled, it was clear from the location that they were now in bed, too. *Just leave, Rebecca. Go to a hotel. Does your self-torture know no bounds? Do you have to picture him naked with her?*

Suddenly she saw him, not with Marci, but back in Athens. He was twenty years old or so, peeling off a sweaty T-shirt after basketball in the intramural gym. Rebecca did not remember now why it had been only she waiting for him after his game — they were headed to some event that had long ago faded in her memory. But she could still feel the bleachers pressing into the back of her thighs as she'd watched him play — wholesome and strong and vigorous. And when he leaned bare chested toward her to throw the soggy shirt into his bag, he had given her a sheepish grin that made his perfect body even more . . .

To hell with it. Rebecca stormed over to her suitcase, flung it open, and retrieved the bag. She held it in her hand, weighing it for balance the way she imagined knights had once done with fine swords.

Why not? she thought again. "Why shouldn't I have a good time, too?" she said out loud, at her normal speaking volume. "It's not like they can hear me," she said a little louder, and waited.

Apparently they could not, because the sounds of lovers in stereo continued on either side of her walls unabated. She considered the thing in her hand, feeling a little aroused and mostly ridiculous. Did women really use these? She knew girls at work who had funny nicknames for their vibrators, and who had no more shame about them than they did a hair dryer. The one Valerie had bought her, the Goddess 3500X, was a rubbery facsimile of a penis (except translucent and hot pink instead of flesh colored) attached to a base of lavender plastic with several buttons and dials. If she held it upright, it looked like an obscene little statue on a plastic plinth.

She paused once more to listen, and it was now clear Jake and Marci were doing more than talking. She looked at the Goddess. "It's either this," she said, "or go sleep on the beach."

Rebecca was not sure what all the buttons and dials did, but she figured out how to make it vibrate, and then discovered that it also spun in wiggly circles on the base, like a short, angry snake trapped in a hot-pink grocery bag. She repressed a giggle, turned off the light, and retreated to the bottom bunk. The buttons glowed! Someone had put thought into engineering this thing. She piled the comforter and every pillow in the room over her midsection to muffle the sound. The extra weight of the covers made it hard to maneuver the rubbery toy under the sheets, but eventually she worked her panties down to her knees and got it into what she assumed was the right position. She turned it on, tentatively trying different buttons and dials until it seemed to be just vibrating.

At first, she barely touched it to the skin over her pubic bone, feeling totally absurd. She stopped and started a few times, nervous but intrigued. And aroused. It was foreign and strange against her body. After a moment or two, though, the vibrations tingled across her lower body. She began to relax, and then, even more. Soon she had abandoned herself to it, and the idea that someone might overhear and come bursting in only added to the excitement. *So this is why all those girls love these things.*

Rebecca slowly began to let her mind wander until it landed on a familiar video montage — there was Jake playing basketball, Jake helping her out of a car somewhere and the way his hand gripped hers just for a moment, Jake tonight on the beach with his hand on her shoulder, and of course, the night four years ago when he had allowed himself to melt beneath her kiss. It had only been a kiss, one tiny moment. She had left his apartment minutes later, dejected and alone.

But in her imagination, there was so much more. Rebecca had a hundred fantasies with that kiss on Jake's couch four years ago as a starting point. And they all ended with her wrapped in Jake's strong, bare arms. Exhausted, happy, and, most of all, safe.

Tonight, however, Rebecca had barely gotten to the good part when she felt herself begin to climax against the weird little machine. It was intense, maybe too much so. She fumbled for the dials to reduce the vibration but just got the squirmy thing instead. Before she knew it, there were fireworks all over again.

Except that she *really was* hearing fire-works, she realized. They were crackling overhead, and no sooner had Rebecca noticed them than there was an enormous explosion right over the house, a boom like thunder. She fumbled with the Goddess's buttons and dials but could not turn the thing off. Meanwhile, the loud noise had interrupted the couples on either side of her, whatever they'd been doing when she was no longer listening. She could hear movement as people got out of bed and came out of the bedrooms. She heard conversation in the hall.

"What was that? Kids, you think?" The sliding glass door opened to the deck.

Rebecca pulled the vibrator up above the covers, still trying without success to find the power button. She figured out how to slow the vibration but it was still making noise. Maybe even louder. Then light appeared under the door and she heard Marci and Kate talking in the hall.

"That really was loud."

"Yeah, what do you think? Maybe some teenagers or drunk college kids with bad aim?"

"Probably. Why fireworks tonight, though?"

"I know — it's not the Fourth of July yet.

Don't they know people are sleeping?"

"Well, not exactly sleeping yet, but close."

A slight chuckle. Awkward silence.

"Do you hear that?"

"What?"

"It's like a buzzing sound."

Oh, God. Rebecca frantically hit every button on the damn thing, and none of them turned it off.

"No, I don't — wait, yeah."

"It sounds like an electric razor or . . . or something. Could somebody be mowing grass this late?"

"I don't think so. Do you think the fireworks hit something, like on the roof, or a power line?"

"I guess. Maybe. But that really doesn't make sense. It sounds like —"

At this point, Rebecca was struggling blindly to get the thing open to simply take out the batteries, but of course, that wouldn't budge either. *I am going to kill Valerie,* she thought. She forced herself to get out of bed, the Goddess in hand. She could think of no other options; it was clear everyone in the house was up, and they would not believe she had slept through the noise of the fireworks, especially with people talking outside her door. She reached for one of the higher baskets on the little bookshelf and tossed the vibrator inside, hoping the sound would be muffled, and then flipped on her light. She buried the velvet bag in her suitcase and grabbed a thin robe at the same time, and then emerged into the hallway, trying to look sleepy and bleary-eyed in the light. She heard Beth's soft snores on the couch and wished she had faked sleep.

"What was that noise?" she said, somewhat convincingly.

"Which one?" Marci said with the trace of a smile.

Thankfully, the guys emerged from the back deck at that moment. "Yep, just a bunch of drunk kids," Jeff announced. "Did Dylan and Suzanne come out?"

"No," Kate said, grinning. "I guess they're assuming we'll come get them in an emergency. Since this is not an emergency, however . . ." She took Jeff's hand and led him back to their bedroom, shooting an impish look over her shoulder as she went through the door.

Now alone with Jake and Marci, Rebecca was beyond uncomfortable. She tugged at her robe, which was already closed, trying to cover herself more.

"Cold?" Jake asked. Then before she could answer, he said, "What is that sound?"

Rebecca tried to look around so that he and Marci wouldn't see that she was now bright red. "Do you hear it, babe?" he said to Marci. "Like a weird kind of buzzing?"

"Oh, that?" Marci said, tossing a glance at Rebecca. "That's just the power lines or something. We heard it last night, too. The landlord says it's normal."

"Normal," Rebecca echoed. She thought there was still a question on Jake's face, but he allowed his wife to lead him back to their room, and Rebecca nearly collapsed in humiliation and relief.

She went back into her tiny cell and stared at the vibrating basket on the bookshelf, regretting ever taking the damn thing out of the bag. When the conversation seemed to have died down in the other rooms, she retrieved the vibrator and located the power button. She had not been imagining things after all. It didn't work. So she pushed, cursing, on the battery panel until it came off its hinges with a snap of breaking plastic. Only then did she notice a tiny release lever on the bottom, now cracked from her efforts. Thankfully, she did not hear any reaction to the end of the buzzing in the other rooms.

For a few minutes, she lay on the bottom bunk, tossing and turning as the house grew quiet around her. She checked her phone — it was 3:45, the time she normally had to get up on workdays, and she could feel her body's energy rising as she lay there. Three years of training for early starts were overriding how tired she felt now. In a way, Rebecca wished she were going back to work today, instead of Tuesday. Between the obnoxiously happy couples flanking her tiny room and tonight's humiliation, there seemed little to look forward to with sunrise and morning coffee.

Rebecca flung the covers off, felt around on the sandy floor for her slippers, and padded to the light switch. It took her only a few minutes to pack and scrawl a note for her friends. "Work called — sorry — catch you guys later!" She sneaked past the sleeping Beth on the couch and was out the front door. She found a cab company on her smartphone and within half an hour, she was sitting in a relatively clean, coconut-scented backseat on the way to the airport. She called the Charleston flight desk and wheedled her way onto the standby list for a five-thirty flight to Atlanta, and then stared out the window at the inky black, dotted with yellow mercury streetlights. It was the same view she'd had on the drive to the beach house with Marci, two nights before.

9

Hours later, Rebecca was walking through the D terminal at Hartsfield-Jackson Airport in Atlanta, wondering what she would do with a couple of free days all to herself, when she remembered the call from her mother. She rode down the escalator and boarded the tram behind a group of teenagers in matching tracksuits before pulling out her phone to see if her mother had called again. She had not. A little surprising, but maybe, Rebecca told herself, the mistake had been cleared up. Maybe Daddy had called the power company and sorted things out. Or perhaps it had not been the power company but just a mortgage payment that got misdirected. Rebecca had heard a horrible news story about a family whose house had been foreclosed because the bank had been applying their loan payments to the wrong account. But surely this would not be the case? Daddy would definitely know. At least, as long as he had been able to disconnect himself from Sonia long enough to pay attention.

"She doesn't need me," Rebecca whispered. "She's fine."

One of the tracksuit kids glanced up at Rebecca, who gave an embarrassed smile in return. She rode back to the main terminal in silence and wheeled her carry-on to the restroom, checking her makeup and washing her hands even though she had not used the stall. She looked in the mirror. "You are entitled to live your own life. Your family's problems do not have to become yours."

But before she was even finished saying the words, she knew they were as hollow and empty as the industrial tile walls around her. She exited the bathroom, waited for the shuttle to her car, and waved her employee pass at the exit gate. The blue interstate signs for the 75/85 connector pointed home to her quiet apartment, soft clean bed, and forty-eight hours of rest before she had to be back here for work.

It was no use. She followed the frontage road around to the signs pointing toward I-285 and then I-20 West. Toward Birmingham, Oreville, and the sinkhole that had once been her whole wide world.

■ ■ ■ ■

Her phone buzzed loudly at ten thirty, breaking her out of an interstate reverie just as she crossed into Alabama and the Central Time Zone. Jake's name flashed up at her from the passenger's seat, and her cheeks burned. For once, she could not bring herself to answer his call. Either she'd forgotten something, which was unlikely, or he didn't believe she'd been called in to work. Maybe no one else did either. She would need to excuse herself; at some point she would have to explain, but not yet. It was all too fresh and confusing.

As miles and miles of I-20 slipped unchanging beneath her Honda Civic, her mind drifted back to Jake and that night four years ago. They had been sitting on the couch together in his apartment, just the two of them. Rebecca had been unbelievably nervous but Jake seemed not to notice, since he was busy grieving for what seemed to be his lost relationship with Marci. He was nursing a bottle of Scotch, and she, her ever-constant desire for him. They were watching *The Philadelphia Story.* Rebecca had known he was in mourning, and that at best she would be his second choice. But he had looked so vulnerable and sad that night, the cloud of anger on his face making him look tortured and — if it was possible — even sexier. His cheeks had been ruddy with booze and the effort of holding back tears, his breath sticky sweet, and his hands lay lifeless on either side of his lap. It was so sad. And so strangely inviting.

She followed the impulse without thinking, downing the rest of her Scotch in one fiery gulp and hoisting herself onto his lap. She stroked his hair somewhat tentatively and he smiled weakly at her. Behind her, the credits were rolling. "It's over," she said softly.

"Yes, it is," he had said. "I think it really is."

Rebecca had leaned forward then, and kissed him. Lightly at first, testing. This was dangerous ground. But then Jake Stillwell had done what she had not dared to hope. He had leaned forward, not to push her away, but to pull her toward him. He had put one hand on the back of her head and the other around her waist, kissing her with desperation, which Rebecca allowed herself to pretend had everything to do with her. He moved one hand beneath her shirt and stroked her bare back, giving her goose bumps. It was this sensation Rebecca had replayed over and over in both memory and fantasy ever since.

In real life, that's where it had ended. "I can't," he'd said, pushing her gently aside and stumbling to his bedroom to close the door without another word. In real life, she had turned off the TV and stared panting into the darkness of his apartment before eventually letting herself out. In real life, he was back with Marci a few months later, and he and Rebecca had never spoken of that moment again.

10

It was after noon when Rebecca pulled into the gravel driveway of the white cinder block house where she had grown up. A quick glance at her cell phone confirmed that there were four voicemails waiting for her. She had put the phone on silent after ignoring the first call from Jake, and she could only assume the others were from some combination of Suzanne, Marci, and Beth. Of course they hadn't believed her note. Who would?

Still, she couldn't deal with the questions now. Not yet. There was too much to explain about the house in front of her, and the woman who lived there. It had been years since she had visited, she realized with shame, and the house seemed smaller than she remembered. The green painted shutters were faded and peeling, and the yard grew high with weeds. There were red-and-black NO TRESPASSING signs nailed to a couple of the trees of what used to be a welcoming, homey yard. Who had posted those? How had her father let the house get this way?

Her mother's old beige Ford Taurus was parked in its usual spot. Rebecca parked behind it and went to the front door. It was still there, the paper her mother had mentioned: bright yellow with official-looking type. NOTICE OF EVICTION. St. Clair County Health Department. Rebecca knocked on the door as she scanned it. *Dear Mrs. Williamson . . . third notice . . . unsanitary conditions . . . multiple violations.* There was no answer at the door. Rebecca knocked again, louder.

"Mama?" she called at the front-room window. "You there?"

The house was dark and silent. Rebecca walked around back, reaching for the rickety screen door to the back porch and finding it locked, too. There was a strong smell of cat urine coming from the back porch. Rebecca wondered how long it had been since the litter was changed. There had been just one old family cat, Harold, when she moved away during high school, but her mother had acquired a few more after poor Harold died. There were often strays roaming up and down this road out of town, and her mother had a soft heart. The last time Rebecca had visited, there had been three cats in residence. She wondered if Mama had found even more since then.

She called again without hearing an answer, and thought about walking across the street to Mrs. Pindergrass's house, in case her mother had walked over there. But there were no cars in the neat driveway facing theirs, and an ominous feeling told her that her mother had not gone on a neighborly visit. For a split second, she considered getting back in the car and heading home to Atlanta. She could be in her apartment and asleep under the covers in three hours flat. Rebecca went back to the car, but instead of getting in, she sighed and unlaced her sandals, tossing them into her suitcase and pulling out canvas tennis shoes instead.

The key was still hidden in the same spot, tucked in a hollow knot of the big oak tree on the side of the house — where she and Cory had had a tire swing as kids. The crevice was damp and mossy, and the key a little rusty, but she found it easily after she had hoisted herself up onto one of the lower branches. When she brought it down, there was moss and bark wedged beneath the nails on her right hand. *What a waste of a manicure.*

The front door was hard to open; once she accomplished it and flicked on a light, she immediately saw why. "Oh, God, Mama."

There were cardboard boxes piled high in the front hallway, hiding what had once been her mother's cherished pink carpet and blocking the door from opening fully. Beyond the boxes were more piles: newspapers, garbage bags, plastic totes, old blankets. Some of them were recognizable — old floral patterns she remembered from childhood. Others were new to her but looked worn and frayed nonetheless. There were also clothes, everywhere. Kids' clothes, piles of jeans, suits still in dry cleaning bags.

There was only a sliver of path from the front door to the kitchen, off to the left, and no path at all into the living room on her right. From what she could see of the living room, it was also full of boxes and bags and papers, piled high and perched precariously on top of furniture. Her grandmother's antique sofa was barely visible beneath the mess, and as she stared at it, a monstrous black cockroach skittered along its soft green cushion to hide itself under a produce box.

But the worst thing, by far, was the smell. There was the same overpowering odor of cat urine she had experienced on the back porch, along with a sour rotten smell like old meat and a sickly sweet note of molded honey — a smell that immediately made Rebecca think of rodents. For a horrifying moment, she thought perhaps her mother had died in the house and was rotting away in another room. Then she remembered that she had spoken to her only the day before.

"Oh, God," she said again, and spun on her heel, bolting back out the front door without bothering to close it. She ran to the bushes on the side of the house and vomited, falling to her knees on the soft earth before realizing that the unmaintained grass all around her was the perfect hideout for rats, snakes, and God knew what else. She wiped her mouth and stood quickly. Her heart raced and her chest tightened. The familiar sensation of panic overtook her — and suddenly every blade of grass felt like the brush of scales or fur or claws against her bare legs. She ran for the open car door, slamming herself in and staring ahead at the old storage shed in front of Mama's car. Rebecca could only imagine what horrors might await in there.

She wanted desperately to cry, but the tears would not come. Her body was brimming with fear and exhaustion, leaving no room for the sadness she knew she should be feeling. Where was her mother? How had the house gotten this way? How could Daddy have let this happen? What the hell was she supposed to do now?

Rebecca gripped the steering wheel and let out an exasperated sound, half moan, half scream. It was an ugly noise but it helped. Some of the panic seemed to be venting itself with each scream, so she continued, slamming her fists into the steering wheel and dashboard for effect. After a couple of minutes, she stopped and stared lifelessly at the back of her mother's abandoned car, having no idea whatsoever what to do next. Absurdly, she thought of her friends at the beach, wondering what they were doing now and whether they were sad or relieved that she had excused herself from their party. In her mind's eye, she saw Marci, laughing with her hand on Jake's arm, and this only made her more miserable.

A sharp rap on the window startled her out of the daydream. Her hand flew out instinctively and locked the doors. She saw a shadowed face beneath a wide-brimmed hat, and finally, once her eyes could focus on it, the starched khaki uniform of a sheriff's deputy. He motioned for her to roll down the window, but with her heart still pounding in her ears, she was nervous. She looked at his name tag. A. CHEN. A quick assessment of his face revealed an imposing cleft chin and serious expression highlighted by soft wrinkles around his mouth and eyes. But the eyes themselves seemed friendly enough, dark brown and more curious than menacing. She rolled the window down partway.

"Ms. Williamson?" he asked. She nodded. "I'm sorry if I scared you. I tried to make noise as I came up, but you were . . . well, you were sort of screaming. You okay?"

His thick, woodsy accent reflected Alabama dirt roads and fishing holes. When she heard it, she was embarrassed to discover she'd been expecting an Asian accent based on his name and features. She nodded again. "I'm fine."

He nodded in return. "Your mama isn't here," he said. "But I reckon you realized that."

"Yes, I — I went inside," she said. She wondered what he was doing here. Apparently he knew something about her mother. "Is she okay?"

"Yes, ma'am, far as I know," he said. "She's up at the county hospital today. Think they have her pretty well sedated. I expect they'll be calling you soon. I was here yesterday when we brought her in, so when the neighbors called in about the disturb—I mean, the neighbors called to say you were here, I figured I'd come out and talk to you myself. I was on my way home anyway."

"Thanks," Rebecca found herself saying, though she wasn't exactly sure what she was thanking him for. "You said you were here? What happened?"

He straightened and moved back a half step. "Do you wanna get out so we can talk? I mean, not that I mind talking to you through the window, but . . ." Rebecca fumbled for the lock as he said, "I promise not to arrest you or anything."

She got out of the car, and they stood awkwardly for a moment, sizing each other up. Finally he said, "Rebecca, right? You don't remember me, I bet."

Dear God. Even at the best of times, Rebecca hated trying to place people from memory, and it was the last thing she wanted to do in the current situation. "Sorry," she said flatly. "I don't."

"I didn't think so," he said. "Alex Chen. I was a couple years older than you, so you probably didn't pay any attention to me in high school. But I . . . I played football with your brother. I remember you used to come watch our practices. 'Course, you were just a skinny little thing then."

"Oh," she said softly. He seemed to be searching her face for something, and she shifted uncomfortably. "So . . . my mother?"

"Right," he said, glancing at the open front door. "Well, I guess you probably saw the inside of the house. I don't know if you've been home much, but it's been getting worse over the last couple of years. Lots of complaints from the neighbors, especially on hot days. The smell —"

"I live in Atlanta," she said, cutting him off. "Home is Atlanta."

"Of course," he said, smiling. "Fun town. Went over there for a bowl game last year."

Rebecca decided the best way to get him to get to the point was to keep her own mouth shut. After a pause, he did go on. "So anyway, the health department finally had to serve her an eviction notice. They gave her lots of warnings, I think. Don't know if she told you?"

Of course not, Rebecca thought. *She's only my mother.*

She said nothing. He went on. "By this weekend, things had not gotten any better — your mama had more than twenty cats in there, some of 'em not too healthy — and we had to come get her. We were sup-

119

posed to take her over to the Super 8 so she could get a room, but she wasn't too happy to go. Anyway, she went a little . . . she got kind of violent. Scratched Deputy Davis up pretty good, right under the eye. Technically that's assaulting an officer, you know, but we all felt kinda bad for her. We called Judge Parker and had her put your mom under a seventy-two-hour psychiatric hold instead. That's why she's at the county hospital now, but if you want my advice, I think you're going to want to move her somewhere else for a while. I'm not a doctor, but I think your mom needs more help than she's going to get in three days at County."

"Thank you for your opinion," Rebecca said coldly. She knew the deputy was intending to be kind, but something about the familiar and sympathetic way he talked to her made her feel infuriated. *You don't know me; you don't know my family,* she thought. "Is there anything else?"

He only looked taken aback by her rudeness for a second. "Well, you can't stay here," he said. "I'm sure you wouldn't want to, but I feel like I should tell you. It'll have to be cleaned out and reinspected first."

"Of course," she said stiffly.

"I don't know if you'd be staying with your dad or not, but the Super 8 has decent rooms. Clean."

"Thank you," she said numbly. She turned back toward her car, not knowing what she was going to do next, only that she couldn't go back in that house right now.

"No problem," he said. "It was nice to see you again, Rebecca. Take care."

Before she could reply, his boots were crunching across the gravel driveway back to his patrol car. She watched him drive away, trying to remember a younger version of his face from high school. Like everything else from that part of her life, it was blank. Just blank.

11

Rebecca checked in to the Super 8 as Deputy Chen had suggested. She left a message for her dad and stripped the dated bedspread from the bed before sprawling across the sheets. She got the number for the county hospital from information, only to discover that visiting hours would be ending in less than half an hour and that they would not provide any information without a signed release from her mother. The nurse would technically not acknowledge that her mom was even a patient there, but suggested gently that Rebecca drop by when visiting hours began again at nine the next morning.

After that, Rebecca stared at her phone, wanting to reach out to someone but not knowing whom to call. She listened to the concerned messages from the beach — the first and the last were from Jake, his voice thick with concern. She felt bad about that, but she still didn't know what to say. The other two were from Marci and Suzanne, both sounding chipper but curious and asking her to call when she got off tonight. *Doubtful,* Rebecca thought. *Soon, but not today.*

She dialed Valerie, realizing as it went straight to voicemail that she would be in the air now. Rebecca left a short, awkward message. It felt as though the whole world were continuing on without her as she sat, helpless and alone, in a motel in rural Alabama. Atlanta felt thousands of miles away. Her life felt far, far away. She threw an arm over her face and tried to practice breathing with the techniques *Calm Your Mind* suggested.

She awoke to darkness hours later. Her stomach growled menacingly, and Rebecca fumbled for her phone, remembering she had not eaten since an early lunch on her way from Atlanta. It was now almost nine. Her body ached from the car ride over and the long, dead sleep in one position on the hotel bed. She pulled herself up, found the light switch, and went to her suitcase. Rebecca had not been back to her apartment since starting her last airline shift five days ago, before the trip to Kiawah Island, and her clothes showed it. She'd been wearing the same jeans since four o'clock this morning. In her suitcase she had her work uniforms, a sandy bathing suit, the wrinkled dress she'd worn at Suzanne and Dylan's wedding, and a pair of white shorts with a large crimson stain where Beth had spilled wine on her. She was wearing her last pair of underwear.

She washed her face, reapplied her smeared makeup, and went to the front desk. A tiny older woman with long gray hair and what must have once been a tattoo of a butterfly on her upper arm gave her directions to Walmart. She also informed Rebecca that the two best options for a late dinner were a sports bar on the edge of town and, of course, the Waffle House next door to the motel. Rebecca thanked her and set out.

She made it to Walmart five minutes before closing, enduring the glares of annoyed cashiers and staff as she zipped past them to the clothing area. With no time to try anything on and not many options available, she grabbed two pairs of inexpensive jeans, an Auburn University T-shirt, and a pack of granny panties. Normally she triple-sanitized new underwear before putting it on, but she decided that since these came in a sealed package it was unlikely they were contaminated.

She paid for the clothes and changed in the restroom — she was too hungry to go back to her hotel room before dinner. Waffle House was a safe choice, she thought, but as she passed by the signature yellow-and-black sign, she could not bring herself to pull into the parking lot. There was something about the glare of the lights and the harsh Formica tables that she couldn't stomach tonight. And she needed a drink.

Dickie's sports bar was on the edge of town, almost halfway to Gadsden on the quiet two-lane highway. A few miles farther and she guessed she might be able to locate some sort of suburban chain restaurant, with fatty appetizers and a predictable grilled chicken sandwich on the menu, but she had no idea how late they would be open, and she was too famished to take chances. She pulled into the gravel drive from the highway, following a blinking arrow sign with crooked letters: WELCOME TO DICKIE S KAR OKE SUNDAY. *Just what I need,* she thought darkly. There were a few beat-up cars and pickup trucks in the parking lot behind the building. Maybe, hopefully, Karaoke Sundays were not a big draw.

Inside, the bar was a little smoky, but homey enough. There was light oak paneling on the walls and booths, and vintage neon beer signs everywhere. NASCAR drivers and country singers grinned or smoldered at her from every wall, depending on the mood their particular poster was trying to convey. The floor even boasted a little sawdust and many, many peanut shells.

On the far wall, there was a rickety wooden stage big enough for two or three singers, or maybe two guitars. A single spotlight shone weakly on a rolled-up microphone, which sat idle on top of an amplifier. Relieved, Rebecca steered herself toward the bar, where a sullen girl in a forest-green Dickie's T-shirt and long ponytail glared at her.

"Do I just sit anywhere?" Rebecca asked.

The girl made a show of looking all around the bar and the thirty or so empty tables before responding. "You got a reservation?"

With effort, Rebecca attempted to laugh off the rudeness. "Okay, then, I'll just be over here." She gestured to a corner booth as far away from the stage as possible. "Do you have a menu?"

Another eye roll, and the girl had retrieved a stained page of cream-colored card stock with about twenty items listed in a simple, centered font. She thrust it into Rebecca's hands with a perfunctory, "I'll be right with you."

Rebecca tried a winning smile and a thank you that dripped with honeyed courtesy. The girl was not to be won over, however, and she spun on her heel to attend to a couple of large men at the other end of the bar. *Why can I never seem to be charming?* It worked so well for Suzanne. Suze could wheedle anything out of just about anyone — male or female — with a graceful smile and an effortless word. Rebecca had studied her for years and tried her best to emulate her style, but to no avail. Even in the air, she could handle nearly any flight situation, but she did not have the gift for disarming angry customers or plying coworkers for favors, the way Valerie and others seemed to.

She made her way to the booth in the back, focusing on what she would order if the girl ever came over. She debated a salad, her usual choice, but decided that a place like this was more likely to offer her wilted iceberg lettuce with stale croutons and a gallon of ranch dressing than anything with nutritional value. Besides, she was starving. She settled on Buffalo wings with celery and carrots and a bottle of Bud Light. This seemed to meet with the tacit approval of the scowling waitress, who at least did not roll her eyes when Rebecca ordered.

The food arrived quickly and the waitress included a large stack of napkins. Rebecca used the hand sanitizer in her purse to convert one of these to a wet wipe for the surface of the table, which had several names and even a few vulgar limericks carved into it. As she ate, she tried to figure out what her plan would be for the next day. She had felt disconnected from her family for so long. It was strange to be thrust back into Oreville under these circumstances, and even stranger to feel that she was supposed to take charge of the situation somehow.

Rebecca nibbled at the remnants of the last wing and debated ordering another basket. She had to admit they were good, especially for a hole-in-the-wall in the middle of nowhere, Alabama. A few more people had begun filing in while she ate — a group of men in fishing vests and muddy boots, some kids in their early twenties dressed in khakis and matching blue polos, and a few stray women in tight jeans and low-cut tops accompanied by guys in various shades of button-up plaid.

When Rebecca was growing up, the town had hardly been able to support the weekend dance hall that only served soda and doubled as a senior activity center during the day. She wasn't sure how long Dickie's had been around, but it seemed pretty popular, even on a Sunday night. They had turned up some music — country, of course; she even saw a cowboy hat and boots glide by the booth next to hers.

She ordered another beer, having nowhere to go and entirely too much energy for ten o'clock at night. This time a young guy in a tight black Dickie's T-shirt took her order. She saw the scowling waitress mount the stage across the bar and drawl into the mike with a sudden enthusiasm, "Hey y'all — it's time to get going on the third qualifying round of our karaoke tournament. Everybody get your ballots up at the bar if Kevin hasn't brought 'em to you yet — remember you can only vote for three singers, and no voting twice for the same person. Even you, Miss Jeanie — we know your hand, so you can only vote for Matthew once."

With this last comment, the waitress leaned toward a spiky-haired woman seated at one of the front tables with a younger man who must have been her son. The comment was met with laughter and a scatter of applause.

The waitress smirked and went back to

her announcements. "All right, let's kick it off with last year's regional champ, our very own Alex Chen!"

Rebecca's breath caught in her throat as the very same deputy who had been in her mother's driveway earlier that day took the stage at a hop. He accepted the microphone from the waitress, who whispered something in his ear before stepping down off the stage. It was the same guy; it had to be. For one thing, there were probably a total of ten Asian men in a fifty-mile radius of this town, and for two of them to be named Alex Chen was way too much of a coincidence. Also, she recognized his boots: the same dark leather ones he'd been wearing earlier. Though now instead of the pressed khaki of the sheriff's department, he wore broken-in jeans and a flannel shirt with a respectable white undershirt, making him look more ruddy and tan than she had noticed earlier.

Near the stage, a group of guys in cowboy hats and girls in halter tops were catcalling and whooping at him. Alex grinned at them and began to sing a lively version of "Santeria" by Sublime. Rebecca had to admit, he wasn't bad. By the time he was halfway into the song, people had begun to clap in rhythm along with him. As he danced and sang his way through the final verse, the entire place was clapping. He could sing, but that wasn't it. There was something about him — his smile, maybe — that just made you want to root for him.

He jumped down from the stage when the song ended, waving away the applause with a gesture, and sat down to join his friends. A couple of the guys clapped him on the back and a girl with spiky reddish-brown hair streaked in blond handed him a beer in a plastic cup. Next up was a middle-aged man with a sandy beard and large beer belly, which was held in by a belt buckle the size of a dessert plate in the shape of the number three. Rebecca was surprised when he broke into a very tender version of "Bridge Over Troubled Water."

Sitting alone in a bar where she knew almost no one, Rebecca found it hard to keep from watching the deputy. He laughed and traded draft beer salutes with the people around him, one or two of whom looked familiar to Rebecca. She assumed they had also gone to high school together — probably with her brother, since she didn't recognize any of them as members of her own class. Then again, she had never been particularly close with anyone in high school. She tried again to remember, without staring, what Alex had looked like back then. In this case, it was helpful that there had been only one Asian family in town. David Chen had been in Rebecca's class — that had to be Alex's younger brother or maybe a cousin. She didn't remember David being so outgoing and personable, though. Or so attractive.

She shook her head and looked down at her nearly empty wings basket. She fished the last piece of limp celery out of a puddle of hot sauce and nibbled it uncertainly. *This is not a fun visit,* she reminded herself. *I have to figure out what to do with my mom. And besides . . .*

Rebecca remembered the pitying look on Deputy Chen's face as he tried to get her to roll down the car window earlier this afternoon and told her about her mother's situation. The idea of sneaking out the Dickie's side door came to mind. But soon the kid in the tight black T-shirt had brought her the second beer. "Did you want a list?"

"A list?"

"Songs," he said. He gestured toward the stage. "In case you want to sing?"

"Oh, God. No, thank you."

The guy shrugged and walked away. Rebecca did not even have a chance to ask him for the bill. She glanced across the room at Alex, who suddenly seemed to feel her eyes on him. He smiled broadly and waved at her, and then turned to say something to one of his buddies, a pasty guy in a cowboy hat with wobbly jowls, who turned to look at her, too.

Great. *That's the crazy girl, you know, the cat lady's daughter.* She wondered if Daughter of the Cat Lady would soon replace Poor Cory Williamson's Sister as her label in this little town. Not exactly a promotion.

She stared into her beer bottle, thinking irrationally that it had something floating in it, and when she looked up, Alex was on his way over to her table. *Too late to run away now.*

"Hey," he said, sliding into the seat across from her without an invitation. "How you holding up?"

"Did it ever occur to you," Rebecca said haughtily, "that maybe I don't want to discuss my personal family business with a total stranger?"

Deputy Chen's smile did not waver. "I'm not a total stranger. You may not remember me from high school, but I remember you."

"I know," Rebecca said. "Cory's Little Sister."

"Not just that," he said. "Anyway, I didn't mean to intrude on your personal business. My apologies."

"No problem," she said, hoping he might get up and walk back to his friends.

"So let's talk about something else. What are you singing tonight?"

"Oh, no. No, no, no. I do not sing. I can't." It was true. She was a terrible singer. Even her roommates had gently asked her to stop singing in the shower junior year.

"Everyone can sing," Alex said.

"I hate that expression. People say it all the time, but I know for a fact it isn't true. I'm living proof."

"I doubt that," he said. He was looking at her in a sort of appraising way, like he was sizing her up.

"So how long have you been a police officer?" she asked, changing the subject.

"I'm a sheriff's deputy," he corrected. "About ten years, off and on."

"Wow. That's kind of a dangerous job."

He shrugged. "It can be, for sure. But this isn't exactly downtown Atlanta. Around here, a couple of people drive off without paying for gas or hunt deer without a license and it's a crime wave."

Rebecca sensed he was downplaying the seriousness of his job, but she didn't press him. She remembered the kind Atlanta PD officer, Bonita, who had helped Suzanne so much the year before, and had been killed by a drunk driver while making a routine traffic stop.

He signaled the boy in the tight T-shirt. "Now your job is kinda dangerous, too, right? Kevin, can you get me another round, please, and one for the lady?"

"No thanks," she said to Kevin. "How do you know about my job?"

Alex smiled, a little sheepish. "Your dad's really proud of you. He and I go fishing together once in a while."

"You do?" How did she not know this?

"Yeah," he said. "Well, not so much since he and Sonia . . ."

He trailed off. Rebecca shifted in her seat. Apparently there were no secrets in this town, at least where her family was concerned. "Ugh," she said. "It's so embarrassing. Are they — are we — the town laughingstocks or something?"

Alex laughed. "Hardly. People do some embarrassing shit in this town. My dad and my uncle once got in a fight in the front yard and threw chicken feet at each other."

She clamped her hand over her mouth in spite of herself. "Not really!"

"Yep," he said. "That was probably the year after you left. I was in Birmingham at UAB, but my brother David was still living here. You remember David?"

"Yeah," she said, hoping he wouldn't press her for specifics. David had always been a quiet kid who hung out in the band room a lot, if she remembered correctly. Rebecca was not even sure they'd ever had a conversation.

"He's in New York now," Alex said proudly. "Music composer on Broadway — I go up to visit him every spring. Thanks, Kevin."

The waiter set down two beers in plastic cups, and two shot glasses with a light brown liquid nearly spilling over the tops. "We're out of Bud Light in the bottle," he said to Rebecca, as if this were the only important piece of information.

She gaped at him, and then looked at Alex, who sniffed a shot glass. "Whew! What's with the tequila, Kev?"

"Oh, that. That's from Grier and them." He motioned with a jerk of his head toward the table where Alex had been sitting earlier. The guy with the jowls raised his own matching shot glass to them in a salute. Alex responded in kind, and downed the tequila in one gulp.

Rebecca smiled stiffly and left her glass where it was. She waited for Alex to chastise her for this, but he simply glanced at her glass and shook his head. "Crazy guys."

"Work friends?" she asked.

"Well, yeah, some of them. Grier's a deputy and Kenny over there is a paramedic. He works in Gadsden part-time and then with the fire department here part-time. Earl drives a tow truck. So we all kind of intersect at work. Off duty tonight, obviously. Plus we all went to Oreville High at one point or another, just different years."

"And the little blonde?" He had named the men but not the women in his company.

"Oh, yeah. Um, Bethany is one of our dispatchers. Kathy, next to her, is her friend; she's a bank teller, I think." He pointed to each one in turn. "And the other brunette is Tanya; she works at the hair salon downtown. You two might remember each other. Actually, I think she was in your class."

"Tanya Boozer?" Rebecca looked again at the brunette in the short-cropped hair with blond streaks, trying to recognize the cheerleader who had overlooked her in high school, even at the best of times. Sure enough, there she was, surrounded by a good bit of hair product and a gratifying extra layer of flesh. "Wow."

"Time changes us all, I guess. I keep forgetting how long you've been away." Alex was talking to her like they were old friends.

"So you go fishing with my dad?"

He nodded. "The post office was down the street from my parents' restaurant, and he used to come in for lunch a lot when I worked there in the summers. They moved the restaurant a while ago, next to the Winn-Dixie on Highway 9. Anyway, when your dad found out I went fishing at sunrise most days at Lake Ofeskokee, he decided to start tagging along. I guess you would say we're friends."

"That's nice," Rebecca said dully.

"He never shuts up about you, though. If I have to hear one more time how many exotic places you get to fly with your job . . ." He nudged her foot gently under the table. It was a boyish gesture. But he had a man's face — full eyebrows and dark, serious eyes. The wrinkles at the corners had been exacerbated, she guessed, by all the time he spent outside squinting in the sun, making his eyes look even more narrow and intense. He had a tiny scar over his lip. She glanced at the untouched tequila and took a fiery sip.

"You'd never know it from my end," she said.

"What?"

"I almost never hear from Dad," she said. "Except when I call him. And even then half the time *Sonia* answers."

"I take it you're not a fan?"

"It's not her, really. Well, I guess it's partly her, but it's just . . . he and my mom aren't even divorced."

"They probably never will be," Alex said. "He loves her too much, even now."

"How do you — You know what? I'd rather not talk about it."

She quickly downed the rest of the tequila and slammed the glass on the table. There was something bubbling inside her — grievous and hollow. Something about Alex irked her — whether it was his presumptuousness to invade her space at every turn today, or the fact that he seemed to be trying — successfully — to replace her father's lost son, she did not know. Kevin the waiter was passing by, and she gestured for him to bring another round. Alex raised an eyebrow.

"Unless you need to get back to your friends?" she said. A challenge. "I mean, you did come all the way over here and start needling me for personal information that's absolutely none of your business. You don't even know me! But now you've got me drinking tequila and running my mouth. So don't tell me the big bad officer —"

"Deputy."

"Deputy. What's the difference, anyway?"

He started to answer, but she plowed on. "Don't tell me you're going to back away now that you're getting what you came over here for. Going to run back over there and get on the stage and sing?"

"I wouldn't dream of it," he said lightly. He was laughing at her, she knew. "Unless you want to sing with me? A little 'Islands in the Stream'?"

She ignored that. "So, let's talk about you, Deputy Chen," she said, as Kevin put two more tequila shots in front of them. She hardly knew who this woman was, talking with her mouth, but she could not seem to stop. "What skeletons are in your closet?"

"That would take a while," he said, still wearing a smile that no longer reached his eyes. "And maybe a few more of these."

He lifted the shot glass and waited for her to clink hers against it. Even though they both drank at the same time, he did not move his gaze from her, even when he put the glass on the table. "You're right," he said. "I was intruding and I'm sorry. I just assumed you and your dad were in touch more. I can tell you don't remember me, which is understandable, given your move to Atlanta and . . . everything. Plus, to be honest, I wasn't that memorable in high school. When you're one of three Asian kids in a basically white town, you try to fly under the radar as much as possible."

"I guess I didn't think of that," Rebecca said.

He shrugged. "It's a little more diverse these days. We minorities are up to like almost four percent or something. At this rate, we'll have a Taco Bell in fifteen years. Fingers crossed."

Rebecca was not sure what to say. She thought he was kidding but wasn't sure. Was he making fun of her?

He grinned, getting up from the table. "Come with me and say hi to everyone. They're all curious about you."

Rebecca had never known anyone to be curious about her. Tonight she had no particular interest in meeting "everyone," or getting closer to the karaoke stage, but Alex stood with his hand extended to her and she could not think of a polite refusal. Her head swam a bit when she stood, but he bolstered her with his outstretched arm.

"Cool?" he asked.

A combination of warmth, giddiness, and utter panic rose in her chest. But between Alex Chen's inviting eyes, guilt about her rudeness, and the smoothing power of tequila, she allowed herself to be led toward whatever disaster awaited. "Cool," she lied. "I'm cool."

12

In the dream, she was swimming. A pool, in the middle of her mother's living room, grown to the size of a football field. She was wearing a cheerleader's uniform, the wet weight of it pulling her down. Giant roaches hissed around her, skittering across her arms and up the back of her neck, through her hair. A man's voice boomed in the distance, like a loudspeaker, but the man was muttering, and she could not understand him.

She tried to reach the side, follow the echoing voice, but she could not move and it faded. An airline mask hung above her, just out of reach. A familiar voice — Valerie, maybe? — was close by now, reciting the safety features of the DC-9-50. Rebecca screamed, but Valerie just got louder. It was all going black. A tiny circle of gray sky was all that remained above her and she gasped desperately for air. It would not come. She was suffocating.

Rebecca sat bolt upright, throwing the pillow from her face halfway across the room. It took a beat to realize that she was back in her hotel room, and that it was 6 A.M. Another beat to realize that she was not alone. He was standing by the door, silhouetted so that she could see he was wearing jeans but no shirt, hunched over and talking softly on a cell phone. She gathered the sheet around her, realizing in the process that she wore only underwear herself. Ugh. The granny panties. *Dear God, what have I done?*

Alex Chen put the phone in his pocket and pulled on a white undershirt before he crossed to her, smiling. She tried to ignore the lovely way the cotton clung to his muscled chest. "Anybody ever tell you that you punch and kick like an Ultimate Fighter in your sleep? It's like trying to sleep in a boxing ring." He handed her a glass of water and a couple of small brown pills from the nightstand. "Take these. You'll thank me later."

She did as he suggested, awkwardly trying to keep her body covered with the sheet at the same time. Her head was splitting and her mouth tasted like a drunk possum had died in it. Alex took the glass back and handed Rebecca her bag. "Here," he said. "I know better than to dig through a woman's purse. Can you get your keys out for me, please? Grier's outside and I'm going to go back and get your car."

Shame filled her as she realized she had almost no memory of what had happened the night before. "I didn't drive?" she said tentatively.

"God, no," he said. "Or me either. I would hate to have to arrest myself for DUI. Bethany dropped us off."

Rebecca had a vague memory of climbing into blond Bethany's car, and laughing. So much laughing. The car had smelled like strawberry air freshener. Memories were coming back to her in snatches. "Did I . . . did we sing together last night?"

He answered her with a decent Elton John impression, perfectly on-key even at this rough hour of the morning. "Don't Go Breaking My Heart."

Oh God. Not only did you sleep with a guy you haven't seen since you were fifteen, you were Kiki Dee. In front of people. Stellar night, Rebecca. Just stellar.

"Did we . . . um, I'm embarrassed to ask." She glanced down at her clothes in a pile on the floor, feeling her cheeks burn.

"Afraid not," he said. "Though you did

suggest it repeatedly. You were . . . hard to resist, I'll say that. But I have a strict policy of not taking advantage of women who are more than four times past the legal limit. I slept on top of the covers, and I was a perfect gentleman. Well, mostly perfect."

His grin made her feel even more naked. He leaned down and kissed her on the forehead. "You should go back to sleep," he said. "I'll get your car and call you later."

With that, he slung his plaid shirt over one shoulder and went quietly out the door, carrying her car keys. She glimpsed the side of a black patrol car in the parking lot before he closed the door. Part of her wanted to get up and eat something, and maybe try to puzzle through what had happened the night before. But a bigger, stronger part of her knew this would be an unwise course of action. She took Alex's advice and lay back down to sleep instead.

When she woke again, she could see before looking at the clock that it was much later in the morning. Bright yellow sunlight invaded the room through the part in the curtains, and she was ravenously hungry. Her mouth still tasted horrible, but the headache was gone; she had Alex to thank for this small grace. On the table by the door, her car keys sat with her room key and a cup of Waffle House coffee that was already cooled to room temperature. A scrap of paper next to it held a phone number with a scrawled note. "Thought it would be less intrusive if I let you call me instead. — A"

The word *intrusive* had been underlined and there was a small smiley face next to it. It gave her a nervous feeling in the pit of her stomach, or maybe that was just hunger and the remnants of last night's tequila. She studied the number blankly for a minute before tucking it into her purse and heading for the shower.

13

After her shower and a greasy, satisfying breakfast at Waffle House, Rebecca drove to the county hospital Monday morning. It was a tiny complex of small buildings, each painted the same institutional slate gray and surrounded primarily by pine trees. There were a few lonely flower beds flanking the front door, and she could see a couple of wooden picnic tables behind one building, where two men sat smoking.

She pressed the intercom at the front door and gave her name and her mother's name. After a moment, she was buzzed in and directed to a small waiting area with burgundy padded chairs and a single magazine rack. She thumbed through last year's Christmas edition of *Woman's Day,* flipping the pages without really seeing them. Soon a woman in hot-pink scrubs with large, poufy red hair came into the room. "For Lorena Williamson?"

Rebecca raised her hand. "That's me."

"Hi, dear, I'm Kathy Winslop, the charge nurse. I was here when they brought your mom in."

"How is she?"

"Well, you know, she's had a rough time. She is up and about today, a little more coherent, and did sign the paperwork giving us permission to speak with you about her treatment."

"More coherent?" Rebecca did not know her mother had been incoherent.

"Yes," Nurse Kathy said, nodding gently. "I'll let Dr. Sussman tell you more. Here's my card, though. We nurses are here more often than the doctors are, and this has my extension if you need to reach me with any questions. One thing your mom really needs is some clothes. Have you been to the house?"

"Yes," Rebecca said. It was almost a whisper.

"Yeah, I heard about the house," Kathy said with sympathy. "Maybe, if you know her size, it will be easier to just buy her a few things. She'll need comfortable pants and T-shirts, and a pair of plastic flip-flops for the showers. We give them slippers, but to tell you the truth, they aren't very nice. You can always bring her some softer ones if you want. She's got a toothbrush, but again, they're nothing fancy. No razors or floss are permitted, no mouthwash with alcohol, no belts or shoes with laces, and absolutely no medications. Not even Tylenol. If they transfer her to Mountainside, she can work her way up to the day unit and they will let her have some of that. But not here. Okay?"

Rebecca could not even process what she was hearing, but she nodded, hoping someone would repeat the list to her later. "When you bring her stuff back, just drop it at the front desk over there, and they'll deliver it. Now, let's go back and you can see her."

Her mother was in a small room that reminded Rebecca of a college dorm, only less optimistic. There were two twin beds, each with a sickly mauve bedspread and grayish-white pillows. Each side of the room had a nightstand and a tall cabinet made of white pressboard. The cabinet had a bar across the top for clothes on hangers, and each nightstand had a large plastic cup resting on it with ALABAMA BOARD OF MENTAL HEALTH printed on the front. The lights were plastic, built in to the walls, with no cords. Rebecca noticed there were no drawers in the nightstands or doors on the cabinets. All open shelving. No place to hide.

Her mother's roommate must have been out in the common area with the other residents, because one of the beds was empty, with a navy sweater draped across it. On the other sat the woman Rebecca had known every minute of her life but now barely recognized. Lorena Williamson was gaunt and pasty. Never a large woman, Rebecca thought her mother must have lost about forty pounds since she had seen her last. Her eyes were sunken and red, her arms bony beneath sagging flesh. Rebecca wanted to cry.

Nurse Kathy spoke from the doorway. "Mrs. Williamson, your daughter Rebecca is here."

"Your daughter Rebecca." In case my mother doesn't know me, Rebecca thought grimly.

Lorena looked up blearily. "Becky?"

"Yes, Mama."

"Did you finish your homework? I told Mrs. Pindergrass you had to do your homework before you could go outside. Where is Cory? Where is your brother?"

A painful lump collected in Rebecca's throat, but she did not want to cry. Not now. "Mama," she said gently, sitting down next to her mother on the bed. "Cory's gone. He died, remember? Years and years ago."

"No," Lorena said lightly. "You're thinking of something different. Don't worry. I'll wait up for him. You go on to bed, now." She patted Rebecca's hand.

Rebecca rose obediently, grateful for an excuse to leave the room, even if it was imaginary. She kissed her mother on the forehead. "I'll be back soon," she muttered. She wished it didn't feel like a lie.

When they were back in the hall, Rebecca turned to Kathy with tears in her eyes. "What is going on? She's never been like this. Is this because of the mess at the house?"

Kathy put a gentle hand on Rebecca's arm. "She's actually better today than she was yesterday. She was nearly catatonic and wouldn't eat. I was afraid we were going to have to send her to the main hospital for dehydration. Dr. Sussman will be able to explain better, but from what I know, this seems like more than just the hoarding issue."

Hoarding. Of course, that's what it was. Rebecca had always known it, that her mother's "collecting" and "saving" things was not normal. She had sensed it was getting worse as the years went on. Wasn't that why Daddy had moved out? But she had never put the word to it. There were TV shows about hoarders and even though Rebecca had never seen one of them, the commercials always made her uneasy. She wondered darkly if her mother would end up on TV, too.

Kathy led Rebecca to an office at the end of the hall. It was larger than many of the rooms they had passed, but not a luxurious office by any means. Three of the walls were swimming with books — on shelves and credenzas and piled high from the floor, with papers sticking out every which way. On the back wall were four imposing filing cabinets, one of which was topped with a wilting plant. On the others rested binders, boxes of office supplies, and a single dusty frame containing the Serenity Prayer against a background of fading watercolors. *Not exactly setting a great example,* Rebecca thought.

Dr. Sussman looked far, far too young to be a psychiatrist — more like a child playing doctor. He wore a checkered shirt unbuttoned at the collar under his white lab coat, no tie. He sat in what had once been a polished red leather executive chair, but it had seen better days and was worn in patches. He was signing forms in a stack of manila folders, and when Kathy introduced her, he smiled tersely at Rebecca and continued his work. He handed Kathy the stack of completed folders, holding the last one on his desk.

"I'll stop back by in a few minutes, Rebecca," Kathy said behind her before departing.

"Hi, Ms. Williamson," Dr. Sussman said formally, reviewing the file on his desk.

"Rebecca, please."

"Sure. I'm Will Sussman. I've been your mother's primary treating psychiatrist since she was admitted. Though, obviously, we work as a team here." He glanced at the door as though including the rest of the staff. Rebecca was not sure if this was for her benefit or in case someone was passing by, so they would not feel slighted.

Rebecca repeated the question she had just put to Kathy. "What is going on? My mother seems very confused. Does this have to do with the hoarding?"

Dr. Sussman shook his head, still looking at the chart. "Good question. Clinically, hoarding should not have anything to do with her orientation to the here and now. Um, the confusion. Anyway, there's some dispute in the research, but most professionals agree that hoarding is on the obsessive-compulsive spectrum."

He fished around for a large binder under some papers on the desk and opened it, flipping pages while he talked. "While OCD and related disorders can sometimes feature delusions or magical thinking among their symptoms, they are not generally characterized by pervasive confusion about time and place, nor the catatonic state your mother was in when she was brought in."

Rebecca wrinkled her brow, trying to wrap her mind around what he was saying. "What does this mean?" she asked meekly.

He seemed to notice her in the room, then. His voice softened and he took a less academic tone. "Sorry. Have you heard of OCD?"

"Yes." She had, though she hoped he would not ask her to give a definition.

"Okay, well, hoarding behavior is pretty much a special form of OCD, which is a pathological response to anxiety. It's not 'normal' behavior, especially when it gets to the point where your mom is, but usually a person who has OCD or who hoards, they are still mostly in touch with reality. They have a skewed view of things, of course, but usually just related to certain rituals, like in your mom's case, holding on to stuff.

"But Mrs. Williamson seems to have something else going on as well. As you pointed out, she's confused about when and where she is. And when she first came in, she was completely dissociative — that is to say, disconnected from reality. She was either unable or unwilling to even speak at first."

"So what does it mean?" Rebecca repeated. "I mean, will she get better?"

"It depends," he said. Then hurriedly he added, "Well, let me say this. I'm very encouraged that she is more lucid today than when she came in, and I'm hopeful that means she will continue to improve. But mental illness can be hard to predict, so I don't want to tell you she'll be fine in a certain number of days or weeks."

Mental illness. He had said the words offhand, but to Rebecca they were as stark and foreboding as though they'd been stamped on her forehead.

"Why —," she stammered, choking back tears, "why is she this way?"

And will I be this way, too? Am I doomed? Thoughts too shameful to voice.

He sighed. "So much about what we do is a mystery," he said. "The human mind is extraordinary and powerful. It can hide itself, protect itself, and sometimes heal itself, and we don't always understand why or how."

Great, Rebecca thought. *I have no idea what's going on and this guy thinks he's Gandalf.* She caught herself twisting her ring, and then gripped the arms of the chair to still herself.

Dr. Sussman did not seem to notice her frustration. "My guess would be that your mom had sort of a predilection toward the hoarding, or at least to some form of OCD. Those things are often at least partly hereditary. But environment plays a role, too, and sometimes a traumatic event can not only trigger a worsening of the OCD, it can cause the kind of psychotic break your mom seemed to experience this week. You had a brother who died, is that right?"

"Yes," she said. "In a car accident."

He was flipping through the chart. "When was that?"

"In 1997. He was eighteen."

Dr. Sussman made a note in the chart. "Thanks," he said. "It's been hard putting everything together."

Poor you, Rebecca thought acidly. She tried to remind herself that this man was helping her, and her mother, no matter what a jackass he might seem.

"Had you noticed the hoarding before

that?" he asked.

She tried to think. "I don't know. I was only sixteen then." Her father used to tease her mother for being a pack rat but it never seemed crazy to Rebecca. She saved silly things like wrapping paper and old sour cream containers, but Rebecca had always thought she was just thrifty. They had never had money to waste, that much was certain.

Will Sussman made a tent with his fingers, sitting back in the chair and looking at her directly. "I can't know for sure, but if I had to guess, I would say that maybe your mom was always a little inclined toward hoarding, which basically means that keeping certain things made her feel less anxious sometimes, but that the trauma of losing your brother caused her to spiral out of control, so that the hoarding behaviors became harder and harder to keep in check."

For a jackass, he was pretty good. This description fit almost exactly with how things had been after Cory died. First it was that her mother did not want to get rid of anything belonging to Cory, not even his old clothes and baseball gear, which were just collecting dust in the shrine she had made of his room. Then she began to collect little things, like magazines she was saving in case she needed a new recipe for something. But she wasn't cooking or even eating much; Rebecca and her dad survived on TV dinners and the Hardee's drive-through.

Then came the garage sale phase, which started late in Rebecca's junior year of high school. Her mother developed the ambitious idea that she would collect and refurbish "antiques" and knickknacks for resale. A well-meaning friend of hers, probably hoping to help Lorena develop a hobby after mourning for her son, had offered her a booth space at the big antique shop in Gadsden. For months, Lorena went garage saleing every weekend and came back with the most inexplicable loads of junk. Broken record players, children's toys, dry-rotted furniture. "I can do something with this," she would say, adding each item to the pile that started in their living room and eventually took over most of the kitchen.

"I can do something with this," Rebecca muttered.

"Pardon?"

"That's what she used to say, all the time. Mom. She would bring home junk and say 'I can do something with this.' It was like her mantra or something."

"Oh, yes." Dr. Sussman sounded distracted. He was scribbling on a pad.

They were the words Rebecca and her dad came to dread most. At first, Lorena would look to them, bright eyed and expectant, for their approval of whatever she had found. She would tell them elaborate stories about where the item came from, or how it would look with a fresh coat of paint. After a while, though, she stopped showing them her treasures when she acquired them, which was often when no one else was home. They would simply appear on the pile or on the back porch, or sometimes even in the back of the closet or the trunk of a car. As the months passed, the quality of the items diminished and the quantity increased. Very few of the items she had painted or refurbished sold at her booth, so the logjam was at their house.

In the early years, Rebecca's dad would help control the chaos. He would insist that Lorena cut back on her garage sales. He would make sweeps of the house: reorganizing, putting the less desirable items in the backyard shed, even throwing things out from time to time. After Rebecca moved to Georgia for her senior year and then went on to college, however, it became harder and harder for him to keep her mother in check. Lorena became defensive and angry when challenged. She retrieved treasures from the trash. And when he put her on a strict budget to curb her garage sale habit, she began accumulating newspapers and food containers in place of knickknacks.

Rebecca had been in her midtwenties when her father got his own apartment. He'd come to Atlanta and taken her out for dinner when he told her. He wasn't divorcing Lorena, he insisted. He never would. He loved her mother always. "I just can't live in a home where there's no place for me," he had said sadly.

In a way, she admired how long her dad had held to this idea. For nearly seven years, he had been faithful to Lorena, scarcely unpacking his suitcase at the new apartment. He'd gone home twice a week to bring food and to sit with Lorena for a meal. Rebecca gathered that he tried to clean up a bit while he was there, and that once in a while he even spent the night with his wife. But how long could a marriage go on that way?

Eventually Richard had rented his own house — the lonely bungalow off a two-lane highway he lived in now — but he was still paying the mortgage and the bills at Lorena's place, without question. Rebecca was not sure when he had started seeing Sonia.

She'd been absorbed in her own life, and resisted understanding her father's relationship as long as she could. But Sonia had kept popping up in conversation, and as it became clear they were more than friends, Rebecca and her dad silently agreed not to delve any deeper.

Richard had not divorced Lorena, but he had left her all the same. His name was on the insurance card she was probably using during her stay here, but it was not Richard Williamson sitting in the chair across from this arrogant guy in the white coat. Daddy would have known what to say, or at least would have asked more intelligent questions than she was. But for now, Rebecca was it.

"So what happens next? What about the house?"

"Well, technically the house part is up to the Department of Health at this point, but I can say, from what I've seen, that if you are able to get it cleaned up within the next ninety days or so, they will allow you to have the condemnation revoked without having to jump through too many legal hoops.

"Normally with hoarding behavior, I suggest having the patient present to help clean out the home. It's more therapeutic that way and more likely to actually help with the disorder. In this case, though, since she's having some comorbid dissociation and obviously needs ongoing treatment for that, you may have to clean the house without her."

"Me? Clean the house?"

"Unless you decide to sell it, as is. You can hire a company to come clean it, if that's the way you want to go. They can be expensive and the challenge there is that they don't know what you might want to save — if anything, I don't know — but then at least you don't have to do it yourself. It might be harder on your mom that way, when she's able to realize what has happened. But you have to do what's best for your situation."

"I have to clean out the house," she said. She did not know why this had not occurred to her sooner. Of course she had to clean out the house. Who else would do it? Dad? Sonia?

"Or you could just walk away and let the bank deal with it."

"What?"

"If she still has a mortgage, you can let the bank foreclose on the home. The mess will be theirs to deal with. Of course, then your mom would need somewhere else to live and you would lose any equity that's in the home. For that, you'll need to talk to your attorney or financial advisor, actually. I can't really advise you on all that stuff."

"Of course," Rebecca said numbly. Lose the house? Where would her mother live?

"In the meantime, I'm going to do what I can to stabilize her medication in the next few days and get her transferred up to Mountainside," he was saying. "Your dad has really good health insurance — someone said he's a mail carrier, right? — so I think we'll be able to get her a spot over there that won't bankrupt her. They really have more to offer long-term residents than we do here. It's a nice campus. You'll like it." He attempted a facsimile of a warm and personable smile. "Flowers and pretty views and stuff."

Until that moment, it had not occurred to Rebecca to consider who would be paying for her mother's care. Her dad? Maybe. For most of his life, there was nothing he would have denied his pretty wife, even after he had moved out. But now? Now it was complicated. There were two house payments, two sets of bills. And Sonia. Now there was Sonia. Rebecca had a fair bit of savings stashed away — one of the few perks of being a single workaholic who rarely spent money — but she had no idea how much her mother might need. And she had to work, she couldn't care for her mother full-time.

It was too much. She stood up. "Thank you." It came out in her airline voice.

Dr. Sussman looked startled. "Um, you're welcome. Kathy's not — well, it's okay, I can walk you out."

He came around the desk, saying something about how he was planning to go to lunch soon anyway. As though this mattered to her. As though anything mattered right now, other than being outside these walls and away from this nightmare. She was in the parking lot before she even realized what was happening, clutching Kathy's card and a tenth-generation photocopy of a list of personal items acceptable for inpatients.

The one thing she was sure of, as she drove away and navigated back to the two-lane highway to Oreville, was that she could no longer pretend none of this was happening. Her dad would have to be in the loop. And it was time to let her friends know what was going on. She pulled over and scrolled through her list of contacts, head swimming.

Before she got to Marci or Suzanne, the name appeared, and she knew it was the right call. "Hey, Jake. It's Rebecca."

14

Rebecca returned to the St. Clair County Mental Health Hospital a couple of hours later, dropping off a bag of clothes, toiletries, flip-flops, and slippers at the front desk. It was the second time in twenty-four hours, and maybe the second time in her adult life, that she had been shopping for clothes at Walmart. Technically it was still visiting hours, but she did not ask to see her mother again. Her head was already spinning — after waking up to a half-naked deputy sheriff in her hotel room and finding out her mother was essentially on another plane of existence, it was surreal. Suzanne's wedding and Rebecca's friends seemed like something from another lifetime. And work . . .

Shit. It was Monday. She had to fly tomorrow. Somehow she had to get checked out of the Super 8 and back to her apartment tonight so she could be at the airport at five in the morning. As she pulled out of the hospital parking lot, her phone rang.

"Hey, doll," Valerie said. "How's it going over there?"

"Hi, Val. It's okay. Well, actually, it's a little overwhelming." She gave Valerie a quick summary of everything that had happened, except the part where she woke up with Alex Chen in her hotel room. Rebecca decided that part was not strictly critical.

"Why don't you take some time off?" Valerie said.

"I can't. I don't want to lose my job."

"Um, sweetie, ever heard of FMLA? The Family Medical Leave Act? You can take up to twelve weeks of unpaid family leave and keep your job."

"Really?" It was a wonder Valerie had never become a lawyer. She could quote Federal Aviation Administration regulations, the HR manual, and half the laws pertaining to property ownership in Georgia. She'd had a couple of disputes with a neighbor that got escalated to the homeowners' association, and Valerie had made sure everyone involved regretted messing with her.

"Hang on, let me text you the number for Trey in HR. He's the only one in that department who's not an imbecile. There are a couple of forms to fill out. Tell him

I'm helping you, that will put you at the front of the line." Rebecca had no doubt this was true but she wondered vaguely if Valerie's were the right coattails to ride at the airline. More people seemed afraid of her than truly happy to see her.

"Okay, I just texted you," she said. "Now, tell me more about this boy."

She did her best to explain to Valerie that Alex Chen was not a love interest. He wasn't even really an old friend, since Rebecca barely remembered him from high school. He was just a guy who had played football with her brother and managed to still be in the Podunk town where they had all grown up. "Still," Valerie said with her usual candor. "He's not your best friend's husband, so that's a plus."

"Okay, then, I guess I'd better go call your friend Trey," Rebecca said through gritted teeth. She didn't enjoy being ribbed about her long-standing feelings for Jake, of course, but something about the motherly way that Val gave her a hard time was reassuring. It's not like she could talk to anyone else about it.

"Seriously, doll," Valerie said before they hung up. "Don't let them give you a hard time. If you need me, call."

Trey in HR turned out to be as nice as

Rebecca could have hoped. She left him a message, and he returned the call before she'd been back in her hotel room for half an hour. He briefly explained FMLA, and that the airline's policy was that Rebecca could use any accrued paid vacation first, and then start up to twelve weeks of unpaid leave after that. "If your mom isn't feeling better by then, we have an outside service that can help you set up home health care, transportation to doctor visits, that kind of thing. Some of it may even be covered by insurance, if your mom is on your policy."

"She's not," Rebecca told him. "But she's not sick, you know, in the traditional sense of the word. She has a . . . a mental health issue. It's not like cancer or anything."

"It doesn't matter," Trey said without missing a beat. "Our leave policy applies to any medical condition, including mental health issues."

"Okay, you're sure? Do I need, um . . . do I have to document everything?"

"Nope," he said. "Just a form for my files here. Do you have access to a fax machine?"

"I think so, the hotel . . . does it have to be notarized?"

"No, just a simple form and a signature."

"I could get something from the hospital, where she's staying? Like a receipt or . . .

something?"

"Not necessary. We've had very little abuse of FMLA, so we more or less operate on the honor system."

Rebecca had not expected it to be this easy. "Thanks," she said.

"My pleasure. So . . . I'm showing that you have seven days of paid leave left this year. It works Monday through Friday for our purposes, even though your actual work schedule probably isn't limited to that. I will fax you the form to fill out and get in touch with your supervisor. You might want to touch base personally since you're sched-uled to work tomorrow."

"Do you think it's late notice? Should I come back and work tomorrow?"

"No," Trey said gently. "It should be no problem. That's what alternates are for. Just go take care of your mom."

Tears spilled down Rebecca's cheeks when she hung up. Only then did she realize that she'd been gearing up for a fight with her employer, and surprisingly, that she had half-hoped she would lose. If her job were on the line, everyone would understand that she needed to pack up and drive back to Atlanta tonight. She couldn't possibly be expected to venture into the disgusting mess that had once been her childhood home, much less be in charge of cleaning it out. And the distraction of serving Diet Cokes at thirty thousand feet might make it easier to ignore the fact that she had not the first idea what to do next.

15

If she'd been wondering whether she would bump into Alex again during her stay, he answered the question by showing up at her hotel door a little after six. He was freshly showered, wearing khaki cargo shorts and flip-flops and carrying a clump of scraggly wildflowers.

"Hey," Rebecca said. She was too tired for formalities. She felt like a slip of paper ready to crumple in a giant fist.

"Thought you might want dinner," Alex said. "I saw that your car was still here at the end of my shift."

"I'm just going to ignore how much that makes you sound like a stalker. Did you run my license plate, too?" It was supposed to be a joke, but he looked a little wounded and memories of Suzanne's horrifying experience with an actual stalker made her shudder. She touched his arm. "That was inappropriate. I'm sorry."

"That's okay," he said. "And you should slow it down, too. Your insurance is going to skyrocket if you keep getting speeding tickets."

Rebecca flushed. "You *did* run my license!"

"A little," he admitted. "Which is totally illegal and could get me fired. So now you have something to hold over my head to make sure I'm on my best behavior. Dinner?" He extended his elbow for her to take.

"Is there anywhere to go besides that place we were last night?"

"Sure," he said. "In Gadsden. A short thirty-minute drive."

"No thanks, I'm exhausted. Where's your patrol car?"

"It's not *my* patrol car. I usually only drive it on duty. Why, were you hoping for the cuffs this time?"

There was an indignant retort for that somewhere, but Rebecca was too exhausted to do anything but roll her eyes at him. She didn't even insist on taking her car when he opened the passenger's door of a slightly beat-up red Chevy Malibu. After the last few days, it felt nice to have someone else in the driver's seat.

They sat in the same booth as the night before. Rebecca ordered a grilled cheese sandwich with a side of fries and coleslaw, while Alex feasted on baby back ribs. The waitress who had been surly the night before was polite, even friendly. Rebecca supposed they had become familiar at some point during her karaoke episode the night before. Rebecca had never been a big drinker, but between Alex and the friendly smiles she was receiving at the bar, she began to wonder if her drunk self was more fun to be around than her real self.

She found herself recapping for Alex the broad strokes of what she'd learned from Dr. Sussman that day. It felt odd to confide in someone she barely knew, but he was here, in front of her. When she'd talked to Jake, he had conveyed sympathies and offers of help from the rest of her friends. She knew they were sincere, but she also knew that their own lives were full to the point of overflowing. Dylan was going back out on tour soon. Suzanne had her charity and her business to run, not to mention the planning of the second, more public wedding. Marci and Jake had Bonnie to look after, a new baby on the way, and each other. And Valerie, the closest thing Rebecca had to a work friend, bless her. Valerie was Rebecca's mentor, and certainly a friend, but she was someone with whom Rebecca had so little in common personally, it was hard to picture their relationship working if they didn't fly together four times a week.

So, she talked to Alex. He listened politely, and asked appropriate questions, and told her what he knew about County Hospital (underfunded and understaffed like everywhere else), Mountainside (nice, expensive, but supposedly good), and Dr. Sussman (not much). As with Trey in HR, Rebecca found herself surprised at how accepting Alex was about everything that was happening with her mother. He'd had to help restrain her on Sunday, to get her into the patrol car and over to the hospital, but he talked about it as though it happened to him every day and was a perfectly normal thing. Maybe it was. She didn't ask.

He told her about his family, too. His father and uncle had owned the only Chinese restaurant in the area for as long as Rebecca could remember. They had moved a couple of times, each time getting closer to the micropolis of nearby Gadsden, which was experiencing population growth while Oreville flatlined and floundered. Alex's parents had hoped he would take over the restaurant, but he had no interest. He had worked there evenings, weekends, and summers while attending college in Birmingham.

"You went to UAB?" Rebecca asked.

"For a couple of years. But I got a little sidetracked," he said, with a grin.

"Oh? How so?"

"It's a long story," he said. He looked down at his basket of fries in silence.

Rebecca sensed his discomfort and fished around for something to say. It came from overhead: not the voice of an angel, but of her friend Dylan Burke. "Baby, this is where Country Rules . . ."

"Hey! I know this guy!" She realized she sounded a little too eager and starstruck.

Alex looked around. "Which guy?"

"This song," she said. "This is my friend Dylan."

"Dylan Burke? You *know* Dylan Burke?"

The impressed tone in his voice pleased her. Normally she didn't publicize her relationship with Suzanne and Dylan, but this seemed like a reasonable time. "Yeah, he's engaged to one of my good friends."

He whistled. "Well, I don't know if I know any celebrities that big," he said. "I'll just have to win you over with my charm."

Now it was her turn to stare down at her food.

"So what are you going to do next?" Alex asked.

"I don't know," she said. "I need to go home, to Atlanta, at least to get some clothes and water my plants. Dad is supposed to be back late tonight, so I guess I'll check out of the hotel in the morning and talk to them on my way out of town." *Them.* Sonia would certainly be there when she went by. Would this woman she barely knew be part of the discussion about her mother? Rebecca didn't want to think about it.

Kevin brought the check, even though she still had half a sandwich and most of her fries left. Alex waved away her hand when she reached for the bill to pay her half. Now she had to say something.

"Listen, Alex, I really appreciate everything you've done for me, and for my family, and it's been great to catch up."

"But?" he said, tossing a credit card down on the bill.

"Yes, there's a 'but,' " she said. She could feel her face reddening as she went on. "I'm not sure what happened between us last night, but I don't want to lead you on. I am not looking for any kind of relationship at this point in my life."

"Which point is that?" he said. The words were challenging, but his eyes were friendly.

"Well, I don't even know, to be honest. I have no idea when I'll be back or how long I will stay if I do come back here. But my life is in Atlanta, and anyway, I'm sort of tied up right now, emotionally."

She was ashamed of it as soon as it came out of her mouth. It was half a lie, which was bad, and the kernel of truth was even worse. There was no taking it back now, though. He was still smiling, but a bit of the light had left his deep brown eyes. "I understand," he said. "Of course I do."

"Besides, we don't even know each other. I know you have wonderful memories of Cory and football and everything, but he and I were always very different. It was so long ago."

"It's okay," he said. "If you don't come back, you don't. I'll live. But if you do, I'd like to think we can be friends. It's not often I get the privilege of meeting someone who hobnobs with celebrities and parties in the big city. I'll finally have something to put on my Facebook page." His Southern accent was extra thick now. He was mocking her, she realized. Worse, she deserved it.

Rebecca threw her napkin into the basket and excused herself to the restroom. She was washing her hands and examining her falling ponytail when the door opened and

Tanya Boozer stood next to her.

"Hi, Becky. You're still in town?"

"Hi, Tanya. I'm still here. Probably heading back tomorrow."

"I guess you probably won't be gracing us with your presence again anytime soon then." Tanya wore a smile so broad Rebecca could almost see her molars, but the tone was less than friendly.

"I'm not sure yet," Rebecca said. "Why do you ask?"

"Just curious. Alex sure seems happy to see you."

"It's been good to catch up. With all of you."

Tanya looked down and swung a black-booted foot back and forth across the tile. "Well, yeah. But Alex, I think he'll be better off when everything is back to normal."

"Normal?"

"Yeah, you know, everybody back where they belong. You in the big city with your rich friends, and us here."

Years of sparring with Marci had given Rebecca incredible self-control in these situations. She kept her expression neutral, friendly even, and turned to face Tanya. *This isn't the high school locker room anymore. You have no idea who you're dealing with now, girlie.* "What are you trying to say,

179

Tanya?"

"I'm just saying I consider Alex a friend. He's been through a lot, and the last thing he needs is to get involved with someone who's not going to be around for him."

Rebecca had no intention of getting involved with Alex, but saying that outright would be admitting defeat. "Don't you think Alex can decide that for himself?"

"Of course he can," Tanya said, her smile wavering just a fraction. "I just wanted to let you know that we all look out for each other here. I don't know how y'all operate in Atlanta, but that's who we are."

"Thanks for the reminder," Rebecca said sweetly. "It's nice to know things haven't changed in my hometown."

She rested her fingers lightly on the bathroom counter and waited, wearing her best "is there anything else I can do for you?" smile. Compared to some of the cat-fights she'd mediated in the sorority house, not to mention your average cranky first-class passenger, this was nothing. Tanya hesitated, opened her mouth, closed it again. She spun on her heel and headed for the door.

"Nice chatting with you," Rebecca called after the stylist.

"Yeah, you too," Tanya said.

Rebecca let the door swing shut and redid her ponytail before leaving the bathroom, hoping to give her old classmate time to cool down. When she walked past the bar on the way back to the booth, Tanya was absorbed in conversation with a man in a white shirt and tie and did not look at her as she passed.

"Tell you what," Alex said, when she slid back into the booth. "I'll make you a deal."

"A deal? I'm intrigued." She noticed he had ordered another round while she was in the bathroom.

"Since we don't know each other anymore, you can ask me three questions the next three times we meet. Anything you want, and I'll answer truthfully. I figure after nine questions we'll either be friends or you can decide you don't want to know anything else."

"You're assuming we're going to meet again. What if we don't?"

He shrugged. "If we don't, the deal is irrelevant."

"And you'll be asking me questions, too?"

"It only seems fair."

"I don't know. You have an advantage. I don't go fishing with your family."

"Fair enough," he said. "Okay, how about this: for every three questions you ask, I only get one."

"Can I decline to answer?"

"The one question? When I'm giving you three? No way."

She laughed. "Fine. But I go first."

"Clearly."

"Starting now?"

Alex looked at his watch. "Sure. I don't have anywhere to be, do you?"

Rebecca fished for a question. It was harder than she'd thought it would be. "You said you went to UAB. What did you study?"

"Ah, a softball to start with. Thank you very much. Civil engineering. I wanted to build cities."

She waited for him to say more, but he didn't. "So . . . why aren't you doing that now?"

"That's number two. Well, I was on a football scholarship my first two years, but then I blew out my knee doing something stupid. I wasn't even on the field at the time," he said, shaking his head. "My parents couldn't afford to pay for my college, and I hadn't exactly been a model student, so I joined the army to pay for the last two years. I ended up coming back here when I got out — my dad was sick — and I just never went back."

"So how did you end up a sheriff's deputy?" she asked. She wasn't really thinking about the questions anymore; she was just curious.

"I knew Grier from football — he's a couple of years older than I am, but he kind of looked out for me back when I was just a skinny kid who was afraid of the ball. And my background in the military makes me a good fit for law enforcement. It's not what I ever pictured myself doing, but I really do enjoy it."

Rebecca was about to ask if he ever thought about going back to finish college when Alex went on. "Okay, my turn. What's your least favorite thing about being a flight attendant?"

"You're starting with that?" she said. "It's so negative."

"Hey, I only get one question a day. I want to get to the juicy stuff quickly."

Rebecca thought about it. There was so much about the airline industry people complained about: the hours, the food, all the off-the-clock duties outside of the flight hours for which she was paid. But those things didn't really bother her as much. "This is going to sound weird," she said, "but I miss seeing people say goodbye at the gate. That was always my favorite part of flying when I was young. I always watched people saying goodbye at the gate — parents sending their kids on a first big trip, or off to college, people dropping off family members after a visit, couples saying good-bye.

"I remember one time this young couple at a gate next to mine held on to each other until the final, final boarding call, when the girl got on the plane, blowing kisses to the guy all the way down the jetway. I could tell the attendants were annoyed with her, rolling their eyes and everything. But I thought it was kind of sweet. And once she was on the plane and they closed the doors, her boyfriend stood there for the longest time and watched out the window. He waited until the plane had taxied away, even though he couldn't see her anymore and she couldn't see him and he was probably paying five bucks a minute for parking. I thought it was so sweet. You don't get moments like that anymore, because after 9/11 people have to say goodbye at the security gate, where it's all hectic. By the time people get to us, they're numb already and just want to know when the beverage cart is coming through."

"So I take it you have never seen anyone chase someone down to profess their love and tell them to stay like they do in the movies?"

"Never," she confirmed. "It's kind of disappointing. Seriously cuts down on the potential for dramatic romantic moments."

Suddenly, a catchy teenybop song rang out between them, and Alex looked embarrassed as he reached for his phone. "Ah, it's my daughter. She picked the ringtone," he said, rising from his chair. "Excuse me for a minute."

"You have a *daughter*?" Rebecca said, incredulous.

"You already used up your three questions," he said, grinning. As he walked away, she heard him say, "Hey slugger. How was school?"

Rebecca ate more fries than she intended, waiting for Alex to return to the table. When he slid back into the booth, he grinned at her. "You forgot to mention that you had a daughter," she said.

"I did? Sorry. I have a daughter."

"How old?"

"She's fourteen, going on giving-Daddy-a-heart-attack," he said. "Her name is Honey."

"Honey," she repeated, still unable to process the information fully.

"Shall we go?" He stood and extended his hand. Then he held the doors for her on the way out of the restaurant, and again getting into the car, whistling "Don't Go Breaking My Heart" as he went. But they said nothing else until Alex pulled up in the parking space directly in front of her hotel room.

"Can I walk you to the door?" he asked. He did not reach to unbuckle his seat belt, however, and Rebecca was relieved.

"No, thanks, I've got it. Thank you again for dinner, and for . . . being a friend." She said it hesitantly, apologetically, but the word felt good in her mouth. There was an absurd impulse to hug him, something she rarely felt for anyone, but she sensed it would not be well received. He would probably feel insulted, since it was fairly clear his intentions went beyond friendship. She knew people sometimes saw her as condescending, and she did not want to make that mistake with Alex. She liked him, despite the awkwardness of their beginning and his overzealousness. He had kind eyes. He listened to her. No one had listened to her like that in a long time.

She waited with the door half-open and one foot hanging out.

"You're welcome," he said. "I'm a good friend. You'll see."

"Okay." She stepped out.

"Wait!" he called, before she could swing

the door closed again.

She leaned in. "What?"

"You keep saying we don't know each other. I do know you, and not just your driving record. You came to almost every football practice we had for two years, except never on Tuesdays. You had piano or Beta Club or something on Tuesdays. Cory tried to act like he didn't care if you were there or not, but if you came late, he couldn't focus until he saw that you were in the bleachers. You always had a dog-eared book on your lap. *Little Women* was your favorite, I think, because you had that one the most. I tried to read it once. Not my thing, at least not when I was seventeen. On the warm days, you wore ratty jean shorts and those white Keds with scuffs all over them. Those were the best days because I could see your legs. I used to dream about those legs.

"Then when it got colder you'd wear jeans, or you had this long black skirt you liked. It always got dusty when you came down to the field, which made me like you more for wearing it anyway. You put your hair up a lot our senior year; you were a sophomore then, if I remember correctly. When the defense was on the field, I'd take an extra water break because from the cooler I could see the sun on the nape of your neck. I waved at you a couple of times — you probably don't remember."

"I —"

"Eleven guys bigger than me were trying to kill me every week, but you were the most terrifying damn thing on that field. I always wanted to come talk to you, but I was scared shitless."

He took a sheepish glance at the steering wheel. "I didn't talk to girls much back then. Believe it or not, I was painfully shy — don't worry, it went away. Plus, everyone knew you were off-limits. Cory was our quarterback and you were his little sister. I'd be surprised if any guys talked to you the whole time we were in high school, even after . . ."

He trailed off.

Stunned, Rebecca could not eke out a word.

"He loved you, you know," he said. "Cory. I'd be willing to bet he didn't tell you a lot, knowing him, but he was so proud of you. Most guys griped about their families and younger siblings — God, I'm ashamed of some of the things I said about David — but Cory never said a word against you. He called you 'my little sis,' even in the locker room, always said you were a genius and you'd be the first person in your family to graduate from college. Maybe that's part of why I was drawn to you. You were his treasure."

"I — I don't know what to say," she said, a lump in her throat like a rock.

"You don't have to say anything, Becky. I just wanted you to know. You may not know me, but I know you. It's okay that there's some guy in Atlanta, and it's okay if your feelings just aren't . . . whatever. I will be here if you, or your family, need anything. Anything. I'm not a romantic, I'll give you that. But I know something about loyalty. Even if I didn't like you, which against my better judgment I do, I owe it to your brother."

Rebecca was still leaning on the open car door, and could not bring herself to speak. He watched her for a minute, his brown eyes intense. "Go get some sleep," he said finally. "You have a lot to worry about with your parents and stuff. Call me if you come back in town. Or I guess, with your record, I'll know you're back when I pull you over doing fifty-five in a fifteen or something."

She laughed, trying not to cry, grateful to him. For giving her Cory back, even for a moment. And then for releasing her to mourn in her hotel room alone.

BY MARCI THOMPSON STILLWELL

BLOG: THE CARE AND FEEDING OF A SUBURBAN HUSBAND
{Entry #175: Sunshine & Sweet Surprises}

Monday, June 20, 2016

Hi, friends! Marci here, back from the beach, refreshed and exhausted. Have you ever noticed how sometimes a vacation is more tiring than normal life? I'll keep this short for now, since I need to go clean the sand out of my suitcase and snuggle with Munchkin, who I missed more than I imagined possible. The good news is, now I know that I can be away from her for a couple of days and not have a nervous breakdown.

And vice versa. Uh-oh.

I guess you could say I am reluctantly thrilled that everything went well, and even more thrilled that I got to combine my girls' weekend and some time away with SubHub. Yep! That was one of my surprises — he and some friends crashed our girls' weekend, and it was so much fun. There were a few more sweet surprises this weekend, some of which I'll be able to share with you in time. For now I'll just say that you never know what might happen at the beach.

Someone else surprised me this weekend, both by demonstrating a generous spirit I never knew she had, and by disappearing abruptly before the trip was over. She left a note saying that she needed to leave for work, and I don't want to call her out on that if she doesn't want to explain further. She doesn't owe me (or the rest of her friends) an explanation. And yet, part of me finds something doesn't quite add up about her departure.

Do you have a friend like that in your life? Someone you just can't seem to put your finger on? I wrote last time about "characters" in our stories that we just can't seem to put in a traditional role — those who seem neither wholly good nor fully evil. I guess maybe some people see me that way, too, maybe even this person who stole away from our beach party in the middle of the night.

I don't know about you, dear readers, but when people in my life behave in ways that are . . . well, let's just call it unusual, I often immediately assume I did something wrong. What does that say about me?

Anyway, if that friend of mine happens to be reading this blog, I hope she'll let me know if I did anything to offend or upset her. No matter what, I'd like her to know that all her friends, myself and Sub-Hub included, are here for her if she decides to reach out and tell us more.

16

Rebecca stared at the endless line of I-20 stretched out before her, foot numb on the gas pedal, every inch bringing her closer to Atlanta. She had crossed the Georgia-Alabama line fifteen minutes before, and she could already feel things changing around her as she drove. The air was different (or was she imagining that she could already see Atlanta's smog line on the horizon?), the trees were different, the names of streets. Her own apartment, and the clean shower inside, called to her from forty minutes ahead like a beacon. Even though she had put on her beach flip-flops, held her breath, and showered at the Super 8 before meeting Dad and Sonia that morning, she still felt grimy.

Tom Petty came on the radio, and Rebecca cranked it. *I'm technically on vacation, might as well enjoy it.* She glanced at the clock. Her flight crew would be in Columbus, Ohio, now, doing preboarding. She'd been tracking their schedule all day without really intending to do so. It was simply the automatic thought that came to her each time she looked at the clock. Even though Val had called to say the alternate was taking her shift and not to worry about anything, not worrying was not exactly Rebecca's specialty.

Besides, being concerned about an airline that had run without her successfully for sixty-odd years was simpler than thinking about the train wreck that was her life. For one thing, her supposedly closest girlfriends were more comfortable reaching out to her via anonymous blog mention than a phone call. And if Rebecca was honest, that feeling was pretty mutual, at least with Marci. Still, it irked her to be called out publicly like that. What irked her even more was the niggling suspicion that maybe she deserved the betrayal, having called and confided in Marci's husband instead of any of the girls.

But Rebecca couldn't analyze the workings of her messed-up friendships now. Her family life was screwed up enough to occupy her brain all the way down I-20. And back. It shouldn't have surprised her, she knew, that her father had not been at his tiny rental bungalow when she stopped by midmorning on her way out of town. She had known, hadn't she, that Sonia had her own huge, rambling house on Grimmer's Lake. Why would they squeeze into Dad's plain, single-bedroom bachelor pad when Sonia's wealthy ex-husband had provided a picturesque home five times as large?

So it was Sonia who had answered the door at Rebecca's second stop, wearing a shiny lavender robe and holding some kind of rat-like dog with its little nails painted hot pink. She had invited Rebecca in with a smile, which Rebecca strained to return. Sonia had put on a pot of coffee, pulled some canned biscuits out of the oven, and then — to her credit — politely remembered something urgent she needed to do in another room.

Rebecca's father wore sweatpants and an old USPS Tour de France T-shirt, a little too comfortable in this strange house for Rebecca's taste. Their conversation was short and tense, marked with lowered voices and furtive glances toward the back of the house where Sonia had busied herself with something and could occasionally be heard talking to the little dog. It was as though they were talking about her father's mistress in his wife's house, rather than the other way around.

"Listen, Becky," Richard said, after she had presented everything she'd learned at the hospital and asked for his help.

"Rebecca," she corrected. "I prefer Rebecca."

"Fine, Rebecca," her dad went on. "You know how much I love you. And your mom, too."

"I can see that," Rebecca said, glancing around Sonia's well-appointed kitchen.

He ignored her. "I will always love your mother, Rebecca, whether you choose to believe that or not. But I've fought this battle before. I have been paying the mortgage on that house since you and Cory were little. It ought to be paid off, except we had to borrow against it when your mother . . . anyway, it doesn't matter. Water under the bridge. In eight more months, it will be paid off. I plan to file a quit claim, giving it to her outright. It's hers."

"How does that help?" Rebecca said.

"It might not help," he admitted. "I'm telling you what I can do."

There was something in his tone, a coldness she'd never felt from her father before.

"You've been there?" he asked.

She nodded.

"Okay, so you see what it's like. Until I moved out, I was fighting that mess every day of my life. I woke up early to bag up trash and throw it in the Dumpster at the post office before I started my route. I stayed up late, after your mother was asleep, throwing things away and cleaning under things. I want you to know, I never expected when we got married that your mother would be an immaculate housekeeper. I didn't care about that. But the way things got, Rebecca. She never wanted to throw anything away. There was always some purpose everything could serve. Everything. Used paper towels and old newspapers, empty syrup containers. We started getting insects and I kept spray in every room.

"You talked to one doctor yesterday. I went to three of them. At first your mom went with me, and we even tried marriage counseling for a while —"

"Daddy." Rebecca put her hand on his, and he shrugged her away, angrily wiping his eyes.

"Your mother didn't want you to know. God only knows why. Anyway, honey, I don't want you to think I'm abandoning you with this, but I have done all I can do. I have cleaned that damn house and pissed into the wind with your mother for years. Even after I moved out, I came back and cleaned. She started screaming at me, and then she wouldn't let me in anymore, or if she did, she'd watch me like a hawk to make sure I didn't 'steal' anything."

"Oh, Dad, I didn't know —"

"Of course you didn't know," he said. His voice was icy. "You were in Atlanta. Living your life away from this town. But now you're back to tell me what my duty is to my wife. Like I don't know."

It would have been better if he had slapped her. He must have seen the hurt on her face, because he softened then. "Sweetheart, I'm sorry. You did what you had to do. I wouldn't have wanted anything different for you, and I still don't. I'm proud of you. I know you want to help, but your mom is a grown woman. She's sick, and she's in pain, but she has to want help before we can give it to her."

"What about the house?" Rebecca asked, staring at her lap.

"I don't know what to tell you," he said. "I poured my life into that house. I still write a check every month so your mother doesn't lose it. But maybe it's time to let it go."

"But then . . ." Rebecca's voice faltered. "Where will she go?"

Her dad squeezed the bridge of his nose and closed his eyes, leaning back in the chair. It was a gesture she remembered from her earliest years, whenever he was faced with something serious. She had seen it the most in the months after Cory died. "I don't know," he said, softly. "I've asked myself that question every day for years and haven't come up with an answer."

"Babe," Sonia called from the hallway. "Babe, I hate to interrupt, but don't forget that we have that meeting today."

"Yeah," Rebecca's father answered, his voice cracking. To his daughter, he said, "I don't have an answer right now. We'll talk more about it later. I want to help you, but I just don't know what I can do."

Sonia entered and put her hands on his shoulders, letting them slide down the front of his chest in a gesture that was nauseatingly intimate and affectionate. But Rebecca saw her father's countenance change then; some darkness lifted from his worn face and he managed a tired smile. She sighed.

"Becky, I hope you don't mind," Sonia trilled.

"Rebecca," she and her dad said simultaneously.

"Oh, right! I guess I always think of you from when you were little. I helped teach your second-grade Sunday school class, remember? I was just a teenager then myself. . . ."

When no one commented on this bit of nostalgia, Sonia went on. "Anyway, your dad and I have a meeting at church to go to this afternoon, and then we're going to play golf. It's the last day of his vacation, and you know how few days off your father gets."

"I do," Rebecca said.

"You're welcome to join us," Sonia said brightly. "I'm sure we could find a fourth."

"No, thanks," she said. "I have to go figure out how I'm going to help my mother." There was just the slightest bite on the word *mother,* but Sonia pretended not to notice. *At least she has some sense in her head,* Rebecca thought.

She pulled off onto the exit for her apartment, and numbly pressed the keys for the gate code. Except for one houseplant that looked wilted, things were exactly as she'd left them. The maid service had been there; they came every other week. The check she always left them on the granite counter was missing and everything gleamed with extra shine. She watered the plant and wheeled her carry-on bag into the laundry room, emptying the clothes into the washer and stripping herself down while she was at it. She had to laugh when she pulled out the velvet purple bag, and was tempted to throw it away. But Valerie had spent at least sixty dollars on this thing. It seemed a shame to just throw it out.

The shower was long and hot and glorious. Clean marble tile walls were a vast improvement over the fiberglass tub and low ceiling of the Super 8 in Oreville, Alabama. Afterward, Rebecca sat on the couch for a long time in her pristine white terry cloth robe, staring out the sliding glass balcony door to the woods behind her complex and the busy highway beyond. The world was moving along down there, everyone about their normal business for a Tuesday afternoon.

While she watched, the beginnings of rush-hour traffic began to accumulate on the northbound side of the highway. In Atlanta, rush hour was more like rush half-day, from six to ten in the morning and three to seven in the afternoon. Thanks to her job, Rebecca was almost never forced to participate. On the days she worked, she was already in the air for an hour when rush hour really started, and by the time she made it home at the end of a shift — usually a few days later — it was long after all those little people in the cars were home, having dinner or putting their kids to bed. She often reminded herself how freeing this was. Not lonely. She would not use that word.

Today she watched the traffic and wondered what life was like inside each of those little cars. She knew they must all have their worries, but she wondered if anyone was dealing with the same problem she had. Was someone else down there thinking that her mother might have gone so far off the deep end, she might never come back? Did one of those drivers worry that his dad had finally left the family for good? She was so hurt and angry with Richard. She kept seeing the way Sonia rubbed his shoulders, and the relaxed way he sat in the kitchen chair. Like he lived there. *Oh, Jesus,* she thought. *He does live there.*

And yet, he had a point. What right did Rebecca have to judge him? Hadn't she run away herself, years ago? Her ambition to be in a sorority at UGA, which seemed so powerful then, now looked like a wisp of an excuse to move in with Aunt Louise and out of her parents' home. Maybe at seventeen she could not be expected to have insight about what was going on at home. Maybe then it wasn't so bad.

But for the last ten years, what was her excuse? Too busy lusting after a man who didn't love her? Her career? Maybe that was valid for the last three years since she'd become a flight attendant, but before that she had usually been free on weekends. Yet she had rarely, rarely used those weekends to make her way out on I-20 West.

Maybe the truth was that she was angry with her father for doing something she herself had already done years ago.

17

When her phone rang early Friday afternoon, it pierced the silence in the condo so suddenly that Rebecca's heart raced for a full minute afterward. She had been alone with only the occasional sounds of the television or her neighbors in the hallway for three days, trying to figure out what to do next, and feeling a little guilty that she was using family leave to sulk around her apartment feeling sorry for herself. She was further surprised when it was Marci's number on the screen; her head was so much in Alabama that she had forgotten about everything else. She wondered briefly if Jake was calling from Marci's phone, but he should be back at work by now.

"Hey, Rebecca." Marci's voice was strained. "Are you busy? You're in Alabama?"

"No, I'm home, for a couple of days. I'm at my apartment."

"Oh. Well, good. I just wanted to say how sorry I am to hear about everything going on with your family. Jake told us."

"Thanks, Marci," Rebecca said. Marci's voice had an edge to it: there was something else. She waited.

"Are you free this afternoon?" Marci said suddenly.

How could she say no? She'd already told Marci she was in Atlanta, and it would soon be common knowledge that she was taking time off work.

"Sure," she said. "What's up?"

"I just want to talk to you about something. Can I come over? My mom has Bonnie."

Somehow, Rebecca did not like this idea. She didn't know what was going on, but Marci's tone was making her nervous. She thought about the weird showdown with Tanya in the bathroom the other night. Wherever they met, she wanted to be able to leave.

"Actually, my place is a mess," she said. "Can we meet for coffee? I'm going to be out running errands anyway."

"That's fine," Marci said absently. Normally any one of her friends would have called her on the lie that her condo was a mess. They knew her better than that.

Something was definitely wrong. "Cool Beans okay? Maybe in an hour? Is that the right part of town for you?"

"Sure, no problem," Rebecca said. She dried her hair and dressed quickly, wondering what was coming next in the weirdest week of her life.

Cool Beans Coffee Roasters on the Marietta Square was an eclectic place to say the least. A shotgun-style store next to a photography studio, it sat just off the main town square. The front faced one of the primary streets through the historic area; the back door led to an old railroad courtyard, where it met the back sides of a family restaurant and a successful dance studio. The shop itself boasted graffiti-covered interior walls and an enormous red bean roaster. On Friday afternoon, every human element that could be found in the suburban city seemed to be represented, with tattooed and pierced youths smoking cigarettes out back, while young mothers in yoga pants pushed strollers among them and long lines of lawyers and clerks spilled out of the nearby courthouses for a caffeine fix before the weekend.

Rebecca had never cared for Cool Beans much. She preferred the clean predictability and cozy dark neutrals of Starbucks. She knew she was supposed to appreciate the character of the indie coffee shop, like her friends did; she had to admit the coffee was usually better than at the corporate places, but somehow she could never see past the cigarette butts on the entry steps and the feeling that everything was covered with a light film of grime that never quite got scrubbed away.

Marci loved the place, though, and when Rebecca arrived, she was already seated in an artsy nook by the window, sipping a hot tea in a paper cup and talking to a large man with a long reddish beard and one of those strange black circlets that made his earlobe look all stretchy. Rebecca went to the counter and ordered a mocha, plus two chocolate croissants. A preemptive peace offering.

"Where is your studio?" Marci was asking the man with the beard as Rebecca approached with pastries.

"Right now it's in the corner of my apartment. Oh, excuse me." He noticed Rebecca and stepped to one side so she could sit across from Marci on a bench with a worn, spotty cushion.

"These pieces are all Tim's," Marci explained, gesturing at the canvases around them, which featured strange combinations of cartoonish little animals, smears of color, and dark, realistic trees in the foreground. Not Rebecca's cup of tea, to say the least, but she forced a polite little smile. Marci turned back to him. "Do you have a card?"

"Oh, shit, I mean, shoot," Tim said, feeling the pockets of his ratty black cargo pants. "I don't have any on me. My sister keeps telling me I should keep them with me all the time."

"Your sister is right," Marci said charmingly. "Napkin?"

"Oh, sure," Tim said, and ran to the counter to borrow a pen.

"Jake loves this kind of thing," Marci said. "We're really into supporting local artists."

Rebecca tried to ignore the affected tone in Marci's voice, reminding herself that for years she had probably sounded just that way. Always trying to be someone better than she was, always trying not to be from Oreville, Alabama. Perhaps that was why it was so grating to hear: it was a reflection of the worst of herself.

The large man returned with a strip of receipt paper on which he had scrawled a few lines. "So that's my email, and my website, and there's my number. I can do pretty much any size you need. Thanks a lot." He nodded to both of them and left smiling; Rebecca was a little ashamed of being surprised that someone who looked like that would have such good manners. She watched out the window as he made his way a few feet down the sidewalk, where he stopped to talk to a girl with a sloppy ponytail of deep purple and a tie-dyed broomstick skirt.

Then she forced her eyes back across the table to Marci and waited.

"I hate this," Marci said with a deep exhalation. "I hate this kind of conversation. I'm not good at them. They make me sick to my stomach, and I'm already nauseous all the time anyway." She put her hand on her lower abdomen.

"Marci, what's wrong? You're kind of freaking me out."

Marci set the tea down on the table between them, next to the croissants that she had apparently not noticed. She looked Rebecca directly in the eye and said, "I need to know what you know about whatever is going on with Jake."

"I'm sorry?" Rebecca was flabbergasted.

"I need to know if my husband is cheating on me, and if so, with whom." Marci's gaze was level, but her face was flushed and Rebecca could tell she was trying to control her emotions.

"Jake . . . cheating on you?" Rebecca parroted.

Her expression must have registered the level of shock she felt, because Marci seemed to relax and she picked up her tea again. Oddly, Marci looked relieved. "So it's not you, then."

"What? No! Marci, there is no way Jake would ever cheat on you." Rebecca believed this. Jake was the most honorable person Rebecca had ever known. Then her mind brought up the memory of his hand on her shoulder at the beach, and how that had made her feel, and she brushed it quickly away. "Never."

"I know. Or at least I thought I knew," Marci said. "My heart says he never would, but his behavior lately . . ." She trailed off, as if not sure how much she wanted Rebecca to know.

Rebecca knew she should feel indignant that Marci had come very close to accusing her of adultery, but she was too focused on wondering if Jake really could betray Marci, and with whom, and what that would mean about everything she had known and believed about him for years. She felt a little sick herself. "What's been going on?"

"Well, I guess you have gathered — and maybe Jake has told you, I don't know —

our marriage has been under a bit of a strain the last few months. It's exhausting having a child, and we — we feel differently about a lot of things, like whether to let Bonnie sleep with us, how long to let her cry in her crib, and even how far apart the kids should be. I know it doesn't sound like a big deal. We both wanted more children, and my feeling is, let's just do it while we're in baby mode, you know? I knew Jake wanted a little more space between the kids, he's so much more reasonable than I am about stuff, but I thought he would just see past that once he found out this one was on the way. I never thought, I never expected him to be so disappointed in me. He's acting like I did this on purpose."

Didn't you? Rebecca thought, but she quashed it. Her opinion on this was not the point.

Marci dabbed at her eyes with a beverage napkin. Rebecca did feel sorry for her, despite their long rivalry. Jake was one of the most easygoing guys alive, and his patience with Marci's quirks always seemed nearly infinite. It was hard to imagine what it would be like to have those kind eyes turn angry and cold. Then again, there had been the broken engagement before they worked that out, and Rebecca had not been so sympathetic to Marci then.

"Don't you think he'll come around?" she said, while Marci collected herself. "He's always seemed so forgiving."

"I've been thinking so, hoping so," Marci said. "But he's been disappearing at odd hours, traveling more with work lately, and I'm pretty sure he has lied to me about where he was going a couple of times. I found some hotel bills that don't match where he was supposed to be for work."

"Oh, no," Rebecca said.

"I knew the two of you sometimes have lunch together, and he calls you sometimes, but he has always told me about that before. I thought maybe, if he turned to you —"

"No," Rebecca said definitively. "He hasn't. The last time we had lunch was three or four months ago. I remember he returned that sweater of mine you had borrowed, so I am sure you knew about it."

Marci nodded, wiping more tears. "I didn't really think it could be you, honestly."

Rebecca couldn't hold back the laugh. "Uh, thanks."

"I'm sorry." Marci laughed. "I didn't mean it like that. I just meant, I think you guys had your chance, you know, back when he and I were apart, and if he had wanted —"

"If he had wanted me, he would have chosen me then, when I was throwing myself at him. But he picked you."

Marci nodded again, looking down. They had never spoken so frankly about what had happened four years earlier. In fact, at first they had scarcely spoken at all. Marci had punished Rebecca's treason by excluding her from the wedding — which for Rebecca was a blessing of sorts anyway. How would she have stood and smiled in some blue monstrosity while Jake married someone else? Then when things cooled, it had been too much of a sore spot, painful for both of them.

"We've never talked about this," Rebecca observed.

"No."

Suddenly it was as though Rebecca could see — after years of fumbling around in a dark cavern — that the way out had been right in front of her. Dangerous, maybe, but necessary. "Marci, you can ask me anything. I'll be honest with you."

Marci raised her head in surprise. Then she hesitated. "I don't know. It will feel like I'm confirming information Jake has already given me. Like I don't trust him."

Rebecca shrugged. "So you brought me here to ask if I was sleeping with your husband because you trust him?"

To Rebecca's surprise, Marci laughed. "God, I am such an idiot, aren't I? I know I shouldn't blame the pregnancy, but the hormones really do mess with you."

"It's okay," Rebecca said. "I can imagine." She held Marci's gaze. She wanted to be done with this: to release herself from the unspoken tension, and the middle school ridiculousness between herself and her friend, once and for all.

"The truth is, it's not Jake I don't trust. It's me. I've been the other woman in a relationship, and I know how easy it is for two people to slip into something wrong, especially when the marriage is in a rough spot."

Rebecca nodded. She never heard the full story, but she had known Marci had an affair with a married man before she moved back to Atlanta, and that the affair was part of why Jake had called off their original engagement. At the time, Rebecca had been of the definite opinion that Jake should run like hell from someone who would get involved with another woman's husband. But she had to admit: at the time, she had been hoping when he ran like hell, it would be into her *own* waiting arms. And that was before Jake had become another woman's husband.

"I just can't help feeling," Marci said, the tears flowing fully now, "that if Jake is seeing someone, that I . . . I deserve it. Like it's karma or something."

Rebecca hesitated. She put her hand on Marci's. "No," she said. "No. You don't deserve it."

She was ashamed, even as the words left her lips. Hadn't she been the one nursing feelings for Jake herself? Would she really have turned him down if the opportunity presented itself? She couldn't say for sure. But Marci's pain was so palpable, the words just came in response. "Life is just . . . complicated. And love is worse. Nothing is as simple as we always believed when we were little."

"You're right," Marci said, wiping her eyes. "I know you are."

Rebecca stared out the window, trying to give Marci a moment to discreetly pull herself together. Tears made Rebecca uncomfortable, and public tears were worse. It was strange to have Marci so vulnerable in front of her. The chicken had come to the fox for advice. *But maybe I'm not the predator after all,* Rebecca thought.

"Thank you. I really appreciate you being so nice," Marci said after a minute. She heaved a sigh. "And you seem to know about relationships. Don't take this the wrong way, but how have you never — ?"

"I don't know," Rebecca said. She didn't want to hear the end of that question. She lived with it every day. For a moment, she felt brave or reckless — she was not sure which. But she said it. "I'm glad we're talking, Marci. I won't be upset if there's anything else you want to ask me."

"Okay." Marci stared at her cup for a moment. Then she said suddenly, "Did you try to seduce Jake while he and I were broken up?"

Despite the redness that was rising in Rebecca's face and the clenching in her stomach, she would not allow herself to drop Marci's gaze. "Yes."

The other woman nodded. "But he didn't —"

"No. We kissed. For a few minutes, I thought maybe . . . but, no. His heart was broken. He loved you. *Loves* you. It's always been you." As she said the words, there was a cavern opening up inside Rebecca's chest, dark and deep, and horribly empty. A truth that she had been carrying around with her for years but refused to acknowledge was finally dawning as she repeated the words. "You two belong together. I never had a shot with him. And I find it hard to believe anyone else does, either. Marci, there has to be another explanation."

"Thanks," Marci said. There was a pause, and then her voice was gentle and tentative. "Rebecca, how long have you been in love with him?"

At first, Rebecca didn't answer. An old instinct told her this was a trap, that she should protect the soft center of her feelings with the same half truths and misdirections she always had. But when she looked at Marci's face, she was surprised to see kindness written there. Sympathy, even. Marci knew something about hopeless love, didn't she? Suddenly, Rebecca felt exhausted. It was a bone-deep tiredness that weighed down her limbs and pressed her into the seat. She was tired of fighting, tired of hiding, tired of trying to do the right thing and never knowing what that was.

"A long time," she said finally. "A long damn time."

18

Early Monday morning, Rebecca loaded her car, dropped off the sad little plant with her neighbor, and headed back to Alabama. This time she had added a large suitcase to her familiar carry-on bag, with enough clothes to get by for two weeks without having to go to the Laundromat. She had packed her cleaning supplies, a giant can of insecticide, and a box of rubber gloves in a laundry basket and loaded her iPod with traveling music for the car. She was not entirely sure what to expect; she had no idea if she could be helpful. She only knew there was nothing for her in Atlanta right now, and she had to at least try to do the right thing, whatever that was.

She had called her dad over the weekend, and he had agreed that she could stay in his house indefinitely so that she wouldn't have to go back to the Super 8. "Rebecca," he'd said before hanging up. "Don't forget you have a life, too. It's okay to live it."

"Thanks, Dad." She had a feeling the permission he was offering was as much for himself as for her. She accepted it without voicing her response. *But what is my life? Is any of it meaningful?*

The hole that had emerged in her chest at the coffee shop was still there, but today the emptiness no longer scared her. It was the place where she'd been cradling a hopeless love, a lost cause. In Alabama, there was a mess to clean, and maybe it wouldn't help anything, but it was something she could do.

She went to her dad's house first, where the key was under the mat as promised. The little two-room bungalow was stark and white everywhere, but basically clean except for a fine layer of dust on the minimal furniture. There was no liner in the trash can, and only condiments in the fridge. She would run to the grocery store later. Richard had not been here in a while, she realized.

The bed was freshly made, however, the sheets smelling of some kind of floral softener. Someone — Sonia? — had at least made sure she had clean sheets. She pulled out a bleach-stained pair of cut-off denim shorts and a ratty gray T-shirt from some long-forgotten sorority car wash. She changed in seconds, folding the khaki pants and button-up shirt she'd worn on the drive, and leaving them across her suitcase on the bed. She felt like a visitor in her father's house, but that was fine. She felt like a visitor everywhere.

When she pulled up in front of her mother's house ten minutes later, she had to gather her courage with a deep breath. "You can do this," she said out loud. "Just stay for ten minutes and you can leave."

With the time allotted, she tried to assess the condition of the house. The piles of detritus that cluttered the front rooms only worsened as she pushed her way into the interior, wearing a mask and holding a can of insecticide in front of her, like a wooden cross in a graveyard known for vampires. She had put vapor rub under her nose, the way she'd seen cops and medical examiners do sometimes on *Law & Order.* It seemed to help with the smell but made her upper lip tingle unpleasantly.

Filling the rooms and lining the walls, there were loaded trash bags and cardboard boxes, and large plastic tubs in a variety of colors and sizes. Piles of magazines and newspapers were everywhere, sometimes in great stacks with strings around them, and other times scattered as though someone had been reading them just before leaving the house. Clippings filled open spaces on the walls — recipes, news stories from around the world, local sports recaps. Rebecca also began to notice that alongside the trash and bins, there were plastic bags from stores, some of which seemed to still have new items in them. Comforters in various colors and men's suits and children's clothes — boys' and girls'. Perhaps Mom had intended these as gifts for someone? She'd heard of compulsive shopping and wondered if that had become part of her mother's pattern.

When she reached the cluttered hallway to the house's three bedrooms, she hesitated. Rebecca tried to remember the last time she had been in her childhood bedroom — sometime during college, she thought. Soon after that, her parents had converted it to an office-slash-"craft" room, which meant that her father had built a small desk in the corner where he played Spider Solitaire and paid the bills, and her mother filled the rest of the space with crap. Now, she could see the glossy white chest of drawers that had been hers since she was a baby still against the far wall, surrounded by an unfathomable amount of junk. An ancient exercise bike with clothes draped across it and hanging from its rusty handlebars, some of them still in dry cleaning bags. A wrought iron chandelier with frayed wires emerging from the top and cobwebs joining most of the spires. A stringless guitar painted a deep red, covered in dust. A rusty metal box of Tinkertoys she didn't remember from her childhood.

It went on and on. There was a path on the stained carpet between the door and the computer, which she supposed her mother must still have used sometimes. Her mom had an email account she used about twice a month, mostly for acquiring and distributing chain mail. Overall the room was cluttered, but more with piles of stuff and less garbage. *This won't be so awful,* Rebecca thought.

Her parents' room across the hall, however, was an unqualified disaster. The minute she walked in, she realized the cats had been more present here than anywhere else in the house. The unmistakable stench of cat piss mixed with a sickly sweet honey smell, which reminded her of Jimmy Banks, who had a ferret in sixth grade. There was rotting garbage everywhere, some of it in bags, some of it sitting out. There was food on paper plates beneath wadded paper towels, and even under the bed. The bed was pushed against the wall; the far side could not be seen for all the newspapers and blankets and boxes, books, beverage cups, and cat toys. Closest to Rebecca there was a sliver of open bed — where she could see the sheet and pillow her mother slept on. Even this area was spotted with clumps of black cat hair. Vomit threatened in Rebecca's throat as she pictured her mother trying to curl up on this tiny space to sleep. She turned and went quickly out, careening across the hall. She stormed into the room she'd been silently forbidden for years to visit.

Cory's room was the worst in the house. Not because of rotting garbage or insurmountable piles, but the opposite. The room was exactly as it had been nineteen years ago. Dusty, but otherwise untouched. The bed was neatly made. Cory's childhood teddy bear, Simpson, sat between the pillows as though waiting patiently for his owner to return. If his owner had not been killed, the poor bear would have been tossed aside two months later when Cory went off to college at Auburn. Of course, their mother would have insisted on keeping the damn thing anyway, in the attic at least, along with some of the countless baseball and football trophies that still lined the walls.

His cleats and shoes were lined up on the floor of the closet, neater than he had ever left them in his life, and all his clothes and uniforms hung in a row above them. She could see a baseball glove rotting to paper on a hook with Cory's lucky number, 22, painted on it. Not such a lucky number if you didn't even live to see it.

Before she had walked in the house today, Rebecca had promised herself she would be strong. She had thought if she could last ten minutes in the garbage and roaches, that meant she could handle the house for half an hour the next day. Then an hour, and then step by step, however many days it took to clean it out. But now she felt defeated; she sat down hard on the dusty carpet of her dead brother's room and cried.

"How could you do this?" she screamed at a picture of Cory on the nightstand, in which he was pointing at the camera with a football extended in his hand. He had the same arrogant grin that always got him out of trouble, plastered there forever. "How could you do this to her? To us?"

She stood, went to the nightstand, and flung the picture against the far wall. The sound of the breaking glass was both horrible and satisfying. She tore down the hook with the glove on it and sent them both hurtling after it. "Why? Why? Why?!?" she screamed again. "You knew this would happen, you reckless idiot. You knew you were going to get yourself killed and ruin our lives. Mama always loved you best. Now she needs you and you're gone. What am I supposed to do without you?"

Tears of rage fell unheeded as she tore down one trophy after another, slamming them on the floor or against the wall so that the fake gold baseball and football players came loose from their marble plinths and hung by the black screws that attached them. She pulled out drawers and tossed them, splintering the wood and scattering clothes around the room. Notebooks full of baseball cards, an old record player, Star Wars toys that were probably worth something on eBay. They might be the only things in the house that were valuable, but Rebecca didn't care. She pulled them off shelves and threw them against the walls, where they left pockmarks on the faded blue cowboy wallpaper.

The tantrum lost its appeal in short order as rage and grief turned to despair. How could her entire family abandon her? She had always been a good girl; why did she get left alone with the mess? They were hiding from her, all of them. Her father at Sonia's lake house, her mother lost in her own mind, and Cory himself in the sweet oblivion of death. Rebecca alone was left to face the pain. She clenched her fist around a small action figure she barely knew she still held, not caring that it dug painfully into her flesh. She flung open the bedroom door with a bang and pushed her way down the hall and back out the front door.

A guttural moan emitted from her as she sat down hard on the concrete steps to the front yard. She allowed her head to sink into her hands in unruly sobs. It was in this state that Alex found her, pulling the patrol car into the driveway so quietly that she scarcely noticed he was there.

He sat down next to her on the porch steps, silent. Rebecca could see his boots on the ground through her hands and the bottom of his pant legs — synthetic khaki with a dark brown stripe up the side. She could feel that her face was a snotty, streaky mess under her hands, but she was helpless to do anything about it. The sobs were convulsing out of her in painful, guttural bleats. She must've sounded like a dying sheep, and she did not want to humiliate herself in front of Alex. But she simply could not stop.

He put one hand on her shoulder, but said nothing. They sat like that for a while, the afternoon marred only by her sobs, until there seemed to be nothing left inside her to cry out. When she was down to heavy breathing, he handed her a white cloth handkerchief, reaching between the crook of her elbows and knees so that she wouldn't have to raise her head. When she had cleaned her face, she raised her head.

"Thanks."

He nodded. "So what did he do to you?"

"Who?" she asked, thinking of Cory. Or her father. Or Jake. Maybe all three.

"The Jedi Master."

She followed his gaze to her other side, where a Yoda action figure lay facedown on the concrete step, a broken plastic cane in his hand. She had not even realized that she brought it with her. "Huh."

"Did he pretend not to be Yoda, and trick you into saying mean things about him, only to reveal that he really was Yoda after all? 'Cause I hate it when that guy does that."

She laughed, sniffled, and wiped her nose again. There was a pause. He was watching her. "Who carries a handkerchief, anyway?" she asked, holding it up. "I didn't realize you were sixty."

He smiled back. "Well, when women crying on doorsteps came back into fashion, I thought this would be a good trend to follow."

He extended his hand to take it back, but she balled it up in her fist. "I'll wash it for you," she said. "It's the least I can do. Did the neighbors call again?"

"Yeah, they said it sounded like someone was breaking things and screaming, and that you seemed to be crying on the front steps. That part, I've verified myself."

"I can verify the rest," she said. She stood up and adjusted her jean shorts. Alex glanced quickly away when she noticed him watching.

"Are you okay?" he said, pushing himself up to stand in front of her.

"Yes," she said. "Just battling a few ghosts."

He put a hand on her cheek, wiping it with his thumb. "Dirt," he said softly.

She turned her head from the intensity of his gaze and wiped the spot with her own hand. "Thanks."

"Well, I'm on duty until three, but if you need anything, just call, okay? And maybe keep the screaming to a minimum?"

"I will, sorry."

"Me, too," he said. He looked behind her toward the house. "I can't imagine what all this is like for you."

He turned to walk back to the patrol car, his boots crunching on the gravel. "Um, Officer — Alex?" she called.

"Yeah?"

"There is something you could do to help, actually."

He brightened. "What is it?"

"Would you have dinner with me tonight? We could do more questions. I could . . . I could use a friend."

He smiled. "That's tempting. But my daughter has a swim meet tonight in Leeds," he said. "I can't miss it. Sorry."

Rebecca waited for him to follow up with some alternate suggestion, but he seemed to have nothing to say. Embarrassed, she settled for saying, "That's okay, another time."

"Definitely," he said, getting into his car. "Take it easy, okay?"

Before she could reply, he was gone, leaving her holding the handkerchief in her fist and twisting her ring.

19

Rebecca could not face the house again that day. Once Alex drove away, she took the cleaning supplies out of her trunk, put them on the floor just inside the front door of the house, locked the door, and left. On the drive back to her father's house, she promised herself she would return the following day to get started in earnest, minus the ridiculous, self-indulgent tantrums. Today would be for phone calls.

Nurse Kathy confirmed that her mother would have a bed waiting for her at Mountainside the following day. Rebecca took down a list of instructions for her father to follow when contacting the insurance company that afternoon. She reviewed everything with Kathy twice. The nurse patiently and slowly repeated each number, code, and phrase Richard was supposed to use when he talked with the insurance company so that Rebecca could write them down. Richard still had not come to the house or the hospital, but he had agreed to advocate for Lorena with the insurance company and to pay any additional bills. Rebecca could only guess how much treatment at Mountainside was going to cost; she tried not to wonder how much her parents had in savings.

She had a short conversation with Suzanne, who was busy making preparations for a big foundation fund-raiser, as well as her public wedding to Dylan, which had finally been scheduled for October. It sounded like being married for real at the beach had freed Suzanne up to allow things to move forward under the glare of the spotlights. She even giggled once or twice after referring to Dylan as "my husband." Suzanne did manage to ask polite questions about what was going on in Alabama. They avoided the topic of Marci and Jake altogether.

Next, she called Valerie to find that the airline had indeed survived a short absence by one of its more junior flight attendants. "Don't worry, doll," Val said. "Take care of your business. We'll be here when you're ready."

After wavering back and forth, trying to consider how her mother would feel about it, she decided that she had no choice but to order an industrial-sized Dumpster, which the company said it could deliver in two days. An old boss of hers had said once that it was "better to ask forgiveness than permission." Today, she finally thought she understood what he meant. She would give herself the following day to collect her thoughts and prepare, and then she would simply set herself to the task of clearing away the trash. She would have to atone for her mother's hurt feelings and embarrassment later.

By five thirty, all her calls were made and there was nothing left to do. After picking up the phone three more times and putting it back down, she located her father's number in the call list and hit Send.

"Hey, Rebecca," he answered. He sounded tired. "Don't worry, I got everything worked out with the insurance and your mother is all set for tomorrow. I even gave them my cell phone number in case there are problems."

Rebecca knew this was a big deal for him. He hated talking on the phone, and guarded his cell phone number the way most people hid their Social Security numbers.

"Thanks, Dad," she said. "I really do appreciate it."

"If anything else comes up, I'll let you

know." He sounded ready to go.

"Um, Dad," she said, still debating whether to say what she was about to say. "I was actually wondering if you're free for dinner. You and Sonia, I mean."

"Oh," he said, and was quiet. Clearly the last thing he expected.

"I mean, if you're busy, it's fine. I could call some friends," she said. The last part was a lie, of course, but he didn't need to know that.

"No, no," he said, recovering. "That would be great, sweetheart. Come over at seven."

Sonia flitted around the kitchen like a hummingbird, with a brightly colored satin robe streaming behind her as she moved. Rebecca wondered how many satin robes Sonia had and whether she ever wore anything else. She pulled out ingredients, put them back, checked a pot roast in the oven, searched for various serving bowls and platters, and checked the roast again. The little dog, which Rebecca had learned was named Bear Bryant, followed her owner anxiously around the kitchen, jumping up and cowering in turns as Sonia whirled. Her little nails made scrabbling noises on the tile floor and the hounds-tooth check collar she wore glinted with what Rebecca hoped were just rhinestones and not real diamonds.

From what Rebecca could see, it must've been a seven-course meal being prepared but Sonia kept apologizing for just "throwing something together," and insisting that she would have done more "if I'd known more in advance." She came to the kitchen table frequently in her travels, refilling Rebecca's wineglass and her father's sweet iced tea each time they took a sip, while the two of them made awkward conversation about Rebecca's former classmates.

"Roger Simon is back in town," Richard said, as Sonia swished back to the kitchen for the twentieth time. "He came into the post office a few weeks ago. Asked about you, of course."

"Yeah, I heard he was back in town," Rebecca said. "Facebook."

Her dad rolled his eyes. He was suspicious of the Internet in general, and Facebook struck him as particularly dangerous and unseemly. "So you know that he's married, then? Can't remember his wife's name. Cute. Blond. Three kids, I think."

"Of course," Rebecca said. Roger Simon had been a good friend of Cory's, and her only high school boyfriend. She did not wish him ill, of course, but his picturesque, professionally photographed life seemed only to make hers look even less desirable. "How's his law practice?"

"He's doing well, I think," her father said. "I hear he still does a lot of stuff for a big paper company in Birmingham. And some of the locals here are going to him now that Beaver Green has retired."

"Great," Rebecca said dully. *We might need him, too, depending on how things go with Mom.* She took a gulp of wine, and Sonia came running with the bottle.

"Is he the one with the ads in the paper? Those cute little girls?" Sonia asked. "He's sure a good-looking guy."

Rebecca groaned.

"He and Rebecca dated for a little while in high school," Richard said. "What was it, your junior year?"

"Sophomore," Rebecca corrected. "He was a senior."

"Right," Richard said. "Of course."

Rebecca watched his face as her father remembered that they stopped dating after Cory and Roger's senior year, because Roger was going on to UAB. And there it was, as real and present as a fourth guest at the table: the always-thought but never-spoken fact. While Roger had gone on to college and then law school and a happy life with cute little blond children, his best friend Cory had gone on to death and nothingness, memorialized forever for breaking the state record for passing yards.

Sonia, however, did not seem to notice that the lost potential of a dead teenager had joined them at the table, or Richard's crestfallen face, which he quickly corrected with a manufactured smile.

"You dated him?" Sonia chirped, setting down a salad bowl in the center of the table. "Wow, honey, how'd you let that one get away?"

"I'm the one who got away," Rebecca said. "I mean, he went to Birmingham for school, but he wanted to stay together. He wanted to marry me, actually."

Her dad raised an eyebrow. "He did?"

Rebecca laughed. "Yes, and I'm sure that would have worked out great since I was not even sixteen at the time. I told him he could be my backup guy if I wasn't married by the end of college, though."

"He didn't want to be the backup guy?" Sonia asked, dishing a large quantity of greens saturated with some dark-colored dressing onto Richard's plate, and then Rebecca's.

"He was okay with it at the time." Rebecca smiled, remembering. "But obviously someone made him a better offer. Besides, I moved to Georgia a year later, and by then I'm sure he had girls lined up outside his dorm at UAB."

"No kidding they did," Sonia agreed, serving herself the salad last. Roger Simon had apparently charmed her, whether she had met him in person yet or not.

"Did we mention he's *married*?" Richard said pointedly.

Sonia giggled and put her hand on his arm. "I know, I know," she said. "Hey, just because I'm on a diet doesn't mean I can't look at the menu!"

Richard pretended to be annoyed with her, and Sonia leaned toward him with lips puckered, making little whining puppy sounds until he relented and kissed her back. When they parted, Sonia brushed a crumb from his beard with her fingertips, and Richard's face turned pink underneath. He shot Rebecca an apologetic glance, and she quickly focused on stabbing the soggy salad with her fork. *If I can make it through this without throwing up,* she thought, *Mom's house should be no problem tomorrow.*

"I never understood that," Sonia said, scooping Bear Bryant off the floor and onto her lap before returning to her own plate.

"Why you moved to Georgia for your senior year."

Rebecca could not tell if she meant she had not understood at the time, which would have been a surprising amount of interest for a young married woman to take in a seventeen-year-old kid, or she had not understood when Richard had talked to her about it more recently.

"Well, I wanted to join a certain sorority, and my aunt Louise was a legacy at UGA. I had to live in Georgia for a year before college to get in-state tuition."

"Wow. That seems like a lot of trouble just to be in a sorority, doesn't it, Bearie? Doesn't it, Bear-Bear? Mommy would never move away from Alabama. It's where we belong. Yes it is!" The little dog licked her face appreciatively in reply.

"It was important to me," Rebecca said quietly.

"I guess it must have been. Good for you, then."

This was the kind of statement Rebecca never knew how to take. Was it a judgment, a compliment, or just awkward conversation? "Well, I was the chapter president my senior year," she said. "And now I'm head of the alumni group for the entire Southeast."

Sonia smiled thinly. "That must be really nice. I never got to go to college, so I always wondered what it would be like to live with all those other women and go to college parties and stuff."

"We also did a lot of charity work," Rebecca said. "I still do — I volunteer more than a hundred hours a year with the Junior League in Atlanta." Why on earth was she defending herself to this woman? Rebecca wished she had never come.

"Do you ever get homesick?" Sonia asked. "For Alabama, I mean? And the country? I hear Atlanta has terrible traffic and pollution. And people shoot each other. Maybe you get used to it, if you live there?"

Finally Richard spoke. "It's no worse than Birmingham. Or anywhere. Just bigger."

"The murder rate went down last year," Rebecca said.

"To tell you the truth," her father said, "I was glad you went to Georgia. Things were hard here, and you had something you wanted to do. You did it. It's always a little sad for a parent to let go of a child who has grown up, and you surprised us by doing that a little sooner than a lot of kids. But who could blame you? I'm proud of you. So is your mother."

Sonia stiffened a bit at the mention of Lorena, and excused herself to get the roast out of the oven. "Dad," Rebecca said. "I didn't —"

"Let's not talk about it now, okay?" he said, barely above a whisper. "I know Sonia can be . . . interesting. But she's a good person. And she's trying so hard to get you to like her."

"She is?" Rebecca said without thinking. "I'd hate to see how she acted if she wanted me to hate her."

Richard gave her a tired smile and nodded to where Sonia stood trying to decipher a meat thermometer in the next room. "Every single thing she's made tonight is something new she found on the Internet. Before you called, we were planning to have hot dogs."

Rebecca glanced back at Sonia, who was looking critically at the overcooked roast. *It's pretty much jerky by the looks of it.* "Mom was a good cook. Before —"

"Yeah. She was," her father agreed. "But she hasn't cooked a meal in ten years. Maybe more."

"And Sonia —"

"Can barely boil water. Yes." He said it softly, but Sonia was busy trying to dig into the carcass and would not have heard him anyway. "But she *tries*, Rebecca. I love that about her. All anyone can do is try."

20

That night she lay restless for a long time, unable to get comfortable or to quiet her mind, no matter how many affirmations she tried. One o'clock came and went, with Rebecca berating herself each time she looked at the small red numbers glowing in the darkness. At this rate, she would be too tired to get anything done tomorrow. But tomorrow was keeping her awake, intruding on her night space, creeping in where it did not belong. The house, and more specifically having to face it alone. Her parents, her friends, Alex, and even poor little Tanya Boozer. Whenever she pushed one away, another would shove in.

Each time she closed her eyes, she saw the different pieces of her life as wild animals she'd kept caged for so long — separate and contained. But now the cages were dissolving in front of her. The animals were pawing at the crumbling walls and snapping bars, breaking free, and she was powerless to stop them. She was afraid, yes. But there was something else — a low, guttural growling sound that could be heard apart from the rest. It was a sound of ferocity and wildness, and as Rebecca tossed and turned, she was beginning to think it was coming from inside herself.

She felt less hesitation this time, retrieving the Goddess 3500X from her suitcase. There were no rooms with listening ears flanking hers tonight. For that matter, there was no one within at least a quarter mile of the quiet little house. No interruptions or humiliating experiences awaited. Just bliss and, hopefully, sleep. The only distraction was that Rebecca found it hard to hold on to her visions of Jake, or even the fantasies of movie stars every girl had sometimes. They were all becoming fuzzy, swirling away from her before she could pin them down in her mind.

Eventually she returned the Goddess to the velvet pouch and her suitcase, pacing the tiny room in unresolved frustration. She threw herself back into bed and forced herself to lie still with the pillow over her head until she eventually drifted off. To her annoyance, even as she fell asleep, the images pushing their way into her brain consistently — infuriatingly — included a white T-shirt, khaki uniform, and those damn brown boots.

Two days later, Rebecca got up and out early, headed straight to her mother's house. She'd allowed herself the previous day to rest and prepare, reasoning that she would be nearly useless with no sleep and there wasn't much point in going to the house before the Dumpster was there anyway. It was nearly July, and would be sweltering all across East Alabama, but she hoped the air conditioner was still in working condition. She promised herself she would stay until noon, no matter what.

She was met in the driveway by the Dumpster Dude, who wore a scruffy salt-and-pepper beard and a rainbow tie-dyed DUMPSTER DUDE T-shirt that almost covered his large belly. She had a feeling, as he thrust the clipboard into her hands with nicotine-stained fingers, that the T-shirt was not his idea. "You call the number on the yellow form when you want us to pick up. Takes a couple of days. They say up to five, but usually it's more like two."

"Thanks," Rebecca said.

"Yes'm," the Dude said.

She unlocked the door as he pulled away,

hydraulic brakes hissing and squeaking. *Wonder if the neighbors will call the sheriff again for all that noise,* she thought. There was a lift in her chest as she thought Alex might be back by. *Jesus. I must be lonely if I am hoping the police will show up.*

By midmorning, Rebecca would have welcomed law enforcement, or any other excuse to take a break. She had begun in the kitchen, thinking it was the most pressing problem in the house because of all the rotting food, and then quickly retreated to the living room. The kitchen would take working up to, she decided.

At least thirty times she had resisted the urge to run out the door. It was overwhelming to think where to start, with so many piles. There was also the risk, which Rebecca deemed quite reasonable, that she might pull out the wrong bag or box and cause an avalanche of trash, so that she would be found here weeks later, being eaten by squirrels. More than once she thought how easy it would be to just burn the place down. The insurance might pay for all her mother's health care, with some left over to put a down payment on a small, clutter-free house. This plan was not viable for a number of reasons, insurance fraud and felony being just the beginning. Still, it had a certain dark appeal.

With thick gardening gloves on over her vinyl dishwashing gloves, she felt as safe as she might digging through the mess, and she talked to herself for encouragement as she moved things around. *This is just a thing. It might be dirty or smelly or rotten, but it can't hurt me. At the end of the day, I can shower and be as good as new. It's a thing, to be moved. That is all.*

After a while, Rebecca came up with a sorting system. If a bag or box was obviously trash, contained anything perishable, or had a strong odor of any kind, it went to the Dumpster. If it was in good condition, somewhat clean, and had clear value, she did one of two things: things she recognized from her childhood went down the hall to Cory's room to be looked at again later; things that must have been recently acquired went out to a tarp she'd spread in the front yard for donation to charity or a garage sale, whichever seemed easier when the time came.

On one of her trips to Cory's room, she found an old stereo that still worked and plugged it in by the front door — the only outlet she could reach. Three stations came in well — country, classic rock, and the station that featured only church sermons. She alternated between the first two every hour or so, and after a while was surprised to find that she had been working for nearly six hours. Her stomach growled, so she stopped to survey her progress.

The living room was not yet clean, but the path through it was close to five feet wider than the sliver of carpet it had been before, and the surrounding trash mountains not nearly as high. Her arms and legs were sore from bending, reaching, and carrying. She put her gloves on the front porch, washed her hands in the bathroom, and went out to her car and applied three layers of hand sanitizer before eating the peanut butter sandwich she had packed for lunch.

Rebecca leaned against her car while she ate. Nothing had ever tasted quite so delicious as this particular peanut butter sandwich. She had promised herself she would stay until noon, and it was now nearly two. Beating her own goal made her feel more exhilarated than she had in a long time. Her body trembled with tiredness, but she was not ready yet to give up for the day. She would work until four, she decided. The sky seemed exceptionally blue and bright today, and Rebecca rested her head on the roof of her car, watching a hawk make lazy circles overhead.

Richard stopped by at the end of his route, still wearing his blue USPS uniform. He looked at her neatly organized piles on the front lawn and smiled at her. "Maybe we should have asked you to do this years ago."

She laughed. "I guess you could say this is my special talent."

"You have lots of talents, Becky."

"Right. I can't sing. I'm not a writer. I have no eye for art."

"I'd be willing to bet that last one's not true."

She gestured at the mess on the lawn. "This is it. This is my masterpiece."

He rolled his eyes. "Want some help for a bit?"

"Sure."

"I can't stay long. Sonia has something at the church tonight we're supposed to go to."

"That's fine, Daddy."

They worked for a while in silence. She was surprised that even though her father owned half the house, he deferred to her for decisions about most things. The couple of times she wondered aloud if he might want to take something with him — a toolbox, old football games on VHS tapes — he just shook his head. Rebecca supposed he had already collected everything he wanted to keep when he'd left. A little after five, he tossed a box of broken Christmas lights into the Dumpster, dusted his hands, and gave her a kiss on the cheek.

"I'm sorry I can't do more," he said.

"There's nothing to apologize for, Daddy."

"We're okay?"

She hugged him. "We're fine. I love you."

"Love you, too, Rebecca Rockstar." He gave her a gentle knock on the arm. "Never think you're not talented, okay? You shouldn't sell yourself short."

Rebecca nodded and watched him pull away in the gray-and-burgundy pickup truck he'd been driving since she was in college. They waved at each other, and she went back to work, wondering momentarily what was going on at church that night.

If Rebecca had been waiting for Alex to drop by, she did not admit it to herself, even though she began glancing up and down the street for the patrol car each time she made a trip outside. By the time she was too exhausted to lift another box, it was nearly eight and getting dark. She had been at the house for nearly twelve hours, three times the goal she had set for herself.

She covered the items on the lawn with a second blue tarp, tucking the edges loosely under, and waved at Mrs. Pindergrass watering her lawn across the street. Her old neighbor gave her a tentative wave back and stared at the tarp with apprehension. Rebecca put an old beach towel she'd swiped from her father's linen closet across the driver's seat in her car to protect her leather seats from the grime and drove back to the little rental house. By nine o'clock, she had showered, fallen into bed, and was sleeping the deepest sleep of her life.

21

Rebecca woke after an astonishing amount of time: twelve hours of uninterrupted sleep. It took several moments to remember that she was in a strange house, rather than the strange hotel room that was her usual occupational hazard. Every muscle in her body ached and burned as she pulled herself out of bed and into the tiny bathroom. She had not been this sore or tired since her first week of training in high heels at the airline. She noticed while brushing her teeth that she had forgotten to charge her cell phone the night before, so she had to stand hooked up to the outlet in the tiny kitchen while the coffee brewed to check her messages.

There was a message from her dad, a generic "checking in" message that was out of character for him, at least for the past several years. The second message was from Marci. "I just wanted to say thanks again for everything, and to ask you to give me a call."

Torn between curiosity and ravenous hunger, Rebecca made toast and ate it standing in the kitchen while she dialed Marci's number. It seemed she was taking all her meals standing up these days. It felt very primitive somehow, but she didn't mind.

"Hey," Marci answered on the second ring. "How are things going in Alabama? I hope I didn't interrupt you — I know you have a lot to do out there."

"No, mmm, that's okay," Rebecca said, swallowing. "I was thinking of taking today off anyway. I'm super sore from all the work I did at Mom's yesterday. I can barely move."

"Ah," Marci said. "Well, I wanted to ask if you are going to the Stillwells' on Monday?"

Jake's parents hosted a July Fourth picnic every year at their large old home in Atlanta's prestigious Buckhead neighborhood. It was Kitty Stillwell's pride and joy, and it seemed like half the city turned out for it. They always invited Rebecca, and on the years she'd been able to go, she'd enjoyed it.

"I hadn't thought about it, honestly. I sort of lost track of the days."

252

"Oh, okay," Marci said. "Well, if you decide to go, I wondered if you'd be up for drinks after the fireworks? Just us girls. Dylan is going to be out of town, and after all day with Jake's entire family, I think I'm going to need a break."

Rebecca had not thought about when she would be back in Atlanta, but she supposed the weekend was pretty reasonable. For the first time in her life, she had no schedule to keep, no boss she needed to check in with. At least for now. "Sure, I think I can do that."

"Great," Marci said, sounding uncomfortable. "I think I owe you an apology. I'd like to buy you a drink."

"No apology is needed," Rebecca said. "But we can go out for a drink."

Rebecca hung up with Marci, blow-dried her hair, and stretched her sore muscles. She wondered what to do with the day off she had given herself. She sat on the couch for a bit and flipped through the channels before snapping off the TV. In her apartment at home, sitting quietly on the couch and watching Atlanta go by below her was one of her favorite activities. But here, the quiet was too quiet. Her father's house had few windows, and the ones that were there were dirty and viewed only the dirt driveway in front of the house or the thick woods on the other three sides.

She paced around the tiny house, opening and closing cabinets and drawers and finding many of them empty or partially so. Either he had not brought much with him when he moved out of her mother's house, or he had moved much of it to Sonia's, or both. There were a few books on the shelves, mostly the spy novels that had always been his favorites. She selected one called *Deadly Games* and flopped back down on the couch.

She was two chapters in, following the main character through a harrowing scene in the South American jungle, when a knock at the door startled her. Being alone in her dad's house in the middle of nowhere made unexpected visitors a nervous thing to say the least. Her heart was still racing when she got to the peephole and saw Deputy Alex Chen standing outside, in frayed cargo shorts and a T-shirt. He apologized as soon as she opened the door.

"I should have called you first," he said. "I don't have your number in my phone."

Reflexively, she smoothed down her hair. "No problem. What's up?"

"I'm off today, so I went by your mom's to see if you needed any help." He gestured at his clothes and she saw he also wore construction-style work boots. "You weren't there."

She smiled. "No, I'm not. Where were you yesterday? I worked my ass off by myself. I'm taking the day off today."

He looked at her thoughtfully, and then up at the sky. "Any plans?"

"Just reading," she said cautiously.

"Go put on some good shoes," he said. "I have an idea."

The waterfall was a fifteen-minute drive from her dad's house. Alex drove them, chatting easily about the area as he navigated down the hilly two-lane highway and a few mildly scary narrow roads. Alex seemed to know everything about St. Clair County, Alabama, from when the railroads had come through to which industries and crops had been prominent at various times in the state's history. Rebecca closed her eyes as she listened. Both windows were down, and she liked the morning sun on her skin and the breeze in her hair.

He parked in a shady gravel lot next to a couple of pickup trucks and an RV with a motorcycle strapped to its rear. There were running shoes and bottles of water in his trunk. He quickly changed the boots and handed Rebecca a water. A trail map behind the wooden fence showed various trails marked in bright colors. "Do you still run?" he asked her. "You ran cross-country, right?"

"I can't believe you remember that. No, I don't. I haven't much since college, anyway."

He pointed to a curvy blue line on the map. "Well, there's an easy path here to the bottom of the falls, for city girls with sore muscles who don't want to chip a nail. It's paved, so if you hurt yourself I could bring a wheelbarrow up for you."

"Or?"

"Or we could take my jogging path — the yellow trail. It goes out through the valley here and then works up the back side of the ridge. You actually get a better view of the falls from this peak. Six miles, round trip. If you think you could keep up."

Rebecca looked at the opening in the trees where the trail started and could see the point about a hundred yards ahead where the yellow blazes split off from the paved path. It was a shady trail with the sun filtering down through the trees, which seemed to curve inward to make a tunnel. The scene looked enchanted, and she wondered how she had never been here before. "Six miles?"

she asked.

"Yeah. You know what? It's okay, we'll do the short path. I know you're tired from cleaning."

She knew he was baiting her, but it worked anyway. She smacked him lightly on the chest and hoped her sore calf muscles would not snap as she took off running for the first time in years. "Try to keep up," she called back at him.

Alex had no trouble whatsoever keeping up. After a half mile of running next to her, he went full speed ahead when she stopped to walk, clutching at her side. She wondered briefly if he'd left her, but found him just around the next bend, coming back toward her down a steep hill like a mountain goat. He was not even sweating. "Show-off." She scowled.

He grinned and returned to her side to walk next to her. "I know, I'm sorry. Cute girls have always had that effect on me."

"I forgot you were in the army," she said. "You could probably do this run in your sleep."

"Well, not asleep maybe, but I did it drunk once," Alex said.

"What?"

"For the record, I do not recommend it. I think I sprained both ankles that night. Of course, that was for a cute girl, too."

"Was she impressed?"

"I think so. She married me. Of course, it helped that I had knocked her up a few months before that."

Rebecca had many questions in response to this, and settled on, "So, you're divorced?" *Thank you, Captain Obvious.*

"Yes. For a long time. My ex-wife, Shondra, had a pretty serious drug problem. Still does, I imagine, if she's still alive."

"You don't know where she is?"

"No one does. Not even her parents. Last time any of us heard from her, she called from Chicago six years ago to ask for bail money. I didn't have it to give her even if I'd wanted to, and my in-laws were just done with it. Not that I blame them. She swore she would never speak to any of us again. So far, it's the first promise she's kept."

"That's awful," Rebecca said.

"Yeah," he agreed. "I knew she had some problems. But she had been clean for a while when I met her. Then our daughter Honey was born, and I don't know. I guess the stress was too much for her. I was still in the army then, and got deployed, and Shondra moved back in with her parents. She was trying to finish nursing school and work at the same time, and . . . babies are really hard. I know it sounds stupid to say that, but I just don't think Shondra was wired for motherhood, you know? She started doing amphetamines, I think to stay awake and study, but then she moved on to crystal meth and it just spiraled from there."

"I'm sorry."

"Me, too."

"So Honey lives with Shondra's parents?"

He nodded. "It started out as a temporary thing, while I was deployed. But then when I got out of the army, I started working for the sheriff, and with the crazy hours and the risky job and everything . . . it just seemed easier if they had primary custody. Honey needed stability, and they had lost their daughter. I couldn't take away their granddaughter, too. Not when I wasn't even sure I could raise her alone."

"That's a hard choice," Rebecca said. "Brave."

Alex scaled a large boulder that jutted out into the path from the side of the mountain and held a hand down to help her up. She glanced at the path's walk-around option, which would take her a good twenty feet to the left and back again to where he stood. She gave him her hand to help her scrabble up the rock.

"You have to do what's best for your kids," he said. "Even if it's hard for you."

"Do you miss her? Honey, I mean. Do you wish she lived with you?" she asked.

"Sometimes, yeah." He ducked beneath a low-hanging branch and held it up for her to pass under. "They've been great, though," he went on. "My in-laws. Ex-in-laws. They love Honey and she loves them, and I see her pretty much whenever I want."

"That's nice." This was so outside her realm, Rebecca was unsure what else to say.

"I take her camping and fishing and go to the Daddy-Daughter dances with her. I try hard not to miss the big milestones. It's not perfect, but she's a great kid. Young woman, really. She'll be a freshman this fall. Softball. Volleyball. Honor roll."

"You sound really proud of her." Rebecca thought of Jake and little Bonnie, and found it was hard to imagine that wobbly little round-cheeked toddler as a "young woman."

"I am," he said. "What about you? You ever wanted kids?"

"Is that your one question for the day?"

"What? You're still counting? You just asked me like forty. I thought we were just having a normal adult conversation."

She laughed. "Fair enough. No."

"Just no?"

They were cresting the top of a rise now, and Alex stepped aside to allow her over the top first. "No," she repeated as she passed him. "Does that make you think less of me?"

Without waiting for an answer, she hoisted herself up and gasped. Before her was a gap in the trees through which she could see the rolling green hills and farms below. They created a hilly little patchwork that made it look like God had spread a quilt over the earth — all shades of green stitched in black asphalt and rusty clay roads. The little river that must flow from the falls to their right emerged to the south and wound through the hills before disappearing on the horizon. "It's beautiful."

"Great, huh?" Alex said behind her. "It's why I'll always come back here."

He led her a few feet along the ridge to a spot where a rock outcropped over the trees and they sat, drinking water and gazing into the distance. She stood and stretched, her left calf twinging, and inhaled deeply of the morning air. She let it back out as a long, slow sigh. "I can't remember the last time I felt so peaceful."

"That's got to be a good thing," Alex said. He took off his shirt, rolled it up under his head, and lay back with his eyes closed to soak up the midmorning sun. Rebecca stole a quick glance at his bare chest before turning back to the landscape. She blushed at the memory of shirtless Alex the other morning in her hotel room. Now she could see more clearly. There was a tattoo on his left arm, lettering she could only assume was Chinese, and he had just the merest suggestion of a late-thirties belly, softened by too many nights drinking beer and singing karaoke. Otherwise, his upper body was smooth and muscular, nearly perfect.

Stop it, Rebecca. This guy has a teenage daughter and lives in the middle of nowhere. Worse than the middle of nowhere — it's the last *middle of nowhere I want to be.*

Still, she had to admit the beauty of the landscape was alluring. She picked her way to the edge of the rock and sat carefully so that her legs dangled over the side. The scene before her was like a painting, or a perfect photograph, except that it was not entirely still. Birds flitted and chirped, and every few minutes, she heard a distant motor of a truck or tractor scaling one of the large hills across the valley. The breeze came periodically and lifted the baby hairs on the back of her neck. She lost herself in thoughts of her mom, her dad, and even poor fluttering Sonia. She wondered idly how crazy

Valerie was making whoever was subbing for her at the airline.

"The answer is no," Alex said behind her.

"What?" She'd thought he might be asleep, he'd been quiet for so long.

"You asked if I thought less of you because you don't want kids. The answer is no." He was still lying on his back with his eyes closed; Rebecca was unsure if he was starting a new conversation or had just remembered the question.

"Okay," she said.

"Everyone is different. Kids are damn hard."

"Yes, they are."

More silence. She could not figure Alex out. He seemed interested in her, and he certainly didn't seem like the type to play games. But he was offering her nothing else; he had not made a move on her. Not that she wanted him to. *Obviously.*

After several minutes more, Alex stood and stretched. He walked to where Rebecca sat and extended his hand again. "You always assume I'm just going to take your hand," she challenged.

"You're right," he said. He withdrew the hand and began walking in the other direction. "See you at the falls."

She gaped at him momentarily, until he

ducked back into the woods on the far end of the ridge and convinced her he was not returning for her. "I have to be careful what I say to this guy," she muttered, as she dusted herself off and set out to follow him.

The falls were another ten-minute walk away, over easy rolling landscape in the woods atop the ridge. She caught up to him about fifty feet in, and kept pace behind him as he weaved among the trees and bounced over roots and rocks. He knew this path by heart, she saw, and even affectionately patted a large cottonwood that had fallen across the path at an angle, forcing them to duck beneath it.

They heard the falls before they could see them — a steady rain through the pine needles. Rebecca was ashamed that the sound reminded her instantly of the white noise machine Valerie used in large city hotels, rather than some other more natural sound. *I should really get out more.*

When they got to the next big clearing, Alex took a step to the side so Rebecca could see for herself. They were on the side of the mountain, with the top of the falls less than thirty feet away. The water rumbled over the top and out a little way into midair before dropping in great white sheets. There was a light spray coming off the falls that hit them when the breeze blew in their direction. From where they stood, she could not see the bottom, but she could hear the water roaring on the rocks below. It awed her that the microscopic droplets she could barely feel, and the powerful mass of water that could easily carry her away to drown, were all part of the same magnificent whole. She thought about all the times she had flown over the ocean without giving a second thought to all the water beneath her — how beautiful, life-giving, and dangerous it was all at once.

"Wow," she said.

Alex did not respond, but he took her hand. She did not pull it away. They stood like that for a few minutes, hand in hand. His was rough and a little calloused, hers soft and recently manicured. *I could love him,* she thought suddenly. *If I let myself, I could fall for him here, where it's beautiful and he's strong and funny and holding my hand. But then what? What happens when we come down from the mountain?*

As though sensing her apprehension, Alex gave her hand a squeeze and dropped it. He nodded back toward the path and she followed him back out of the clearing, into the trees and upward again. They scaled another little hill and emerged onto a black asphalt path that led to a bridge over the top of the falls. There were teenagers in brightly colored church group T-shirts scattering around them — some still lingering on the overlook bridge, others following the asphalt path back to a small parking lot. Rebecca could see a small white bus through the trees.

"You're kidding me," she said. "There's a road up here?"

Alex grinned. "Well, yeah. But this way is more fun."

She glared at him and walked toward the bridge, where the last of the kids were being hustled away by a tired-looking chaperone in a large, floppy hat. Alex stood beside her as Rebecca leaned just slightly over the rail, watching the water cascade down toward the rocks below. "See?" he said, gesturing at a boy and a girl who were play-fighting behind the others, as the chaperone threw up her hands and walked on. "You appreciate this more than they do because you *earned* it."

"And because I'm thirty-four, not fourteen."

"That too, I guess." He bumped her gently with his hip and she relented with a smile. He pointed down to the right at a patch of rocky hillside. "That's where we were a minute ago."

"That is actually pretty cool," she admitted.

"Once in a while, Rebecca," he said, taking her hand and leading her back to the trail, "it pays to have a little faith."

22

Mountainside Wellness Institute was situated in a rural suburb of Gadsden, past four-way stops and school zones at the top of one of East Alabama's most picturesque hills. *It's as good a place for a mental hospital as any,* Rebecca thought on her first visit to check on Lorena. In terms of scenery, it was not so very different from her trip to the waterfall with Alex two days before. It had the same natural feel and sweeping views of the patchwork countryside: just more houses, fewer trees, and no waterfalls or confusing social situations.

She checked in at the front reception area, which had more the look of a log cabin than a hospital. A black woman with long braids wearing a long black skirt and animal print blouse introduced herself as Dawn, the social worker on her mother's case. She guided Rebecca through sunlit rooms with high ceilings and walls of windows to a deck in the back overlooking the hills.

"I'll give you a few minutes," Dawn said kindly. "If you need anything, I'll be right inside."

Lorena was sitting at a metal patio table in a soft pink cardigan, staring into the distance. In the sunlight, her gaunt face showed more wrinkles than Rebecca had ever noticed before. Rebecca had to clear her throat twice to get her attention.

"Becky," her mother said warmly, taking her hand. "Sit down."

"Hi, Mom," Rebecca said tentatively. She was searching for a polite way to gauge where Lorena was today: whether she would know Rebecca as her teenage self and be looking for Cory, or if she would see reality as it was. "So you know . . . what's going on?"

Lorena sighed and held Rebecca's gaze. "You look good, honey. Tired, but good."

"Mom," Rebecca said with a slight squeak. She tried to say more, but nothing would come, so she threw her arms around Lorena instead. "Oh, Mom. Please be okay."

Lorena patted her back. "I'm trying, sweetheart. I really am."

"Do you know . . . what's happening?"

"With the house? They told me you're cleaning it up so I can go home."

"Yes. I am." Rebecca said it with more conviction than she felt. She had worked at the house for nearly all the previous day and left feeling as though she had barely scratched the surface.

"Just listen, sweetie — don't move too many things around. It may not look like much of a system, but I have it pretty well organized. No one else can find things there, but I can. And you're taking care of the cats?"

Rebecca had not even thought about the cats, and had not the first idea where they had ended up. "The cats are fine," she said gently.

"Watch out for Archie. He'll claw you if you're not careful."

"Okay."

"You won't throw too much away without me?"

"No." Rebecca wished someone had prepared her for this conversation, told her what to say and do. She hated lying to her mother, but Lorena seemed so fragile. It seemed as though a strong breeze might blow her away; Rebecca could only imagine what the truth would do. She was afraid to even mention Cory.

"How's work?" Lorena asked amiably. "Flown anywhere interesting lately?"

"It's fine. I have a few days off."

"That's nice," Lorena said. She turned back to look at the hills below. Whether she was confused by the situation, afraid of what Rebecca might tell her if they talked any more, or simply content to be quiet, it was hard to say. This process was going to take some time.

Rebecca stood after a moment and patted her mother's hand. "You should eat more, Mama," she said.

"They don't have chocolate doughnuts," Lorena said.

"I'll bring you some."

"Thank you, dear. Your father and I are so proud of you. You know that, don't you?"

"Yes."

Rebecca went back inside and asked the social worker about her mother's attending doctor, who was not due back in for rounds until later in the day. "So how do I handle the house cleaning with her?" she said. "How much should I tell her? Can I mention Cory? Does she understand?"

"Hard to say," Dawn said gently. "She'll have to face reality eventually, but she needs our help giving it to her in a way that her mind can digest. Sometimes that's just about following her lead, or your own instincts."

Rebecca found this less than helpful. "What if I don't have any instincts?"

The social worker laughed. "Then you're in more trouble than she is. You better follow her lead."

As she drove back down the mountain to go back to what had once been her childhood home, Rebecca felt further from understanding than ever.

Saturday night, she was back in Atlanta, snug in a booth at an Irish pub with Suzanne and Marci. The dark walls were covered in flags, vintage Guinness advertisements, and soccer memorabilia in shadow boxes. The corners of their wooden table had been rounded and polished by years of use. Rebecca resisted the temptation to wipe it down with a bar napkin, and instead savored her rum and Coke while the other women sipped their drinks. After her time in Alabama, and all day today surrounded by kids and the Stillwells' inebriated neighbors, it felt like a return to civilization.

"When are you going back?" Suzanne said, eyeing Rebecca's glass. "Not tonight, I hope."

"No, no. Tomorrow night. Maybe Monday. I have to have a couple of days off."

"So what exactly is going on with your

mom, if you don't mind my asking? You've only given us bits and pieces."

"I know, I'm sorry." Part of her wanted to spill out everything that had been happening, with the house and her mom, even Alex. Part of her wanted to change the subject entirely.

"Maybe if you tell us, we could help," Marci said.

Rebecca took a long swig. "Have you ever seen one of those TV shows about the hoarders?"

Suzanne wrinkled her nose. "You mean those people with houses full of stuff?"

"Yeah. Well, I guess my mom has had this problem for a long time, but since I've been away from Alabama, things have gotten much worse."

"You didn't know."

Rebecca sighed. "Sometimes you don't want to know, I guess."

"Is it awful?"

"Well, yes. I mean, I've watched a few episodes of those shows and done a little research, and I think there are worse, but Mom's place is still pretty bad."

Marci patted Rebecca's arm. "How are you handling it?"

"I've just started. Honestly, I think it would have been much worse if Dad hadn't been doing damage control for years."

"So we'll come help you," Suzanne said.

"No."

"Why not?"

"I just . . . I don't know. It's embarrassing. And gross. And really hard work."

"Rebecca," Suzanne said. Her voice had that stern, teacher-like quality she used when keeping wayward vendors in check for her events. "We're your friends."

"I know that."

"So let us help you. I'd love to come see where you grew up."

"No," Rebecca said, too quickly. "You wouldn't find it interesting. And, seriously, I'm not at a point where I would even know how to tell other people to help."

Marci looked thoughtful. "For some reason, I always thought you were from Birmingham. Where is Oreville, exactly?"

"It's close to Birmingham. Well, sort of. Forty-five minutes away. I always just said Birmingham when I met people in college because it was a place everyone knew."

"Huh," Marci said.

Suzanne raised an eyebrow but said nothing else.

"So, how is Dylan?" Rebecca asked, changing the subject. "How is married life?"

"He's fine. Really good, actually. He's

been asked to record this year's NFL theme song."

"Really?"

"Yeah. It's a whole little bit he gets to do with some of the players and cheerleaders. He was so excited. I think I'm going to have to let him go back on tour soon, or he's going to go crazy."

"Do you think you can handle that?"

Suzanne stirred her drink. "Maybe."

"Of course she can handle it," Marci said. "She's just worried about all those girls in the teeny-tiny shorts throwing their bras onstage at him."

"And showing up backstage afterward," Suzanne added.

"But you don't really doubt Dylan?" Rebecca said. "He seems absolutely devoted to you."

"He is. I think it's more about my general discomfort with the whole situation. I've never had this much to lose before, and there are literally millions of women ready and willing to take him away from me."

"Wow," Rebecca said. "I guess I'd never thought of it that way."

"Ready and willing, maybe," Marci said. "But not able. None of those little groupies can hold a candle to you."

Suzanne shrugged. Dylan was several

years younger than any of them, a fact that had always been a little tough for Suzanne. They sipped in silence for a while. Rebecca took in the sounds of the pub and reflected that even the most perfect-looking relationships felt fragile to the people in them.

"Rebecca, I really should apologize," Marci said after a while, breaking the silence.

"Seriously, it's not necessary," Rebecca said. She stirred her drink. "If I thought my husband was . . ." Rebecca did not want to finish that sentence, out of respect for Marci's feelings. Was it worse to have a man like Jake in your bed and be unsure of him, or to have no man in your bed at all? She did not know. Being alone felt awful sometimes, but maybe Marci's situation was worse.

"Well, I implied that you were having an affair with my husband," Marci said. "And I had no evidence for it. That's not cool."

"No," Rebecca said. "You didn't have evidence, but you had a reason. You know how I've felt about him for so long, and I did try to steal him before you got married."

"It wasn't stealing. They were broken up," Suzanne said. She looked at Marci with mild defiance. She was getting a little tipsy. "You were broken up."

Marci rolled her eyes. "Anyway, that was a long time ago and we weren't married then. I should have given you more credit."

"Honestly, Marci, I don't know if I deserve any credit. But thanks." She lifted her drink in Marci's direction, and then followed nervously with, "So, do you know anything . . . more?"

"Well, I found the file where he keeps his business credit card, and I started looking through at the dates when he's supposed to be working or out of town. He's been going to this one hotel near us, I think, even when he says he's somewhere else."

"Un-fucking-believable," Suzanne said. "I never would have thought this about Jake. It just doesn't fit, somehow."

"I agree," Rebecca said.

"Well, I'm going to find out," Marci said. "Next time he's supposed to be working, I am going to follow him and we'll see exactly who he has been seeing."

Rebecca and Suzanne exchanged a look.

"Marci," Suzanne said, steadying herself with an elbow on the table. "Do you think that's really a good idea?"

"No," Marci admitted. "But what else can I do? We're going to have another baby and I can't bring him or her into the world, I can't pretend with Bonnie that everything is fine, not knowing if their father is screwing some slut on the side."

Rebecca bit her lip. Though no one would dare mention it at this moment, at one point not so very long ago, Marci herself had been the "some slut" in question, when she had had a relationship with a married man. *I guess perspective is everything.* The table was quiet for a moment; the three of them sat sipping their drinks and listening to the sounds of the busy pub around them. Glasses and plates clinked in the kitchen; conversations murmured steadily, punctuated by laughter. A group of soccer fans let out a cheer at a table near the bar. Then, true to pregnant lady form, Marci set down her Coke and burst into tears.

23

For the next few weeks, Rebecca's days formed a predictable routine, which would have been comforting if it had not been so sad. Each morning she woke up in her father's stark white bedroom, dressed, and picked up a small box of chocolate doughnuts on the way to see her mother. Lorena was always happy to see her, and especially the doughnuts, but she seemed to waver in her ability to anchor herself in time and space. Some days she seemed to think Cory was still alive, and others she did not mention him at all. Always, she spoke about Rebecca's father as though they were still married, and Rebecca didn't correct her because it was technically true. Lorena had only the foggiest notion of where she was and why, and each time this notion seemed to crystallize a bit in her awareness, Lorena became sad and — if this was possible — even more distant.

"I think some days it's just too much for her to process," Dawn said one day. "Reality can be just awful, you know, and sometimes the mind just needs a break from it."

Intellectually, Rebecca understood this. She would be lying if she said she had never wanted a break from reality herself. Emotionally, she wondered when, if ever, her mother planned to return from this little vacation. She could see the appeal: The grounds of Mountainside were lovely and well-kept, the views spectacular. The staff were kind and approachable, and the food seemed better than average. Better, at any rate, than what Rebecca ate when she worked on meal flights.

"Why don't you come in for a family therapy session?" the social worker asked.

"What? No, I don't — I don't think I need . . ."

"It's your choice," the social worker said kindly, "but it would probably help her recovery. What's your work schedule like? Maybe we can schedule it at a time that's convenient for you."

Rebecca thought briefly about lying, but decided against it. "No, that's fine. I'm on family leave. I should come in."

The truth was, she missed work. At least,

she missed her paid job — being on the move and the tidy routines of the airline. As for labor itself, she had never done so much of it. By ten thirty each morning, she had kissed her mother gently on the forehead, smoothing the gray that had begun to gather around Lorena's tired face, and was on her way back to the house. She arrived each day to find the blue tarp neatly folded on the lawn, so the grass could breathe in the mornings before she began.

She had worked out an agreement with a couple of local guys who worked at the Goodwill in Birmingham — they stopped by first thing two mornings a week on their way to work and cleared away the items she had left on the blue tarp, while a red tarp nearby served as a resting spot for things that might be salvaged or sold. At least twice a day, Rebecca caught herself shifting items from the red tarp to the blue one and back again, or the other way around. She found it was easier not to buy things in the first place, as Rebecca had done for so long, than to have to decide which possessions were worth keeping.

There were moments when she understood something of what her mother must have been thinking. *This is such a cool thing,* or *I bet this has a neat story to it,* or *it seems*

a shame to throw away something so new. . . .
Those were the moments when things got shifted to the red tarp — an unopened hand mixer (even though no one in the family baked), a neat lamp shaped like an elephant that reminded her of her grandmother, a box of collector's bottles of Coke. Then she would spend another few hours in the house and feel ready to burn the damn place down. Back to the blue tarp, all of it.

The relief she would feel leaving the driveway, sometime after dark, would fade into sadness and even regret as the clutter on the blue tarp disappeared into the darkness of the rearview mirror. What would her mother be without all these things? If her family's history and the junk that her mother loved meant nothing, then what meant something?

She had left all these things behind her long ago, when she left Alabama as a teenager. It was easier to leave things behind when someone else was curating them. But Rebecca had sensed, even then, that there was something unhealthy in the way her mother clung to each piece of matter around her. It was as though by holding on to the everyday items that came and went across her fingertips, somehow she could hold on to Cory, too.

In her mother's eyes, everything in that house had infinite possibilities, potential so great it might never be tossed aside. How could Rebecca compete with that?

She couldn't, and even at seventeen she had recognized her defeat. So, she had cast off the world of reused sandwich bags and aluminum foil balls and a closed-off room at the end of the hall. She had replaced it with a senior year trying to fit in with the kids from a rich Atlanta suburb, trying to live up to other people's potential. Then the sorority at UGA, for which she was still the regional alumna vice president at large, where she hoarded social connections the way her mother hoarded garage sale furniture.

Rebecca loved her clean, orderly life. She loved being the kind of person who could be a blank slate, a smile that reflected back what people wanted to see in themselves. She had no pets to provoke allergies, no glaring artwork for someone else to see as tasteless, no low-cut blouses or profanity to offend a potential suitor's mother. She had built her life on being girl-next-door clean, an asset to any man of wealth and reputation. And yet, she slept alone. The men of wealth and reputation wanted blue-blooded women like Suzanne, who could wear high heels and silk scarves, and still manage to make "motherfucker" sound feminine. Rebecca had never been able to pull off either scarves or cursing. Both hung on her with the same ill-fitting awkwardness.

BY MARCI THOMPSON STILLWELL

BLOG: THE CARE AND FEEDING OF A SUBURBAN HUSBAND
{Entry #182: Do You Feel Like a Grown-Up?}

Monday, July 25, 2016
True confessions time: When I was younger and I imagined what life would be like in my midthirties, I thought I would feel, well . . . a little more grown up than I do today. Sometimes I look at my lovely home in the suburbs, my beautiful baby daughter, and our amazing life, and think, "Jeez, they're trusting me with all this? Are you sure you have the right girl?"

I have to be honest, I always imagined I'd feel more self-assured and confident at this stage of my life, the way my mom always did when she was this age. Or at least she seemed that way to me. But

---

when I hold Munchkin in my arms, I don't feel like the mature, nurturing protector I remember Mom being. I feel like the half-crazed, exhausted, confused, and often childish pretender to the throne of adulthood. I don't know about you guys, but I'm operating on the "fake it til you make it" philosophy of marriage and motherhood. Every day I'm expecting someone to realize that I'm not really cut out for this life, knock on my door and deposit me back where I belong, working as a temp and living in a tiny apartment in Texas next to a crappy punk band.

For me, this issue is about motherhood in particular, but in talking to my friends, there is a common theme. Like my friend who recently married (squeee!) a much younger man who happens to be a public figure. Under the spotlight and under pressure to be perfect, even the most talented, beautiful, and self-assured woman I know can feel the strain of long-past insecurities pulling on her. She's amazingly successful and gorgeous, but sometimes it's as though she were still an awkward kid in middle school. As someone who was even more awkward than she was in middle school, I can sympathize.

We have another friend who has returned to her hometown after leaving years and years ago. She is doing some work at her childhood home and trying to renegotiate a relationship with her parents, which I can only imagine makes her feel like she's back in high school again. We always think our parents are going to be these bastions of wisdom as we navigate adulthood. You don't expect that they are going to hand you the reins and wish you luck.

So my question is this: When are we going to feel like grown-ups? Is this a generational thing? Maybe those of us in the "me generation" raised on MTV and Nintendo are destined to be dazed and confused forever. We do seem to have the luxury of more time to gaze at our own navels than previous generations. Or maybe people in every age feel this way, and our generation simply whines more.

All I know is that I wish I'd spent more time enjoying being a kid, and even a teenager and college student. While I wouldn't trade my current life and family for anything, this growing up stuff is not nearly as clear-cut and freeing as I expected. I don't know what adulthood means, but I do hope I get there while I'm still young enough to appreciate it.

24

One Wednesday night in late July, Alex invited her to an out-of-the-way seafood place for dinner. "Just as friends," he'd said when he dropped by her mom's house earlier in the day. "I promise, there will be no hand-holding, canoodling, or other tomfoolery. Just fried shrimp and the best hush puppies in the South."

"Who could turn that down?" she'd said.

By the time Rebecca had returned to her dad's after a day of inspecting, moving, throwing away, and (once) running screaming from the house after discovering a family of mice had taken up residence in a closet, no shower had ever felt so good. She couldn't remember being hungrier, either. She put her long brown hair in a wet braid rather than taking the time to blow it dry, and waited on the front steps so that Alex would not even need to come to the door.

"Maybe I should have made a reservation," he said, when he saw her. He opened the car door for her, and waited for her to get situated before closing it and walking around to the driver's side.

"Do you think it will be crowded?" she asked. Her stomach growled.

"Shouldn't be too bad on a Wednesday. But I think there's half a protein bar in the glove box if you're starving."

"That's okay." She wrinkled her nose.

"You sure? It's only a few days old. I don't want to get my arm chewed off if there's a wait at Abelle's."

"I think you're safe."

"You *think*?" He raised an eyebrow.

"I'll keep you posted."

He grinned at her and turned onto the two-lane highway that ran in front of her father's rental. "Lucky for me we're already on the south side of town. That will save us a few minutes."

"Where is this place, exactly?"

"It's down 231 and a little ways east. About twenty-five minutes. Basically the middle of nowhere. I can't believe you've never been there."

"We didn't usually drive far to dinner, I guess. Dad was kind of a creature of habit, by the time Mom stopped cooking."

They were quiet for a minute.

"Want to ask me anything?" he said. "You've got three questions for tonight if you want them."

"Okay. . . . Um, where do you live?" she asked. She was surprised she had never wondered until now.

"The old Pickney Place downtown," he said.

Rebecca searched her memory for why this name sounded so familiar. "The haunted house? Seriously?"

He laughed. "Everyone says that. It's not really haunted, though. I just use a projector and an old tape recorder to keep Scooby-Doo and his friends from discovering where I've hidden the money from the bank robbery."

"I thought that place was ready to collapse."

"It pretty much was," he said. "I bought it four years ago at an auction on the courthouse steps. Old Ruth Pickney had been in a nursing home for years, and when she died, there was no one to leave it to. It was pretty run-down, but I've been fixing it up. Hoping to sell it, maybe buy another one and do the same thing."

Rebecca remembered walking past the Pickney Place as a kid when she visited her dad at the post office. Even then, she'd thought the creepy old house was ready to fall down, and that had been more than twenty years ago. Ruth Pickney must have spent at least two decades in the nursing home, because the house had never been lived in that she remembered. There were whispers that it was haunted, of course, fueled by the fact that all the other Pickneys had died suddenly during a smallpox outbreak in the 1930s, leaving only little Ruth behind to be raised by an unscrupulous aunt and uncle, who squandered her family's fortune and ran away to New York as soon as Ruth was sixteen.

"People say Ruth was an odd bird," she said.

"I never knew her," Alex said. "But she certainly could have sold the house years ago and been better off. Lucky for me she didn't, though. It's been kind of a labor of love to fix it up. I only use salvaged materials, pretty much."

"Salvaged materials?"

"Yeah, you know. When they tear something down, I'll go talk to the demolition crew and try to find things that can be used again. It's recycling, basically. Green building. But in my case it's mostly because I'm broke."

She made a face. "Wouldn't it be . . . I

don't know, safer or whatever, to use new materials? How do you know you're not bringing in some kind of nasty bug or something?"

"What? Like termites? I check for those."

"Yeah, or mold, or bacteria or whatever."

He laughed. "Bacteria?"

Rebecca hated when people laughed at her, and Alex seemed to do it more than anyone, except maybe Jake. "Never mind," she said, sulking.

"You still have two more questions."

"I'll use them later."

"Can I use mine?"

"Sure."

"Do you see yourself staying in Atlanta? I mean, long-term?"

Rebecca wished she had asked him more questions instead. She twisted her ring and looked out the window. "I don't know. I guess I haven't really thought much about the long term."

Alex did not respond, but kept his eyes on the road. He put the car into fifth and they hummed along quietly for a while. Hungry and cranky as she was, Rebecca was grateful for the quiet.

She tried to ignore her hunger pangs as they drove down seemingly endless country roads, with their innumerable dirt road tributaries and bridges over dribbles of muddy creeks. She hoped she would not have to find her way back to Oreville from here — they were in the middle of nowhere, and they had crossed two county lines that she'd noticed.

Finally, just before the millionth four-way stop, Alex turned in to a short gravel driveway surrounded by a grassy field full of cars and trucks. There were more vehicles parked here than they had seen during the entire half-hour drive. The restaurant itself was little more than a clapboard shack with faded paint on the windows advertising seafood specials and blue plate dinners. There was a bug-light zapping mosquitoes and flickering ominously near the door. An old man sat on a rickety bench out front, staring at the road.

"Evening, Elmer," Alex said as he opened the door.

The man grunted in response.

"Good chat," Alex said.

Inside was the quintessential hole-in-the-wall country restaurant: Formica tables and old padded brown chairs — half of which were losing their stuffing — linoleum floors, flickering fluorescent lights, and — she couldn't help but notice — a layer of dust thicker than a magazine on the air vents next to their table. In her other life in Atlanta, she would have taken one look at this place and walked right back out again. But she was thirty minutes from nowhere, and so hungry she could eat her own foot. And Rebecca had to admit that the hush puppies frying smelled amazing.

"Do you have a drink menu?" she asked the middle-aged waitress who came to take their orders.

"Coke, tea, water."

"It's a dry county," Alex said. "No booze."

"Oh," Rebecca said, and the waitress rolled her eyes. "Unsweet tea, please."

"We're out of unsweet. Be about ten minutes."

"Sweet is fine, thank you." When the waitress shuffled away, Rebecca said. "Jeez, I forgot dry counties even existed."

"You're in a whole 'nother world now," Alex said, amplifying his already-thick Southern accent. "But at least they have a seafood sampler."

They were halfway through dinner, and Rebecca was greedily licking the grease from her fingers while debating a third cheddar biscuit from the basket between them, when the little teenybop song rang out from Alex's pocket. "Excuse me," he said. He got up from the table and took the call outside.

The waitress came back to the table with a pitcher of unsweetened tea to refill Rebecca's mason jar glass and to take away the now-empty bread basket. "Everything good?"

"Oh my God," Rebecca said to her. "This is amazing."

"It'll put meat on your bones," the waitress said. "Not that Alex will mind. He's a good man. Doesn't focus on appearances like so many do."

Before she could protest that she and Alex were only friends, the waitress was gone again. *He knows everyone in a ten-county radius,* she thought. *If I broke his heart, I wouldn't even be able to fly in and out of the state.*

Alex returned a few minutes later and put his phone on the table, smiling.

"I'd love to meet her," Rebecca said, surveying her corn on the cob for any remaining kernels. "You guys seem to have such a great relationship."

"We do," he said. "She's a good kid. But you can't meet her."

Even though her suggestion had been offhand, Rebecca was taken aback by his refusal. "Why not?"

"Nothing personal, but I don't bring

women around my daughter." He used the last of his biscuit to guide a bite of coleslaw onto his fork. "Her life has been chaotic enough without a parade of potential stepmothers in and out of it."

"A parade?"

Alex grinned. "Well, not a parade, I guess. More like a small tea party, but still."

"But we're just friends," she countered. "Don't you think she would understand that?"

"Well, there's a fine line between friends and 'friends.' " He made air quotes with his fingers. "I think when teenage girls hear their dad introduce a beautiful woman as a 'friend,' they are going to jump to the same conclusion anybody else with a bit of sense would."

Rebecca wanted to dispute this characterization of their relationship, but she thought about her own father. He had referred to Sonia as a "friend" for several months, too. And she hadn't bought it either. "I guess you're right."

"Besides," Alex said, wiping his hands on a napkin before dropping it on his plate in defeat, "I haven't given up on the idea that you might promote me from friend to 'friend' yet. So I want to make sure the timing is right when you meet Honey."

Rebecca wished she had not said anything about it. She became engrossed in straightening the red checkered tablecloth so that it lined up with the edge of the table. The waitress returned with the check. "Here you go, darlin'."

Alex threw down two twenties and pushed back his chair. "Ready to go? I'm assuming you don't want peanut butter pie. It's supposed to be good but I'm always too damn full to try it."

"No, I'm stuffed," she said. He stood and she followed him toward the door. "You didn't have to buy me dinner. Thank you."

"As long as you know I'm expecting sex in return," he said as he walked out into the night. He was kidding, she knew. It was the same to him as Scooby-Doo and the haunted house, and the ten thousand other jokes he had made since they met. But the smile felt brittle on her face, and her stomach churned.

They navigated the grassy, unlighted parking lot in silence. There were thousands of stars in the sky, more than she could ever remember seeing before. He followed her gaze upward as he unlocked the passenger's door for her. "It's the country. You can't see them near the city because of all the light pollution."

"Oh," she muttered. She climbed into the car but kept her focus on the sky, even as they drove away.

A memory floated back to her. She was with her dad and Cory beside the creek one summer night, watching a meteor shower. She did not remember where her mother had been, why it had been just the three of them. But she and Cory had been squabbling for half the night — probably he was picking on her about her braces because he knew that drove her crazy. And she was calling him stupid because it was her only defense, his only perceived weakness. Their dad had put one arm roughly around each of them and said, "Hush, you two. Don't you know the stars are magic? You can't be angry when you look at them. Stars are for wishing, and you never know what might come true underneath them."

They had quieted then. Not so much because of the magical stars, but because Richard was not one to tolerate disobedience, not back then. Rebecca had still been angry with Cory and made a hasty wish on the next meteor she saw flare across the sky. *I wish he would just leave me alone.* For years after Cory's death, Rebecca had half-believed that it had been her wish that caused it.

"You okay?" Alex said. They had been driving for several minutes in silence.

"I'm fine."

"You sound fine."

"Sorry, I think I just ate too much."

"Me too," he said, patting his belly. "It's worth it, though, don't you think?"

"It was really good."

"Hey, do you want a beer?" he asked. "I know a great spot."

"I thought it was a dry county?"

"It is, but I happen to have a six-pack in the trunk. It's cold, or at least it was two hours ago. There's a beautiful view of the river down one of these back roads. And an angry old man who shoots trespassers on sight down another. I'm pretty sure I remember which is which."

"That sounds great, Alex, but I think I just want to get home tonight. Can I take a rain check?"

"Oh. Okay, sure."

"I'm sorry. I just realized how tired I am, and I really did eat too much."

"Definitely. No problem."

They went back to being quiet as he navigated down the darkened highways, and Rebecca watched the stars appear and disappear over the silhouettes of the trees. Alex began to whistle. At first it was sort of a

299

tuneless whistling, and then she recognized "It Had to Be You," among other things.

25

Alex stopped by the house on his lunch break Thursday, bringing her a turkey sandwich and a Coke from a little insulated lunch cooler in the passenger's floorboard of the patrol car. Since his radio was quiet, he even helped her reach a few boxes that someone had managed to wedge into the upper reaches of her former bedroom closet.

"So this is where all the magic happened," he said, dusting his hands and looking around at what had become the "office," but still had a faded border by the ceiling of pink and blue bows with a couple of sections missing.

"Not in here it didn't," she said. "I was a good girl."

"Never let Roger Simon have a peek under your Beta Club T-shirt?"

She blushed. "No! I didn't think anyone remembered me and Roger, besides my dad."

"Oh, yeah. I was so jealous of him back then."

She felt suddenly uncomfortable. "His wife now seems lovely, from the pictures I've seen."

"She is. I had dinner with them a few weeks ago. Great kids, too. Honey played with them in the backyard for hours."

"You had dinner with Roger?"

"Sure. I mean, raging jealousy over you aside, we're old football buddies. Besides, we're sort of in the same industry. I mean, at least we both have 'law' in our job titles."

"Well, yeah, at slightly different levels." She regretted it as soon as it was out of her mouth.

His smile faded. He took a step toward the window and looked out in the direction of the patrol car. "I don't know. I like to think what I do is just as important as what Roger does."

Regret crept up from her belly. Why had she said such a stupid thing? "I'm sorry, that's not what I meant. Of course your job is important."

"But you think I could do better."

She hesitated. "Not better, no."

"But?"

"To be honest, I have wondered why you gave up on becoming an engineer. You talk about rebuilding that old house with such passion."

"I wonder that sometimes, too," he said quietly. He turned back to her. "Who knew you were such a snob?"

"I don't mean to be," she fumbled. "I have no room to talk. Most people think I'm just a waitress who works in the air."

"What's wrong with being a waitress? Lots of my friends are waitresses. They bring food and that makes people happy."

She thought about the lady at Abelle's the night before and felt even worse. "No — nothing is wrong with it, I just meant . . ." *Jesus. Who else can I insult?*

"Do you think less of my parents because they're just restaurant owners? Is your dad just a mailman? These jobs make the world go around and they're not appreciated."

"I know, that's true. I don't mean — I —" She was flabbergasted. How had this conversation gone so wrong so quickly?

Alex stared at her for another minute before his face broke into a wide grin. "I'm just messing with you, Williamson. You need to learn to relax a little." He smacked her ass playfully as he walked past. "We'll work on that later. For now, I gotta get back to work."

She stood unmoving, listening to him go,

and did not let out a breath until she heard the patrol car leave the driveway.

Rebecca worked until nearly nine that night. This was partly because she had a purging fit, during which she put more than half the items in her "unsure" pile out on the blue tarp for donation. And partly, she had to admit, because of the nervous energy left over from her conversation with Alex. He did not call her that afternoon, which was certainly not unusual, but she wondered all the same if he was angry with her.

It's totally unfair for him to call me a snob, she thought, carrying an unopened under-the-cabinet microwave to the blue tarp. *I am not a snob. I mean, what's wrong with want-ing something better in life?* There was a box of brand-new, artificial white poinsettias she'd contemplated saving in case they came in handy for the Junior League Christ-mas gala. Blue tarp, she decided. *If everyone were satisfied just doing any old job, we wouldn't have music to listen to, or art, or inventions. We wouldn't have the Internet.*

I can't believe I said that about his job. He's so brave to do what he does, and I know I sounded like a jerk. The elephant lamp with the red tasseled shade. *What was I thinking?*

Maybe I'm embarrassed about my job? I

don't have my own company like Suzanne or a book deal like Marci. I'm never going to be featured on PBS like Jake. There was an old typewriter from the 1970s, still in its blue plastic case. It clanged as she placed it on the tarp next to the lamp. *I'll never be asked to be a keynote speaker for anything.*

Next came a set of colorful melamine mixing bowls. She liked them, but remembered that she never cooked. *Then again, most people are never asked to be keynote speakers. Most people have normal jobs where they work for someone else, and they raise their families and live their lives and try to be happy. I see rich, powerful people in first class all the time and they don't seem happier than anyone else. Less, even.*

This went on for a couple of hours, with no resolution, until it was full dark and the blue tarp was overcrowded with items for Goodwill to pick up early the next morning. Finally Rebecca stopped, staring.

"Oh, crap."

She must have been through twenty boxes of clothes, toys, and knickknacks, plus many small appliances and miscellaneous items. In her frustration, however, she had lost track of what she was doing. There were several piles of things she'd intended to save that were now on the blue Goodwill tarp, and half of what she'd put on the red tarp to keep actually belonged in the Dumpster or the donation pile.

She considered calling the Goodwill guys and asking them to skip tomorrow, but a missed pickup would mean the yard remained crowded with junk for an extra three days. "Alex," she breathed, shaking her head, and went back to work resorting everything she had just done.

By the time she left the house that night she was ravenous, and stopped at the Git up N' Go off Highway 9 on her way to her dad's. A toothless old man held the door for her, and she went out of her way to give him her most genuine, not-snobby smile.

She could not be sure, but Rebecca thought he let out a wet-sounding whistle as she brushed past him. She glanced down at herself, in filthy jean shorts and an ancient white tank top, sweaty and rank from the day's work. There was an odd line of grayish dust across her midsection from something she had carried, and she could feel a matted curl of hair hanging across her brow. Commercials and *Flashdance* had taught her that men had fantasies about sexy women doing hard labor in skimpy clothes, but she was almost positive she could never live up to those images in her current state.

"People are *weird,*" she said aloud.

"You tellin' me," agreed the old black man behind the counter. He was counting a stack of bills at the register and did not look up at her.

She contemplated an egg salad sandwich in the cooler, but decided she did not trust the expiration date on gas station egg salad, no matter how hungry she was. In the end, she returned to the counter with a stick of beef jerky, a bag of sour cream and onion potato chips, and a large Diet Coke to wash it down. It was a far cry from the juicy burger and mixed green salad with balsamic vinaigrette she was craving, but it would have to do.

"Have a blessed night," the cashier said when he handed her the change from her rumpled five-dollar bill.

"I'll try," Rebecca said.

She was almost to her father's house when she slammed on the brakes and put the car in reverse. It only took ten minutes to get back to her mother's house, but she felt inexplicably panicky the whole way. *What if it's gone? What if I'm too late?*

But there it was, exactly where she'd left it on the blue tarp, in all its tacky glory. She loaded it into the backseat, thinking how ridiculous the red tassels and eclectic design were going to look in her sleek, modern apartment. "Maybe it's time to make room for some weirdness in my life," she said. It was too late that night, she decided, but she would call Alex tomorrow and set him straight.

26

That Saturday morning, for the first time in a month, Rebecca got up at 3:30 A.M. On purpose. She put on jeans, a light jacket, and a baseball cap, along with the old tennis shoes she cleaned in, and headed out the door.

"I can't believe I let you talk me into this," she told Alex when she found him, using her phone as a flashlight. He was about thirty yards from the parking lot next to Lake Ofeskokee, sitting in a folding camp chair.

"Shhh," he said. "You'll wake the fish."

"Can you catch them if they're sleeping?"

"No, but you'll scare them away. Did you bring coffee?"

"Yes," she whispered dramatically. She fumbled carefully to get the foam cup into his hands in the dark. His fingers were warm and lightly calloused as they brushed against hers. "Can I get you anything else?

Blanket? Pillow? Beverage napkin?"

"You really do miss your job, don't you?" She could hear the smile in his voice.

"I don't miss getting up before dawn to bring people coffee, no."

"This was our deal — I bring the gear and you bring the coffee."

"I don't understand why we couldn't do something during daylight hours. Or something with other people around. How do I know you're not going to strangle me and dump me in the lake?"

"It's still a possibility," he said drily.

"Or worse, I'll be eaten by some wild animal out here in the wilderness."

"Hey, you're the one who asked me what you could do to prove you weren't a snob. This is it. Well, it's this or pig wrestling."

"Fine. Where's my pole?"

"Here. I even baited your first hook for you. After that, you're on your own."

"After that, I'll probably just go back to bed."

"Okay, fine. I'll bait all your hooks. Jeez, girl, you'd never know that you were born and raised in Alabama. You've gotten all prissy and citified."

"Yes, I can see how the fact that I have some minimal hygiene standards and basic

310

literacy would make me seem like an out-
sider."

"Whoa, now. That's harsh. This is your
town, too. And we're not *that* bad. We have
a library. I've even been in it. Nice clean
bathrooms."

She gave his arm a gentle shove and
lowered herself carefully into the second
camp chair. "So what do I do next?"

"Put the hook in the water."

"Yeah. And?"

"Wait."

"Just wait?"

"Just wait."

She waited. And waited. Fifteen minutes
went by, and then twenty. Alex pulled three
decent-sized bream out of the water and
tossed them in a bucket between them
where they thrashed and rested in turns. He
caught a few smaller fish that he threw back.
But Rebecca got nothing. Once in a while
she felt a tiny bumping sensation at the end
of her line, but each time she pulled it out,
the worm was gone and Alex had to hook
another one on. She watched him do it the
first time, piercing the short yellow mealy
worm with the point of the hook so that a
bubble of white blood formed around it
while the poor thing squirmed helplessly.

She felt all the blood rush out of her face so that she was nearly sick. From then on, he baited her hook while she looked in the other direction.

The sun began to rise behind the trees, painting the sky in glorious warm pastels. She wedged her pole between her knees, the leg of the chair, and the bucket so that it would not move, and allowed herself to sit back and watch the sky beneath the brim of her cap. Slowly the world came into being around them, from gray outlines of predawn to orange light like flame, and finally a muted version of full daylight. Alex materialized next to her, too, in an army sweatshirt and black jogging shorts, with his eyes closed and head leaning back against the canvas of the chair. His jet-black hair was a rumpled mess, sticking out in every direction. She felt a sudden impulse to run her fingers through it, and then something stirred between her legs.

"Ah!" she yelled, forgetting the early hour and Alex's orders to be quiet. "I think I've got something!"

The pole jerked sideways, nearly knocking over the bucket next to her; it almost got away from her before she could get out of her chair and get her hands tight around it. Alex jumped from his seat to help her as the pole bent under the weight of whatever was at the other end of the line. He reached around her to grab the pole and widened his stance to give them stability. She was aware of his body behind her, close and warm, his arms around her.

"Here," he said, "anchor your right foot back and put your left foot forward." She did so just in time, as something tugged mightily on the other end of the line and nearly pulled her over.

"I hope it's not an alligator," he said.

She turned to glare at him. "Don't even play like that."

"Kidding. I'm kidding. It's almost totally impossible that it's an alligator."

"Almost? Alex!"

He laughed in her ear, finding the reel with his right hand and beginning to spool the line in. "You just hold on, okay? I'll bring it in. It's fine."

She could not believe how strong a fish could be, as she struggled to hold the pole steady while he turned the little silver handle on the reel. The pole looked like it was in danger of snapping in half at first, and when the fish finally broke the surface, they both reeled backward. She thought she would fall and the fish would end up halfway to the parking lot. Alex held her up, though, and managed to swing the pole back around so that the fish finally dangled in front of them, shimmery green and silver. She'd never thought a fish could show emotion, but this one looked *angry*.

She squealed in half-squeamish, half-victorious delight as Alex moved carefully around her to lower the fish into the bucket. "Oh my God! I caught one! And it's huge!"

"It really is a beauty," Alex said. "Looks like a red-eared bream."

"Do you see how big my fish is?" she said, ignoring the specifics and doing a little jumping dance. "I caught a really big fish!"

"I knew you could," he said. He threw his arms around her and jumped with her while they hugged in celebration. She felt giddy, and a little silly. But she thought she was beginning to understand why her dad liked fishing so much.

Alex stopped jumping and grinned at her, hands still on her shoulders. "See? I told you." And then something in his eyes changed, and he leaned into her with a gentle kiss that tasted like stale coffee. His face was rough with stubble and prickled her chin. For a moment, she was swept away. She closed her eyes and let her hands rise to his shoulder blades and her mouth press against his kiss. He pulled her closer.

She trembled just slightly — whether from the chill of the morning, the excitement of catching the fish, or Alex, she could not have said. But she felt his warmth against her, and moments later, a hardness stirring in his jogging shorts. This brought her back to reality.

"Oh, no," she said, pulling away from him and nearly falling over her chair. "No, Alex, we can't —"

"What?" he said. The bright smile was still on his lips but fading from his eyes. "We can't . . . what?"

"It's me," she said. "I'm sorry. I can't do this anymore."

"Can't do what? Fishing? Or kissing me?"

"Any of it. This . . . us. This relationship, or friendship or whatever it is . . . I can't do it."

His smile was feigned now, but he kept it. He raised his palms to her. "Was it something I said? Do I need a breath mint? I might have some gum in the car."

"No."

"What, then? I thought that kiss was kind of nice."

"It was, but . . . look, Alex. It's obvious that you think of this as more than friendship, and I know you had a crush on me in school. But it's not that simple. That was

315

almost twenty years ago. I'm not that little girl in the bleachers anymore."

"I know who you are, Rebecca."

"I don't think you do, questions or no questions. You don't want me — I'm a mess. I'm going to end up completely crazy just like my mom, and I am hopeless with relationships. You've been great, and I like you —"

"You *like* me."

"Yes, I do. But I can't stay here much longer. My life is in Atlanta. My job. My friends. I can't live in Oreville."

"What about Birmingham? It's basically West Atlanta." His tone was playful, but it was clear he'd been thinking about it.

"That's not the point." She was getting frustrated.

"What is the point?"

"It's that I just don't . . ." The next part came out in a rush. "Alex, I just don't return your feelings. I'm sorry."

"Oh, come on, you're just saying that because —"

"I am not just saying it," she said. "I know it sounds like a bad line, but I don't think I'm good for anyone right now. My life is a disaster, my family has fallen apart, and what I feel most of the time is numb. Just numb. I have nothing to give you. I'm not what you need."

He looked at her for a moment, his face unreadable, ashen. He went to the bucket and began to work at unhooking her fish. When he spoke, his voice was neutral, steady. "Yours is probably two and a half pounds. You can keep it if you want. Cook it."

"Alex," she said gently.

He did not look up from his work, but released the fish in the bucket and began winding up the line. "I'm going to throw mine back. They're a little iffy, and to be honest I just don't feel like cleaning them today."

"Alex."

No answer. He quietly packed up the tackle and folded his camp chair, watching intently what he was doing as he wrestled it into the sling that fit around it. She sighed and did the same with the other one and handed it to him. He shouldered them both and bent down to get the tackle box. "Please talk to me," she said.

"It sounds like there's nothing much else to say, Rebecca," he said, looking at her briefly, finally, and then turning toward the car. "Listen, I have to go. Do what you want with the fish."

"Alex, I —"

"I need to go," he said. "Thank you for being honest with me."

Rebecca had never seen him angry. She did not want it to end this way. "Look, I'm sorry. I shouldn't have said that the way I did. We can still be friends —"

"I have friends."

The words landed like a slap across her face. The implication was clear. *Unlike me . . .*

Rebecca sensed that trying to repair the damage with Alex would only make things worse. Her eyes were stinging and her hands fell to her sides as he walked away, her only friend in Alabama, hating her.

When the taillights of his car disappeared onto the road, she walked in a daze back to the bucket of fish. The three Alex had caught were mostly still, except for the slow, regular movements of their gills flexing in and out. They seemed resigned to their fate. Her fish, however, still thrashed about absurdly with delusions of escape. He threw himself against the walls of the bucket and his companions, splashing water out onto the dirt where the camping chairs had been just minutes before.

"Give it up," she said to the fish. She had a brief, morbid fantasy of what it would be like to pour out the bucket on the ground and watch the fish flounder around. How long would they struggle and flop around before realizing there was no hope, that they could not survive outside their environment? Instead, she grabbed the handle, straining a little at the awkward, watery weight of the bucket, and staggered to the edge of the lake. "At least you have a place to go," she told the fish as she returned them to the water. "At least there's somewhere you can breathe."

27

When Rebecca arrived at Mountainside the next morning, the charge nurse led her to an office where her mother sat with her legs crossed beneath her, facing Dawn, the social worker. She heard their laughter before she could see either of them, and her mother's laugh sounded both familiar and foreign — like a song she had loved and long ago forgotten. They seemed to be talking about art.

"I always wanted to paint, you know," Lorena was saying. "I was pretty good when I was younger, before I married Richard. We had the kids right away, and then, you know, who has the time?"

Mom painted. Did I know this?

"I know, right? I'm lucky if I can get my pajamas on and fall into bed at the end of the day," Dawn said, and then acknowledged Rebecca with a broad smile. "Hello, Rebecca, glad you're here. Thanks for joining us."

"Hi, Becky," Lorena said amiably.

"Hi, Mama."

Her mother's expression was clearer again today, she noticed. The smile was new, too. Not the perfunctory response to social expectations that sometimes crossed Lorena's gray face when she knew it was called for, but a real smile. Rebecca tried to remember the last time she had seen it, but nothing would materialize.

"So," Dawn said. "We're here to talk about your mom's recovery. To start with, I'd like to say that we think things are going well." She patted Lorena's hand. "What do you think?"

Her mother's mouth flexed downward in an involuntary grimace before she brought back the smile. "Yes, I think it is. Becky, I'm so sorry about all this. I never meant . . . I never wanted you to have to go through this."

Rebecca's throat was tight. She should say something, she knew, but the feeble "It's okay" that wanted to roll automatically off her tongue felt inadequate to her mother's emotions.

And was it okay? Rebecca didn't know. She managed a smile and put her own hand on Lorena's knee.

"Well," Dawn began again. "I don't know how much you've been told —"

"Nothing," Rebecca said. "I've been told almost nothing."

"Essentially, there are two issues your mom is dealing with. Well, that you are dealing with, too. One is the dissociative episode she seems to have had a few weeks ago, probably from the trauma and fear of being evicted from her home. That seems to be largely improving now, which is our main concern here. On the one hand, the best place for her to get better is the real world, her home environment. On the other, we don't want to discharge her until we know she's grounded in reality and safe."

"I'm doing much better," Lorena said. "Better than even before all this."

Dawn nodded. "The other issue is the hoarding, which is a longer-term issue and what you've been seeing firsthand."

"I am so sorry, Becky. I knew it was getting bad, but . . ." Lorena choked on the words. The social worker waited patiently. She made no move to comfort Lorena or to continue on with her speech. It was as though she were creating a space for something to happen and was in no particular hurry. Rebecca twisted her ring, wondering if she was supposed to say or do something

322

to fill the silence. Her mother struggled for words and Dawn just looked down at the folder on her lap, her face neutral.

Rebecca was on the verge of asking what she should do when Lorena swallowed hard and went on. "I knew it was getting bad." She put a fist over her heart. "I knew, somewhere in here, that I was being selfish, driving you and your father away. But I couldn't stop. It's hard to explain."

"You don't have to explain," Rebecca said, though she realized as she said it that she really did want to understand. It was unfathomable. All that trash.

"Well, I'm learning, here, that what I was doing — hoarding — was because I was worried about not having enough. We always worried about that growing up. You may not remember your grandparents very well, but they were farmers who lived through the Depression and they knew what it was like to not have enough. We were pretty poor when I was growing up, too, and they were always very careful with everything.

"I always said I would never be like that, but I guess I was like that, more than I realized, and then when your brother —"

"You don't have to do this," Rebecca said. She wanted to be anywhere else right now.

Dawn intervened. "She doesn't need to

be rescued, Rebecca. I know that's tempting when you care about someone, but it's not helping her."

"Dawn's right. I need to say it. When Cory died, I lost a part of myself. A mother loves all her children, Rebecca, and I love you more than I can say, but Cory was . . . he was my little star. You and your dad were always extraclose; you had a special relationship. Even when he was little, Cory always — well, it might sound silly, me being a grown woman and him just a child, but he looked out for me somehow." She put her face in her hands. "I know it sounds ridiculous."

"No, Mama," Rebecca said, standing to put a hand on her mother's shoulder. "It doesn't."

Rebecca should be angry, she knew. She'd been cleaning out that goddamn house for weeks, including the stupid shrine to the star of her mother's heart, the boy she could never have been. She'd been living in his shadow for her whole life, and the shadow had only gotten bigger when he died. In death, everyone is perfect, and Cory was the most perfect of all. And now her mother was saying it, the truth she'd had written on her heart for decades. She should be angry; she should walk out of that room, get in her car, and drive back to Atlanta.

But what she felt was pity. Rebecca had run away from all this long ago, and while her attempts to build her own life might have been shallow or desperate at first, she'd built it anyway. She had a college degree. She had an apartment and a job she loved. She had friends, imperfect though she and they might be. It didn't matter that she wasn't the star of anyone's heart. She was the star of her own life.

"It's okay, Mama. Everything is going to be okay. We'll get through it. You're going to be okay."

Lorena was sobbing now. She reached for Rebecca's hand and turned awkwardly in her seat to embrace her daughter, clutching her around the waist and crying into the T-shirt Rebecca was wearing. Unsure what to do — she had never seen her like this — Rebecca put her hands tentatively on Lorena's head. They stayed like that for a long time, mother and daughter, comforter and comforted.

When she left Mountainside an hour later, she was surprised to find that she felt lighter. She drove back to her mother's house with the windows down, letting the wind whip her hair and looking up at the bright-blue Alabama sky.

BY MARCI THOMPSON STILLWELL

BLOG: THE CARE AND FEEDING
OF A SUBURBAN HUSBAND
{Entry #185: (Untitled)}

Tuesday, August 2, 2016

Sometimes love is not at all what it seems. Sometimes things happen that lead you to question not only your own judgment, but the people and relationships that have been central to your life for what feels like forever. I've come to believe that part of our natural state of being in relationships is to take other people for granted. Most of the time, we don't even know we're doing it. We meet someone, and we begin to love them. Sometimes it's a powerful attraction at first meeting that is simply undeniable. Other times, it's more like a slow boil: a thousand little things that add up, day by day, to someone being absolutely indispensable to our lives.

That's weird, isn't it? Indispensable. You were alive and breathing before you met this person, weren't you? But then something happens and you become so dependent on them that you are not sure you can live without them. Unfortunately, many of us realize someone's importance in our lives only after they are gone. A part of ourselves that we didn't even notice had taken root until something — circumstance, betrayal, death, loss of feeling — takes it away again.

At what point do we begin taking someone for granted? Is it the same moment that we realize we love them? Or is it later, when they have become a fixture in our lives, like a favorite rug or lamp, and after a while we don't even see them in the room? People talk a lot about how to keep things fresh in a marriage, to keep it stable, but sometimes I think fresh happens most naturally when things are fragile. When we're just getting to know someone or trying to win them over, we keep it fresh so we don't lose it. But once we think we are secure, we stop worrying about "fresh" because we're too busy worrying about everything else.

In some cases, maybe we take people for granted because we give ourselves too much credit, and them, not enough. We think that we're the ones creating the light in our own lives without noticing the everyday luminaries around us. We assume that we are deserving of love and happiness without giving a thought to how much love and happiness we create for others.

And then . . . the consequences. More about this later, maybe, but when someone in our lives — whether it's a coworker, family member, friend, or spouse — feels unappreciated or unloved, do we deserve what happens next? How do we respond to their anger, indifference, or lashing out in retribution?

I'm aware there are no clear answers here. First of all, you don't know the details of this particular case. And every relationship is different. But even if you knew all there is to know, I'm not sure the answers would be clear then, either. Every relationship is made up of thousands of compromises and betrayals, millions of affectionate gestures and moments of implicit trust, and countless mundane moments. . . . When things go wrong, who can say which moment is the tipping point? How can we possibly assign blame?

28

When the doorbell rang a couple days later, Rebecca was still in bed. *Go away,* she told the helpful neighbor or newspaper salesman or lawn mower man at the door. *I'm asleep.* She had already hit the snooze button a couple of times, but her body was refusing to obey the commands of her brain.

Maybe I can skip one day of everything, she thought. *Sleep til noon. Drive to Birmingham, go to a museum, eat a real breakfast for once instead of prepackaged doughnuts and the bad coffee at Mountainside. . . .*

The bell rang again. *Damn.*

Rebecca pushed herself out of bed, every muscle screaming resistance. She had worked harder the past few days than ever before. How did people do this for a living? She made a mental note to tip all future moving men very, very well. She went to the door in the oversized T-shirt she'd slept in, without stopping to tame her pillow-dried rat's nest of hair, thinking that maybe it would increase the guilt for waking her of whoever was on the other side. Only after she turned the knob did it occur to her that it might be Alex.

When she saw Jake standing there, she shrieked and slammed the door.

"Oh my gosh!" she yelled through the door. "Jake, I'm sorry, I had no idea. I'm not dressed."

"It's okay," he said. "I didn't see much."

Even with two inches of solid wood separating them, she could see him smiling. "I'll be out in two seconds," she said. "Let me just put on some clothes."

"Okay, but hurry," he said. "I've had to pee since I crossed the state line."

She ran a brush through her hair and gargled mouthwash, slipped on jeans and shimmied a bra under the T-shirt before letting him in. Jake kissed her on the cheek, and said, "Bathroom?" as he brushed past her. She pointed to the short hallway that led to the bedroom and bathroom. The smell of his deodorant — so simple, so familiar — sent her head spinning. Even at nine in the morning.

While he was in the bathroom, she paced around the tiny living room, frantically moving the few things that had gathered here and there during her stay. Her curiosity was so powerful it was almost a physical feeling, like an itch. She flitted to the kitchen to stash away some Lean Cuisine trays she had rinsed for recycling.

"Bet you're wondering why I'm here," he said when he returned.

"Well," she said, trying to think of something witty. Nothing came. "Yes, to be honest. Not that I'm not thrilled to see you."

"Marci sent me," he said. "I'm sort of in the doghouse."

"I'm sorry," she said reflexively. Then what he said registered. "Wait a minute, she sent you to me? I'm the doghouse?"

He smiled. "Well, I guess technically, your house is the doghouse."

Rebecca searched for the words. "I guess I have to say I'm surprised that Marci trusts me, I mean, that she would want —"

"You're surprised she would send me to someone who has acknowledged romantic feelings for me," he said gently. His clear blue eyes were looking at her, unflinching.

Rebecca felt herself turning crimson and looked down at the dishes in the sink. "Well, yeah."

"That's actually part of why I'm here," he said. "I think we need to talk about a few things. And also, I would like to offer you my services as manual labor for the next several days. My wife and some of our other friends will be along on the weekend to help, too."

She was in shock. "Marci sent you to help me?"

"Yes."

"Is this your punishment?"

He laughed. "Not exactly. Mostly it's that we all realized you were out here on your own and none of us had done a damn thing to help you. We've been assholes, Rebecca, especially me. I've been a terrible husband to Marci and a terrible friend to you and it's time I start making it up to both of you."

Rebecca did not know what to say. She had turned down their offers of help. She had never thought of them as shirking some kind of obligation to her. And yet, when he pointed it out to her this way, she realized she'd been hoping they would insist.

"Thanks," she said softly.

"Where do we start?" he asked. "What can I do?"

"Honestly?" she said. "You can start by buying me breakfast."

The Waffle House in Oreville, Alabama, wasn't much to look at from the outside, but after several days of eating food she had to unwrap, microwave, or both, Rebecca greeted the greasy smells and dingy booths like an old friend. It had been nearly a week since her seafood dinner with Alex, and she had been eating Lean Cuisines, standing in the empty kitchen most nights since then. It was nice to have a meal sitting down, with another human.

She and Jake found their way to a booth near the back, where they could hear the call-and-response of the waitresses and line cooks, speaking a language that was uniquely their own. If you couldn't hear the bacon frying and the old country music playing in the background, you would think you were on a football field, listening to a quarterback calling plays.

"On two, on two . . ."

Jake ordered a Cherry Coke and a patty melt plate, with hash browns "scattered, covered, smothered, chunked, and topped." It was his standard order; he didn't even glance at the menu. Rebecca debated for a moment and went with a cheese omelet, grits, and raisin toast, with coffee and an ice water. She was so hungry she thought about ordering more, and then decided this was unladylike. For a minute, they sat in a silence made more awkward by the noisy activity all around them.

"So . . . ?" Rebecca said. They had to start somewhere.

Jake nodded. "Yep, okay. So, I don't know how much Marci told you . . . I know you guys talked. I'm sorry about that, by the way. It was totally unfair of her to accuse you of trying to steal me away or whatever — why anyone would think I'm worth stealing, I don't know — but ultimately that was my fault and I apologize."

"Don't be ridiculous," Rebecca said. "She apologized already, but there is no reason for either of you to apologize at all. And you know I have always known what you're worth."

He blushed. "Anyway, I guess I was a little freaked out about the new pregnancy. I already feel like a lousy father to Bonnie sometimes —"

"But you're a great dad!"

"Thanks. It's hard to tell when you're exhausted all the time. People say how much kids change your life, but you never really understand until it's 5 A.M. and you have to be at work at seven, and you've been up all night and the baby's crying and you just want some friggin' sleep. I didn't know how much I would love my kid — I love Bonnie so much it hurts. But I guess I wasn't really prepared for the fact that my life would not be mine anymore."

His eyes dropped to the table where he was fiddling with a straw wrapper. In a low voice, he went on. "And I didn't realize that I'd resent her for it. And Marci. Not all the time, of course, but now and then when I can barely hold up my camera, or I screw up interviewing some prima donna athlete, I would think —"

"You would think how Marci is supposed to be taking care of the baby so you can work," Rebecca said. She was voicing her own opinion without knowing that she'd held it.

"We don't work that way," he said quickly, shaking his head. "And it's fine. Really. Marci has her career with writing; I have mine with film; our parents help. We make it work. There are . . . charts. Lots of charts and lists. I wouldn't want it different, really."

He seemed to be trying to convince Rebecca of this egalitarian family view, as though she represented all women. Like if he said the wrong thing, she would call up *Feminist Weekly* and report him.

"I can only imagine how hard it is," she said truthfully. "I can see that it would be hard both ways. This way, you are constantly juggling and you both make sacrifices in every area so you can have family and career. And the other way —"

"The other way," he said, "Marci wouldn't be Marci, and there would be no point to any of it. I love her, Rebecca, every bit of her. If I can't help structure our family so that she can be a writer if that's what she wants to do, then I'm a crappier husband than everyone thinks I am."

Rebecca bit her lip. It was hard, even after all the years, to hear him profess his love for Marci so clearly. Even though she had been trying to let go, part of her had been nursing a quiet, guilty hope that perhaps his feelings were at least not as pure as they seemed. To what end? The little voice in her head chided her for the millionth time. The waitress brought their plates.

Jake went on, digging into a pile of steaming chili and toppings that surely must have been covering hash browns, somewhere underneath. "Anyway, I kind of forgot all that in the last few months. I did some stupid things, and I guess I never thought about covering my tracks. I don't know if I underestimated Marci, or if I was just trying to convince myself that I wasn't doing anything wrong."

"You mean the hotel bills?" She nibbled at the raisin toast.

"Yeah," he said. He didn't seem surprised

that she knew. "It was this little place a few miles from our house, mostly. And also, one overnight trip — not far, just to Knoxville. I said I was doing something on the University of Tennessee athletics director, but somehow Marci managed to find out that he was on vacation with his wife that week. I'm telling you, she could be a private eye if she ever gives up writing."

"And you were with . . ." She finally could hold back no longer. "Who?"

"No one," he said. "I was not cheating on my wife. There has never been anything like that. Not since we got back together. Never."

She believed him, despite the very damning evidence. Lying had never been his strong suit. "So, what were you —"

"Sleeping."

"Beg your pardon?"

"I was sleeping. Like I told you, Bec, it's exhausting. My career was suffering, I was getting sick every other week, and I noticed that whenever I had an out-of-town project for work and got to stay in a quiet hotel room by myself, I was so much better focused the next day. At first, I just started trying to book more long-distance gigs, or add on an extra night. And then one day, I had about a three-hour break between a lunch meeting in Athens and an afternoon shoot with the women's gymnastics team, and it was this nice clear day, so I just parked in the student lot and slept for a couple of hours in my car with the windows down.

"It felt so good, I started trying to build those gaps in my day, so I could nap in the car, and after a while I found this one hotel that is pretty clean but does hourly rates — I know it sounds awful —"

"It sounds worse than awful," Rebecca said.

"I know. Marci wants to have me tested for diseases just from sleeping on the beds, but it really wasn't that bad. Then I could sleep without getting sweaty or worrying someone was going to carjack me or something, and I didn't have to wrinkle my clothes. And from there it just got out of control, I guess."

"How did Marci react to all this?" she said.

"She is beyond pissed," he said.

"She doesn't believe you were alone in these hotel rooms?" She raised an eyebrow. She didn't think he would lie, but it really was an unbelievable story.

"Oh, no," he said. "She believes me. She said this is worse than cheating."

"How can it be worse?" Rebecca said.

"That's what I said!" For a second, he was more indignant than dejected. "But Marci says, and I guess she's right, that it's a betrayal because all that time I was sleeping in hotel rooms, she was working and cleaning the house and taking care of Bonnie, and that she's just as tired as I am. And I guess she has a point."

"She does," Rebecca had to agree.

"I think I really crossed the line when I started changing my schedule around. My mom and Marci's mom are pretty pissed off, too, since they were the ones who always had to come pitch in when I was working late and Marci was on a deadline."

Rebecca stared at her half-eaten omelet for a moment. Inexplicably, what rose in her throat at that moment was laughter. At first it was a sort of forced, whispered chuckle, but soon she was laughing hysterically, with tears rolling down her cheeks.

Jake smiled tentatively at her. "I don't get the joke," he said.

"You were sleeping!" she managed, between gasps. "Your wife thought you were fucking some hussy. For a minute, she thought you were fucking me, and you were by yourself, sleeping!"

Rebecca pulled paper napkins from the

dispenser to wipe at her eyes, but the laughter would not stop. Jake laughed nervously, glancing around at the other patrons, a couple of whom clearly disapproved of Rebecca's newfound mastery of the word "fuck." He looked utterly lost, for the first time since she'd known him, and for some reason this was even funnier. Her already sore sides began to cramp, but she could not stop.

"You okay?" he asked her.

She shook her head. "You're a jerk!" she squealed, still laughing and gasping for breath.

"And that's . . . funny?"

"Yes, it is! My brother is dead, my mom has no idea what year it is, my dad is shacking up with a lunatic who only wears satin robes, I'm on a leave of absence from my job. And my fantasy guy, the man I have been in love with since 2002, is not only married to someone else, he's not even a good husband! Even my vicarious life sucks!" People were staring openly now, and she knew she should stop, but the laughter was turning to convulsive sobs and there was no end in sight.

"Want to get some air?" Jake asked, throwing cash on the table to cover their bill.

She nodded, covering her face with her

hands, and allowed him to lead her out. Even behind her hands, she could feel the stares of the Waffle House patrons, mostly an older crowd at this time of the morning. Jake muttered some kind of courtesies as they exited, but she knew everyone was still watching her through the glass. He led her to his truck, the same one he'd been driving for years, and leaned against it, pulling her to him. She allowed him to wrap her in his arms while she fell apart. Jake stroked her hair and shushed her softly while she cried. Until a few weeks ago, she had not cried in years. Now it was becoming her thing.

After a moment, she gathered her breath and pulled back from him, where she'd left tear stains on his dark-blue T-shirt. He handed her one of the paper Waffle House napkins and she wiped her face, taking deliberate deep breaths as she did. Jake brushed her hair back from her face. "Okay?" he said.

She nodded.

"I really am a terrible husband," he said, with a sad smile.

She shrugged. "I still think Marci could do worse. You love her so much."

"I do," he said. He was looking at her kindly. "I owe you an apology, Rebecca."

She shook her head.

"I have to say this," he said. "I've known for years how you felt about me, and I've never really acknowledged it, because I value our friendship —"

"Oh, God, don't say 'value our friendship,' please."

"It's true, I do. I care about you. I love you, Rebecca. Not in the same way I love Marci, but I do love you and you deserved to hear from me exactly what my feelings were, and were not."

"I think it was pretty obvious when you married someone else," Rebecca said. She was trying not to draw the parallel between this conversation and what she had said to Alex on Saturday. "I'm not stupid, Jake."

"You are not stupid," he agreed. "But you have been holding on to me, to the idea of us, even when you knew it wasn't possible. And I . . . I have to admit that I've let you do it."

"What?" she said.

He shrugged. "I told myself I was sparing your feelings, being a gentleman."

"But you weren't?"

"Not entirely. I was also being a coward, not wanting to disturb the waters. Once Marci and I had worked it out, I figured it would just sort of resolve itself. Plus, if I'm being really honest —"

"Why stop now?" she said.

"I liked the attention."

"You did?"

He looked at his feet. "Sure. What guy wouldn't enjoy a beautiful woman directing her affection at him? And it was kind of flattering, the way I could always make you laugh. Not to mention how Marci always got a little possessive when you were around."

"Jesus, Jake."

A sly, embarrassed grin crossed his features. "I know. I'm ashamed to even say it. Needless to say, I think Marci is going to be pretty possessive all the time for a while. I'll be lucky to get out of this without having to wear an ankle bracelet."

Rebecca gaped at him. "I was wrong," she said. "You're not a jerk. You're a complete asshole."

"Yeah," he said, shuffling his feet. "But the good news is, this asshole is at your service for the next few days."

"Well, thanks," she said. "And I have to say, I appreciate your honesty about . . . us. I know that's not easy to say to someone you care about."

He nodded. "I really do care about you, I hope you believe that. I do think you're beautiful. And I would be lying if I said I wasn't tempted four years ago, that one night at my apartment, do you remember?"

"Are you kidding? Of course I do."

"If I had never met Marci — ," he began.

"You'd be lost and miserable," she finished for him.

"Yes, I would," he said. "But whoever ends up with you is going to be a lucky guy."

"Oh, God, don't say that either. It's such a cliché. You're making it worse."

"Okay, fine," he said. "If I ever were going to cheat on my wife with some hussy, you would be the first hussy I would call. How's that?"

She punched him in the arm, hard, and they both laughed. He pulled her to him in a rough hug, the way Cory used to do when she was a kid, right before he'd give her a noogie on her head with his fist. This playful violence was perhaps unfortunate, since at that moment, a patrol car pulled up next to them, lights flashing.

29

Jake was still tousling her hair as Rebecca turned to see Deputy Alex Chen and his familiar boots exiting the patrol car. Of course it was him. Didn't Grier respond to any calls? She gently clasped Jake's hand and removed it from her head, realizing before he did that Alex thought Jake was hurting her.

"Everything all right here?" he said to the two of them. "I was just driving by — Rebecca, you okay?"

"Hey, Alex," she said. She tried to sound friendly. "I'm fine. Just an emotional morning, that's all."

Alex's face was ashen and stiff. His hand touched the handle of his pistol lightly, and he glanced down at Rebecca and Jake's linked hands. "Are you sure? You look like you've been crying."

She pulled her hand from Jake's and

sniffed. "I'm fine now. I was just . . . venting."

Alex nodded stiffly, looking at Jake.

"Oh, sorry!" Rebecca said, as though this were a cocktail party and not a police incident in the Waffle House parking lot. "Deputy Alex Chen, this is my old friend from college, Jake Stillwell. Actually, Alex is kind of an old friend, too."

"Kind of," Alex muttered.

"Pleasure," Jake said, extending his hand. "Sorry for the trouble."

"As long as everyone is fine," Alex said. His words were polite but the tone was wary. "I'm going in for some coffee. Rebecca, you know I'm right here if you need me."

"I do, thanks, Alex. Really, I'm fine."

He glanced back at Jake, nodded, and walked away.

"Wow," Jake said, once Alex had swung open the Waffle House door and stepped inside. "That is one scary Asian redneck."

Rebecca laughed. "I guess he is, when he wants to be. He probably thought we were fighting. He's actually a good guy."

"He seems to think highly of you," Jake said, nudging her with his elbow. On the other side of the glass, Alex glanced back at them while he waited for the waitress to get his coffee. He gave Rebecca a slight wave as he exited. Jake went on. "I didn't see a wedding ring on the deputy. Did you find yourself a boyfriend out here and not tell anyone?"

Rebecca shrugged him away. "Shhh! He'll hear you. He is not my boyfriend," she said. When Jake raised an eyebrow, she added, "He was a football teammate of my brother's in high school. He's been . . . helpful."

"Uh-huh, helpful. I bet."

"It's not like that. He has a daughter."

"Oh, yeah," Jake retorted. "I can see how that instantly makes him less attractive."

"Shut up," she said. Rebecca was aware both that she was blushing and that she sounded like she was back in high school herself, so she turned and headed for the passenger's side of his truck.

Jake said no more, but he continued to look like the cat that ate the canary until they were almost at her mother's house.

He pulled into the familiar gravel drive at her direction and parked next to the Dumpster. "So what are we doing?"

"What?" Rebecca had been thinking of Alex, and the look in his eyes when he saw her with Jake.

"I'm here to help. What are we doing?" Jake exited the truck and pulled work gloves out of the bed.

"Well, basically, there's a lot of junk to clear out. I mean, a lot. And it . . . smells awful in there. I'm sorry."

"Hey, I've been in the Georgia football locker rooms after the third week of two-a-days," Jake said. "Trust me, I'll be fine."

Inside, Rebecca explained her system and Jake got to work cheerfully. He started in the kitchen she'd been avoiding since her arrival, but none of what bothered her seemed to make him squeamish. Jake was energetic and patient, and carried piles of seeping, smelly trash to the Dumpster as though everyone's home were just like this one. As though there were nowhere else he would rather be than Oreville, Alabama, carrying urine-soaked cat cushions to a rented Dumpster.

The work also went more than twice as fast as it had been going, because he could carry much more than she could at once, and instead of huffing and puffing in and out of the house between each load, Rebecca had more time to spend sorting. Never once did he question her decisions, or comment on the squalid state of the house. He didn't ask intrusive questions about her mom.

Normally she had to remind herself to eat

while she was working, but by one o'clock Jake had already run out for grilled chicken sandwiches from the tiny cafe in town, and he picked up Gatorade as well. They sat on the front steps, chewing quietly, while the classic rock station played in the background. "So this is where you grew up?"

"Until senior year," she said. She knew Jake was from old money, and had grown up in a seven-bedroom historic house that was basically an old plantation. This must have looked like hell on earth to him.

"And that's when you met Marci and Suzanne," he confirmed.

"Yes. I moved in with my aunt. I wanted . . . I really wanted to go to Georgia."

He swallowed the last bite of his sandwich and washed it down with the Gatorade. "I'm glad you did," he said, play-punching her gently on the arm as he rose. He went inside the house as though he'd grown up here, too. "I think we're going to need some different trash bags soon. They make contractor-grade ones that will hold a lot more stuff and you don't have to worry about sharp edges poking through them."

"Oh," Rebecca said, feeling stupid she hadn't known this.

"I'll run over to Gadsden this afternoon

and pick some up."

"You don't have to do that," she called in to him, as she crumpled up her sandwich wrapper and stood up to straighten her shorts.

He reappeared in the doorway. "I know I don't have to, Rebecca. I'm your friend. Let your friends help you."

"Okay," she said softly.

Alex came by at three fifteen, while Rebecca was sorting things in her mother's bedroom and Jake was on his way to Gadsden for the superpowered trash bags. When she first heard the knock on the door, she thought Jake had forgotten something and yelled, "It's open!" from her spot behind a stack of plastic tubs.

"You've made real progress in here," Alex said a minute later, his deep voice making her jump as he stuck his head in the door to her mother's room.

"Thanks," she said. "I didn't expect to see you again today."

"My shift just ended," he said.

"Oh," she said. "Great."

He stood as though he were too big for the hallway.

"Sorry there's no place to sit," she said. Then, sheepishly, "I have a half bottle of

Gatorade over here if you're thirsty."

"No, thanks. I just wanted to make sure you're okay. After today."

"I'm fine," she said. "Jake is just an old friend."

"From college," Alex said. "You said."

"Yeah. His wife is a good friend as well, from my Georgia high school." She felt defensive but she wasn't sure why. "I just had a little breakdown about my family and he was helping me through it. Really, it was nothing."

"I was worried about you," he said. "You can't blame me for that."

"Of course not. It's just that everything is —"

"Fine," he finished.

"It is fine. Alex, there is nothing between me and Jake."

"Hey, you don't have to explain anything to me."

"I want to. And I want to talk about Saturday," she began.

"Forget it. I get it now."

"What is that supposed to mean?"

"Nothing. Doesn't matter."

Rebecca could not tell what he wanted her to say or do. She hated that. It was so much easier when people just pushed the button and asked for what they needed.

"Jake just showed up on my doorstep this morning to help. I couldn't exactly turn him away. His wife sent him."

Alex nodded. "I can see that he — that you are good friends."

"Yes. We are."

"I have to run," he said. He gestured vaguely toward the door.

"Of course," she said.

He hesitated, and left.

30

Jake and Rebecca worked the rest of the week together at her mother's house. She had not realized how lonely her work had been until she had someone helping her. Even when they went for hours without speaking, just the sound of his whistling in the other room or the door opening and closing as he went in and out was comforting. They worked well into the evenings, surviving on peanut butter, Waffle House, and a couple of trips to Dickie's for burgers and beer. On both these occasions, Rebecca looked around the bar for a sign of Alex, but he never appeared.

Rebecca was so tired by the end of the week that she was sure she could sleep for a full twenty-four hours if it were not for Jake's loud snoring on the couch. She caught him rubbing his back and neck a few times when he thought she wasn't looking, but he never complained. What they accomplished, however, was astonishing: by Friday afternoon, when they were joined by Marci and Suzanne, Jake thought the Dumpster was close to ready for pickup.

"It looks like there is more in here than in the house," Suzanne said, looking doubtfully into the Dumpster once Rebecca had given them a tour. "This must have been awful, Rebecca. I'm sorry we didn't come out sooner."

"That's okay," Rebecca said. "I told you not to."

"Next time, I'm not taking no for an answer," Suzanne said. "Sometimes we get caught up in our own stupid lives and don't pay enough attention. You shouldn't have to ask us to be there for you, but sometimes . . . well, sweetie, *ask.*"

"Really, it's not such a big deal," Rebecca said.

"Everything is a big deal for Suzanne the last few days," Marci said. "Dylan has been out of town and she is lost without her new husband."

"Shut up, Marci," Suzanne said. "That has nothing to do with it. I'm just sorry that Rebecca didn't tell us how bad this was. We could have come sooner."

"I was a little embarrassed, I guess," Rebecca said. She gestured at the Dumpster

354

and the ramshackle house behind her. "This isn't exactly the Atlanta Country Club."

Suzanne put her hands to her mouth, and then stepped forward and wrapped Rebecca in an unexpected embrace. "Oh, honey," was all she said.

Sunday afternoon, the Dumpster Dude returned. Suzanne, Jake, and Rebecca had spent the day before and all that morning carting things from the house, while Marci opened boxes and bins using Rebecca's mask and gloves, looking for obvious trash. She took frequent breaks for fresh air but never complained about the smell of the house and her sensitive pregnancy nose.

Even once the Dude had parked in the driveway and was directing a team of unhappy-looking young men in tie-dye, Rebecca continued to pull things out of the bedrooms and toss them on top of the pile in the giant metal container.

On her third trip, Jake stopped her in the hall. "Let it go, sweetheart. You still have trash service, and maybe your mom will want to keep some of what's left. I'll bring the truck back in a few weeks and help you take more to the dump if you need it, okay?"

Rebecca nodded and joined the others on Lorena's front steps. The four of them stood and watched more than a decade of squirreled-away items and rotting trash be lifted onto a large flatbed truck for disposal at the county landfill. *If I'd had more time,* Rebecca thought, *I could have recycled more of it, or gone through some of those moldy boxes to see if anything in them was salvageable for charity. . . .* That road led nowhere, and she knew it, but her brain could not turn it off.

"Has your mom seen any of this?" Marci asked as the Dumpster Dude drove away, and they turned back into the house.

"No. I don't think she can handle it."

"Do you worry what she'll say when she does?"

"Every minute."

They walked in silence from one room to the next. The living-room furniture and floor were now visible, including her mother's antique couch with the green cushions, which seemed to have been spared most of the cat urine by being the first piece of furniture Lorena had covered with boxes and newspapers. Except for a couple of boxes in the middle of the floor, the kitchen looked almost usable again thanks to Jake. As he wiped the scratched wood of the kitchen table with a rag, Rebecca had a sudden, vivid memory: sitting with Cory and her parents, playing rummy one rainy afternoon. The smell of microwave popcorn, and the delightfully fizzy-soggy feel of it on her tongue, soaked with orange soda. Cory's favorite. For a span of several years, every memory of her brother included the soft line of an orange mustache.

In a true gesture of friendship, Suzanne had bleached and scrubbed both bathrooms. There was a pile of musty towels in a basket ready for the Laundromat. The master bedroom still had a fair number of plastic bins in it, but they had been sorted by the girls into type and size of items and meticulously labeled by Marci, using multicolored sticky notes she'd pulled from her purse.

Cory's room had been the hardest. After Rebecca's outburst of throwing things against the wall weeks earlier, she had still found it difficult to decide what to do with her brother's things. Jake had boxed up and labeled a few of the surviving trophies, and whatever he had done with the things she'd broken, she did not know. He had set aside the toys and baseball cards he thought might be worth something on eBay, and a couple of Cory's football uniforms. Everything else they had thrown into boxes and piled near the closet, ready to donate to charity. The bed, however, was still made, and the teddy bear her brother had loved since early childhood still sat in his spot.

Rebecca picked it up. "I think I'll keep Simpson," she said. "He's a bit dusty, but he can be washed."

"That's sweet," said Marci.

"Next time you guys come over for dinner, he'll be around in case Bonnie needs someone to cuddle with. Or the new baby."

"You've never had us over for dinner," Marci said gently. She was definitely showing now, Rebecca noticed. And she looked tired.

"Let's add that to the list of things that need to change when I get home. And that's enough work for today."

"When are you coming home?" Suzanne asked.

"Soon, I think," Rebecca said.

They made their way out, turning off lights as they went, and discussing the limited dinner options for the evening. Jake led the way, and he was the first to the front door.

"Bec," he called, as Rebecca located the house key on the kitchen counter. "There's a car pulling into the driveway."

He came, Rebecca thought. *He's finally over being mad. He'll make some terrible joke.*

We'll all go out to dinner and he'll get to know my friends, and . . .

What? What are you hoping for? She found that she did not know the answer but her smile widened as she moved past Suzanne and Marci toward the door. But it was not Alex Chen getting out of the car in the driveway. It was her dad.

Richard Williamson shook Jake's hand and nodded a greeting to the women, while Sonia tittered and fussed over introducing herself to everyone as "Richard's friend." Rebecca could not help but think of her conversation with Alex on this subject and tried not to smile. She noticed that Sonia was keeping her eyes carefully away from the house, as though it were haunted. *She may not be wrong,* Rebecca thought darkly.

"Hey," she said to her dad. "We were just leaving for the night."

"I thought that might be the case." He slung an arm around Rebecca's shoulders. "Rockstar mentioned y'all were here, and we came by to see if we could have you all over to dinner to celebrate."

"And," Sonia added, "we hoped maybe y'all would spend the night with us, too. I know it must be crowded with all four of you wedged into Richard's little old place."

The four of them answered simultaneously. Rebecca said, "Oh, Sonia, thanks anyway," shaking her head, while the other three said various forms of "yes, please," "thank you," and maybe even "Oh, thank God."

Rebecca looked at her friends, who all looked carefully away, and realized she couldn't refuse them a little comfort their last night here. Since she'd been sleeping on the floor for two nights herself, she had to admit that even one of Sonia's guest bedrooms sounded like an improvement. "Thanks, Sonia, that's really generous."

When she turned to see how her dad felt about the sleepover, Rebecca saw that he had gone into the house. "Why don't we wait out here?" Sonia said. "Rebecca and her dad might need a moment."

She stayed a few steps behind him as he went through the house, examining little cracks in the walls and the condition of the windowsills as though he were considering the house for purchase. Rebecca realized he and her mom must have done this together, nearly thirty years ago, when she and Cory were still little and they were moving up from the even tinier house she'd been born in. She knew they had put every penny they had into the down payment on this place back then, and that her dad had taken pride in maintaining it for years. Rebecca felt her anger dissipating as she realized why it was so hard for him to be here anymore.

Richard looked in the office that had once been her bedroom, and the master that had once been his. "Wow," he said. "You got a lot more done than I thought you would."

"Thanks," Rebecca said. She noticed that he hesitated for a moment in Cory's doorway, and wished she had remembered to close the door. Then he went in.

"The high school might want these uniforms," he said to her. "They asked for them years ago but your mother wouldn't part with them. They'd probably take a couple of the trophies from his senior year, too. The others, just leave on the floor here. I'll take them to Sonia's."

"To Sonia's? You're officially moving in?"

He sighed. "I figure it's time. She's already putting up with me most of the time anyway. I'm going to retire in January, and Sonia wants to travel more. Be easier to have one less house to worry about."

"That makes sense," Rebecca said uncertainly.

"It never ends like you think it will," he said. He sat down hard on Cory's bed and Rebecca saw a little puff of dust rise in the late-afternoon light from the window behind him. "You make all these plans, you know? And God laughs. When I was your age . . . no, younger, even. We had plans, your mom and I."

"I know, Daddy."

"When you take out a thirty-year mortgage, the end of it seems so far away, and all you can picture is how happy you'll be. You imagine the promotions at work that will make the payments easier to bear, and you think of watching your children grow."

"You don't have to explain —"

"You don't think about burying a child. You don't think about letting go of the house with eight months left on the mortgage. You don't think that the woman you love with all your heart will become a stranger, and that you'll be too weak and selfish to help your baby girl take care of things. . . ."

"Daddy. You're not weak."

He smiled at her. "You going to see your mom tomorrow?"

"After everyone leaves, yeah."

"I'm filling in for Route 3 tomorrow, so I'll be done early. Want some company?"

"Sure, Dad."

31

When her friends left for Atlanta the next morning, Rebecca was genuinely sorry to see them go. For the first time in as long as she could remember, she felt comfortable with her place in their little circle.

They had sneaked out of Sonia's house early, not long after they heard Richard's car leave the driveway, stopped off for a quick breakfast at Waffle House, and returned in Suzanne's car to Richard's little bungalow. Rebecca's own car was there, and Jake's truck as well. He transferred his wife and her bags to the truck while Suzanne complained in advance about being lonely on the drive home.

"Don't you have your husband's CDs in the car?" Jake asked. "Can't you listen to those?"

Suzanne was already tearful, which was uncharacteristic, especially when sober. Jake's teasing seemed to make this worse, and she gave Rebecca more hugs in a half hour than she had in the past year. "Don't tell me you're pregnant, too," Rebecca said. "Based on the pictures you sent, I don't know if you have much room to grow in that wedding dress."

"No," Suzanne said. "Maybe in a year or so, after I figure out what it's going to be like having Dylan back on tour. Then we'll see."

Marci hugged Rebecca so tightly that she could feel the hard little lump of her pregnant belly pressing against her. The sensation was strange, but Rebecca did not pull back from it. Her relationship with Marci had improved exponentially over the last few weeks, and she didn't want to risk putting a damper on it.

"You'll call us as soon as you're back?" Jake said. "Or if you need my help again?"

"Yes," she said, accepting his side-arm hug. "But I think I'll be okay. Dad said he would help me finish things up. And I'll be home soon."

She stood in the driveway and waved as they pulled out, noting with amusement that Suzanne already had her hands-free headset on and was talking animatedly to someone before she even got out of the driveway. Rebecca smiled and went back inside, feeling full and hollow at the same time.

She called Valerie on impulse, and was surprised that she answered the phone almost immediately. "Hey, girl."

"Hi, Val, I was just going to leave a message. I figured you'd be working today."

"Nope, I'm stuck in Toronto," she said. "Stomach bug."

"Oh, I'm sorry."

"Me, too. If I'm going to have to call out sick, I'd rather be at home in my own bed instead of some hotel room. Did you know room service charged me fifteen dollars for some ginger ale and stale crackers? Like it's not bad enough I've got it coming out both ends, I have to lose it from my pocketbook, too."

"That's terrible," Rebecca said. "I wish I could help."

"Eh, that's all right. It's good to talk to you. How are things in East Bumble?"

"Getting better, I think. I was thinking about coming home soon."

"That's great, hon."

Valerie was beginning to sound distracted and Rebecca worried she might be feeling ill again. "Well, I'll let you rest," she said.

"You were just calling to say hi?"

"Yeah. Well, I wanted to ask you about

something, but it can wait until you're feeling better."

"I'd argue with you, but I feel the demons moving around again, so I'd better hang up."

Her father came around one thirty. Rebecca found it funny that he knocked on the door of his own house when he arrived. "I like what you've done with the place," he said. Of course she hadn't done anything, but she accepted his attempt at humor with a smile anyway.

"I guess you'll be letting this place go soon, too," she said. "When is your lease up?"

He laughed. "I haven't had a formal lease in a couple of years," he said. "I guess technically it's month to month, but the lady who owns it is real nice, so I'll give her a few weeks' notice at least."

Richard held the car door for her, just like Alex always did, and they drove in silence to Mountainside. The nurse on duty was a quiet redhead Rebecca had seen once or twice, and she gave them a tight smile as she led them to the art studio, where Lorena was sitting in the corner by the window, holding a paintbrush. Rebecca went to her first, while Richard hovered in the doorway.

Her mother did not seem to hear her approach. She was staring out the window at the valley below, or maybe somewhere else beyond sight.

"Hey, Mama," Rebecca said gently, not wanting to startle her.

"Becky," Lorena said softly. "Rebecca. I'm glad you're here."

"You are?"

"Yes. Isn't the landscape here beautiful? I've lived here more than half my life, but I feel like I'm seeing it for the first time."

"I know what you mean," Rebecca said.

Lorena looked up at her, and then focused her attention over Rebecca's right shoulder.

"Richard?"

For a moment, Rebecca thought her mother had become confused again; then she heard her father's voice behind her. "Hi, Lorie."

Lorena's bottom lip trembled almost imperceptibly, and Rebecca saw her grip tighten on the paintbrush. "Richard. You came to see me."

"Yes, honey. I did. Let's go sit outside. It's a nice day." He held out his arm to her, and Lorena took it gingerly. Rebecca had a sudden memory of a Christmas morning long ago, when she was eleven or twelve years old. Her father had bought her mother a new food processor as a surprise, something she had wanted for years. He made her close her eyes and led her into the kitchen so he could see the surprise on her face.

As they passed her on their way to the double doors going out to the patio, Richard said, "Rebecca, honey, go get us some coffee, would you?" *In other words, get lost.*

Rebecca went to the coffee area and took the time to brew a fresh pot. While she waited for it, she refilled the sugar and sweetener packets and the cup full of stirrers, and then wiped down the counter with a paper towel she wet in the ladies' room. *I really do need to get back to work,* she thought.

Even with all her stalling, by the time she reached the patio with three coffees in hand, she still could not bring herself to interrupt. She stopped at the door and watched her parents, the first time she had seen them together in years. They sat in metal patio chairs facing one another, hands clasped tightly together. Her father was leaning down with his forehead pressed against hers, talking softly. She could see tears on her mother's cheeks, but could not make out what was being said.

As she watched, Richard put his hand beneath Lorena's chin and lifted her face to his. He kissed her gently on the lips, and then leaned closer and whispered in her ear.

Watching this tenderness between them, a hope welled in Rebecca's chest. She knew it was a child's hope, but she allowed it to fill her nonetheless. *Maybe, maybe . . .* How could two people who shared such intimacy ever really part? How could her father give up this kind of love for a silly little thing like Sonia? As if proving her point, he sank slowly to his knees in front of his wife, and Rebecca saw the flash of a sheepish grin before he placed his head on her lap. Lorena held his head in her hands, comforting him.

After a few moments, Rebecca could not stand there with the hot coffee any longer, so she went out the open door and walked softly toward her parents. "Hey, guys," she said awkwardly.

Richard stood and walked to the edge of the patio, away from Rebecca, and leaned on the railing to look over the countryside. She knew he did not want her to see the emotion on his face, so she turned to her mother. "Sit down, baby," Lorena said, patting the chair next to her. It was the most motherly she had sounded in years. "Your dad and I talked. I've . . . we've decided that I am going to live with Aunt Jo and

Uncle Larry in Mobile. They have an apartment over their garage. It's real nice. And your father and I are getting a divorce."

32

Over the next few weeks, Lorena's recovery seemed to gain traction. Rebecca visited her daily and was able to observe the change herself, as well as hear about it from the Mountainside staff. It was as though Richard's visit had sped her return to reality — too late to save her marriage, but perhaps not too late for whatever else might come. She no longer had periods of total disconnect from reality, and each day she seemed stronger and happier. She, Rebecca, and Richard had all been in touch with Lorena's sister Jo, who had cleaned out the small apartment over her garage in Mobile and was readying it for her sister's arrival. One of the therapists at Mountainside connected Lorena with an art therapist in Mobile, and she had already registered for a painting class that started in October.

By early September, she was deemed ready to take a short leave from Mountainside to go to her house. She could not stay there; everyone involved agreed this was not a good idea. But she would be allowed to go through her remaining things with Rebecca and choose a few items to take with her to Mobile. She would be meeting Rebecca at the house on a Friday afternoon after therapy, accompanied by Dawn, in case there were any emotional setbacks or problems.

Rebecca fretted about the visit all morning. She drove to her mother's house early to rearrange boxes for the thirtieth time, trying to emphasize what she had saved rather than what she had purged. After that, she paced uselessly around the house, cataloging in her mind everything she had been unsure about throwing or giving away, trying to remember her reasoning for each item so she could defend her choices if her mother was angry. She even picked up the phone to call Alex, still her only friend in Alabama even though he was no longer speaking to her, but she hung up after one ring. She could only see the hurt look on his face by the riverbank.

When Dawn and Lorena pulled into the driveway in a small maroon coupe, Rebecca stepped out of the house to greet them, wiping her dusty hands on her jeans. Her mother looked pale as the social worker helped her out of the passenger's seat. She took a tentative step toward the house as though she were walking on the moon, rather than the gravel driveway that had been hers for decades. She stopped before reaching the porch.

"Mama?" Rebecca asked.

"I can't," Lorena said.

The kind social worker put a hand on Lorena's back. "You don't have to, Lorena. Remember, we talked about it? It's going to be very different, and if you don't feel ready to face it, there's no shame in that."

"No shame," Lorena echoed. Then, to Rebecca, "You cleaned it all up?"

"Yes, Mama. I'm sorry. They were going to condemn the house, the health department, and you weren't able to help."

"Was it hard to do? Was it hard on you?"

Rebecca did not know how to answer. She glanced at Dawn for help.

"Your daughter loves you, Lorena. She did what needed to be done. Families help each other."

"I don't think I can go in," her mother said. "Becky, don't be mad. I just can't."

"I'm not mad, Mama," Rebecca said reflexively.

Dawn's voice was comforting. "It's okay,

373

Lorena. Understandable. The house is probably very different than what you remember, and it's okay if you don't want to see it this way. Maybe you can tell Rebecca what items you would like to take with you to your sister's house?"

Lorena began right away. She had been thinking about this, preparing, Rebecca supposed, for the possibility she would not be able to go into the house. "The pictures, the family albums, I need those. And my clothes, you can choose the ones that are best." To Dawn, she said, "Rebecca has a wonderful sense of style.

"That writing desk in the living room — it was my grandmother's. When I'm gone, that will be yours, Becky. Don't forget. And one box of Christmas ornaments. I'll want my own little tree at Larry and Jo's, I think."

Rebecca was dumbstruck, but Dawn had produced a pad of paper from somewhere and was taking notes. Apparently everyone but Rebecca was prepared for this contingency.

"My iron skillet and the record albums. All the pictures. Did I say that already? It's a small apartment, but I think I can use the small table in the kitchen and a few of those chairs." Rebecca noticed her mother's voice was becoming thick, and a tear ran down one cheek. "Becky, just use your judgment on the rest of the stuff. I trust you."

She turned back toward the car. Rebecca could still hardly believe she'd prepared for this all morning, all summer, and her mother was not even going to set foot in the house before saying goodbye.

"Mama. What about Cory's room?" she asked as gently as she could.

Dawn put a hand on Lorena's arm. "Would you like something to take with you? From his room?"

Lorena seemed frozen. She shook her head mildly. "I can't go in there."

"I saved some of Cory's gloves and footballs and trophies, and the uniforms — Daddy thought the school might like some of them, but you could take a jersey with you. There are his books and —"

"I'll take that," Lorena said, pointing. Just inside the open front door, the Yoda action figure lay discarded on a stack of boxes, where Rebecca had left it the day of her temper tantrum. She had intended to throw it away but kept forgetting.

"Mama, that's just an old Star Wars toy."

"Yes."

"But it's broken."

"I am broken, too," said Lorena. "So we'll be good company."

She turned again and opened the car door herself. "I'm ready to go, Dawn," she said to the social worker.

"That's it? That's all you want to take with you?" Rebecca was incredulous.

"Here's the list," Dawn said. "You might want to wait a day before you do anything. It's possible she could change her mind."

"I won't change my mind," Lorena said. "I've held on to too much for too long. It's time to go. Becky, you can keep anything you want. Dawn, could we stop by Walmart on the way back? I want to pick up some painting supplies and toiletries for the trip to Mobile next week."

Rebecca felt strangely panicked that her mother was leaving so soon. "I'll take you. Can I take her?"

"Sure," Dawn said. "Just check in at the nurse's desk when you are back."

Rebecca had become very familiar with the Gadsden Walmart in the past three months. She did not wipe down the cart with sanitizer anymore, and even Lorena was impressed that Rebecca knew where to find the shampoo and deodorant her mother liked. They filled the cart with toiletries, acrylic paints, paintbrushes, and a couple of inexpensive canvases. "These will do until I can get to a real art store in Mobile," Lorena said.

"I didn't know you'd become such a connoisseur of canvas," Rebecca teased her.

"You're not the only one in this family who can be a snob," Lorena said. "I mean, where do you think you got it from, girl?" She playfully flipped her long gray hair back in a motion of exaggerated self-importance.

Rebecca couldn't remember the last time she and her mother had laughed together, much less been shopping or even to the grocery store. *Who is this woman and where has she been?* She found herself thinking of things she suddenly needed, wanting to stretch their time together a little longer. She had the vague sense that this would be it for a while.

They were on the music aisle, where Rebecca was showing her mother one of Dylan's CDs and telling her all about the beach wedding, when her keys slipped from her hand and clattered to the linoleum floor. As she bent over to retrieve them, a familiar pair of boots came into view behind her. Accompanied by a pair of very tan feet in sparkling pink flip-flops.

Rebecca stood up so fast she gave herself a head rush and had to steady herself on the CD shelves.

"Alex," she said, stunned. Next to him was a dark-eyed, dark-skinned beauty in frayed jeans and a pink T-shirt, who could only be one person. "And you must be Honey."

"Hi," Honey said. "Do you work with my dad?"

"No, I'm —"

"An old friend," Alex finished for her. He wore a smirk that seemed something between bemused and annoyed. "Honey, this is Rebecca; Rebecca, my daughter. Hello, Mrs. Williamson. How are you feeling?"

"Hello, dear," Lorena said. If she remembered that Alex had been instrumental in having her taken from her home and put in the hospital, she didn't show it. "I'm much better. How's your family?"

"They are all fine, thank you."

"David's still in New York? He's eating?"

"Yes, ma'am. He's doing fine, thank you."

"And your dad? No more trouble with his heart?"

"No, ma'am. Dad's great, cranky as ever. He's driving Mom crazy, of course."

"Good." She turned to Honey. "Are you ready for school to start back?"

"No, ma'am," Honey said. "But I guess when it does, I'll survive. I've heard freshman year can be really hard."

"Sure, it can. But you'll be fine — sweet,

smart girl like you. Playing volleyball again this year?"

"Yes, ma'am."

"Good girl," Lorena said. "I saw the story on you girls in the paper last year — making it to the state finals is a big deal."

"Yes, ma'am."

Rebecca was floored that her mother knew all this. She supposed that even confined to the house, Lorena had kept up with the local news. So even her mother knew more about Alex and his family than she did.

Honey was very polite and exceptionally pretty, Rebecca noticed. She had smooth, dark skin and almond eyes that were unquestionably Alex's. Rebecca did not know why she should be surprised that Honey's mother was black, though Alex had not mentioned it. She spent a moment adjusting her mental images of Shondra and her parents, and of the romance she had imagined between Shondra and Alex.

The four of them stood for a minute in silence. Honey shuffled her feet the way teenagers do when confronted with dull adult interactions, and cast a longing glance at an endcap display of brightly colored cell phone accessories.

Lorena said, "Well, nice to see you both. I need to go find something." She turned abruptly, and took the cart in the general direction of sporting goods, where everyone knew damn well she didn't need anything.

"Mom's just on a break from Mountainside for a few hours," Rebecca explained. "We're heading back there shortly. She'll be moving in with her sister in Mobile in a few days."

"That's great," said Alex. "I mean, it's sad that she has to leave town, but maybe it's for the best."

"I guess I should catch up to her," she said. "Before she wanders away."

"Of course."

"It was nice to meet you, Honey. Your dad is really proud of you. He talks about you all the time."

"You, too, Rebecca. He talks about you a lot. I mean, a *lot.*" Honey was grinning.

"All right, that's enough," Alex said. He steered Honey away. "Let's go buy you a new phone so you can talk to your friends instead of mine."

He threw an embarrassed glance over his shoulder as they walked away.

It was nearly a week later that Lorena was discharged from the hospital, on a Thursday afternoon. Rebecca picked her up, waiting in the main common area for almost an hour while the attending physician got around to signing all her release forms. Dawn hugged them both and wished Lorena luck at the door. Rebecca carried a small suitcase with her mother's things and a blue folder with all the discharge information, including an appointment card for Lorena's new therapist in Mobile.

Uncle Larry waited at the house with a small U-Haul, on which he and Rebecca had already loaded the few things Lorena had chosen to take with her to Mobile. On top of what Lorena had requested, Rebecca had gone through the various remaining bins and boxes to locate all the arts and craft supplies and added those to her mother's piles. Richard and Sonia had come by to collect a few more of his things, and everything else had been sold on eBay or picked up by Goodwill. Rebecca had taken Cory's teddy bear, the elephant lamp, and a single bin of her yearbooks and other souvenirs from high school. The house was now empty, clean, and on the market.

When Rebecca pulled into the driveway for the last time, Lorena took a deep breath but made no move to remove her seat belt. "Ready, Mama?" Rebecca asked.

For a minute, she worried that her mother had gone back into a catatonic state.

"Mama?"

"I'm ready," Lorena said, her voice froggy. She took her time unbuckling and getting slowly out of Rebecca's car.

"Do you want to go inside?"

"No." Lorena looked at the FOR SALE sign in the yard. "No, I don't."

"Are you sure? This may be the last —"

"I'm sure."

The three of them stood there, looking at the little white house as though they were looking at a fresh grave. Larry was the first to break the surface of the silence. "It's gotta be hard for you, Lorena," he said.

Lorena nodded. Rebecca put her arm around her mother's thin shoulders.

Larry glanced at his watch. "No rush, but I think Jo is making spaghetti and meatballs for dinner."

"Yes," Lorena said at last. She turned to embrace Rebecca in a sudden hug, squeezed tightly, and let go just as abruptly as she had taken hold. She hurried to the cab of the truck, where Larry helped her in and Rebecca handed her the blue folder and her purse. The goodbyes were quick, as though they would all be seeing one another in a few days, rather than some unknown quantity of weeks or months — whenever Rebecca made time to travel to Mobile, probably. And then they were gone.

Rebecca stood in the quiet driveway in front of the house, wondering what the appropriate length of time was to stand here and say goodbye to her childhood home. She had been away for seventeen years, and had spent more time here in the last few months than the rest of those years combined. She expected the moment to have gravitas or some kind of emotional weight to it, but as she stared at the white concrete walls and fading green shutters, she realized she had already said goodbye years ago. "Bye, house," she said, to make it official. Then she got in her car and drove away without so much as a glance in the rearview mirror.

33

Back at Richard's rental house, Rebecca fidgeted for half an hour or so before deciding she was more than ready to say goodbye to this place, too. Her dad had already informed his landlady of his plans to move out, and she had surprised him by suggesting that she had a tenant in mind who could move in as early as October. "I guess she knew I wasn't spending much time here and figured it was only a matter of time."

Rebecca had reactivated at work, and they had her back on the schedule starting Monday morning. She had the weekend, then, to get home and reacclimate to life outside Oreville before she was back in her old routine. She had no idea if she was looking forward to it or not.

By the time she had showered and packed her bags, it was nearly seven thirty. She sat on the couch in an old oversized flannel shirt she had grabbed on her last trip to

Atlanta. She had pulled on a pair of cotton gym shorts and twisted her wet hair up into a loose knot to keep the shirt from getting damp. She was debating whether to lock up and go home tonight or wait until morning, when there was a soft knock at the door and Alex Chen waiting on the other side.

He wore faded jeans and a button-down black shirt. Simple black leather shoes had replaced his usual work boots, and if Rebecca was not mistaken, there was product in his black hair. Was he coming from a date or something?

"Hey," she said as she opened the door.

"Hey."

"You look nice," she said. She leaned closer. "Are you wearing *cologne*?"

"You sound surprised."

"No, not surprised. Just . . . you look nice."

His eyes took in her flannel shirt and she crossed her arms in front of herself, feeling suddenly slouchy. "You always look nice," he said. His expression was dark and unreadable.

"What's wrong?"

"Nothing. I just heard your mom left today. I thought you might be on your way out, too."

"Yeah, originally I was leaving in the

morning."

"Originally?"

"I was just entertaining the idea of throwing the bags in the car and being in my own bed before midnight tonight."

"Ah," he said. "I can see the appeal."

"Do you want to come in? Want some . . . toast?"

He smiled and stepped inside. "Sure, but I'll pass on the toast."

"Sorry, I don't have a lot to eat here."

"Understandable," he said. "You're going home tomorrow. Or tonight."

"I'm glad you're here, actually," she said, gathering herself.

"You are?"

"Yes. I wanted to, before I leave, I wanted to thank you for being such a good friend to me. While I was here."

A bitter smile crossed his features. "Good friend."

"And I wanted to apologize for my behavior at the riverbank. This has been a really hard time for me, but that's not an excuse. I should have told you sooner that I didn't want to get involved with anyone."

"You did."

"What?"

"Tell me sooner. You did. I chose to ignore

386

it. I'm the one who wouldn't let go. I asked for it."

"That's not how I would put it," she said.

He shrugged. "The important thing is that you still feel that way. Not wanting to get involved, I mean."

Alex took a step toward her. His closeness, the seriousness of his expression, thrilled and terrified her. But she refused to back away. "I don't really know how I feel, Alex. All I know is that I have to go back to Atlanta tomorrow. My life is there."

"You have to? Your life couldn't be anywhere else?"

She sighed. "I just don't want to live in Oreville. I worked too hard to get out of here. I can't —" Rebecca could hardly believe the tears forming in her eyes, the catch in her throat that stopped her words. "Please, I can't talk about this right now."

"It's okay," he said. "I'm sorry."

Alex put his hand on the back of her neck and pulled her to him, kissing her forehead softly, just as he had the first morning — after the karaoke she didn't remember. "It's okay," he said again.

She shook her head, her brain resisting, but nuzzled closer to him anyway. She felt the closeness of his chest, the strong arms wrapped around her. She could smell the familiar scent of his deodorant beneath the cologne. "I'm sorry," Rebecca said. "I wish I —"

"Shhh . . . don't."

"Alex, I want to be able to give you what you've given me, but —"

He lifted her chin so that she was looking up at him. "Rebecca, please shut up. Please."

She obeyed. He kissed her gently on the jaw. Everything she'd felt at the riverbank came rushing back; unlike that morning, however, tonight she had no resources to keep it in check. This was wrong, she knew. It would never work. She should push him away, ask him to leave. Stand on her own two feet, keep things clean. But she was so tired. Her legs seemed to cave beneath her, and his arms around her felt like her only connection to the world.

He put his hand on her head, tangling his fingers in her wet hair and working it out of the bun so that it fell in damp chunks to her shoulders. *No, no, no.* She said it, she was sure she did, but the words would not come out of her mouth. He leaned in to kiss her, and she found herself kissing back. She felt him fumbling with the top button of her shirt, loosening it so that he could push it off one shoulder. Rebecca opened her mouth to protest but only a soft moan came out.

"I don't want you to doubt me," he said into the hollow of flesh near her collarbone. "I can't offer you the life you want, but at least I can show you how I feel about you. Maybe you don't feel the same, and that's okay. Just look me in the eye, and tell me you don't want me here. I will leave and never bother you again."

He pushed a stray hair back from her face with his thumb, and then held his hand on her jawline. His expression deepened, his dark eyes like liquid pools of onyx. His voice was a hoarse whisper as he let his hand trail down her neck and over her bare shoulder. "Say it, Rebecca. Tell me to go. Just say the words."

He kissed her again before she could answer, skillfully working her shorts down with the other hand and tracing lightly over her belly. Her body shuddered and she thought she might collapse. "I can't," she whispered. "You know I can't."

"I know, sweetheart. You can't say it, and I can't do it. I'm in love with you, Rebecca. I can't leave you. Not tonight." He lifted her as though she weighed nothing and carried her to the bedroom.

Before she knew what was happening, he

was placing her gently on the bed. "I can't," she said again, barely audible. Though this time, she was not entirely sure what it was she couldn't do.

"I know," he said. "It's okay."

He kept his eyes on hers as he reached under the shirt to retrieve her panties. Her traitorous hips rose to help him. There was a half smile that flitted over his features as he pulled the lacy red bikinis over her knees. She wondered if he was remembering the Walmart granny panties she'd been wearing that first night. He had been a gentleman then, and every day since. He had given her space and listened to her sorrow and given her his affection freely. He had let her push him away, let her break his heart, and he was back.

But now something had changed. He was calling her bluff, and this was the point of no return. Rebecca knew she could ask him to leave right now, and this good man who loved the law and was friends with her father would respect her wishes. He would go home to a cold shower in his haunted house. And she would never see him again. The thought was unbearable.

He tossed the panties on the floor and put his hands on her knees, which she had instinctively pulled together. "You're shaking," he observed.

She had not noticed. "I guess so," she said.

Alex applied a gentle pressure, the lightest push outward on her knees, and Rebecca watched her last chance to refuse him melt away as her legs relaxed apart, against her brain's receding advice. He disappeared beneath the soft plaid flannel and within seconds she was awash in a cloud of pleasure. His tongue was rough against her, like the hands that were now holding her arms down against the bed, and like those hands, skilled and strong. She had scarcely resigned herself to enjoyment when she felt her body bucking and rocking against his face, and from a distance she heard herself shrieking in pleasure.

Deputy Alex Chen chuckled a bit as he unbuttoned his own shirt and removed his jeans, enjoying her embarrassment. It must have been gratifying to him, she thought, and this vulnerability before him only heightened her breathlessness. The voices in her head explaining why this was a terrible idea and a recipe for emotional disaster had all been drowned out by his tongue between her thighs. Now he unbuttoned the remaining buttons on her shirt and flipped it open, and for a long moment, he did nothing but look at her. He wore boxers, she noticed.

Red plaid.

He kissed her nose, and then the top of her head, her cheeks and neck. He smiled at her before tracing his warm breath across the skin of her chest, where he sucked lightly on each nipple and left her covered in goose bumps. He kissed the center of her torso down to her belly, smiling as his nose grazed her pubic hair and her body shuddered again in memory. He kissed her thighs, her knees, even her shins and ankles and toes. It was exquisite and maddening. She closed her eyes, swirling with feeling, teetering on the edge of a dark oblivion. She put an arm over her face to help her feel more grounded.

He pushed her thighs apart with one hand and stroked her belly with the other, causing her to arch reflexively. Then he was inside her, strong and insistent. He lowered himself to kiss her passionately on the mouth, thrusting and clutching and even pulling her hair as he rocked into her. She gave herself over to him, kissing him back, returning the passion with her body that she could not express with words. He cried out softly in her ear when he came, and then lay there, still inside her, kissing her gently until she felt him get hard again. This time she wrapped her legs around him and clawed at his bare back, feeling her own pleasure rise again, too, with even more urgency and depth than before.

They climaxed together, which had never happened for Rebecca, and collapsed on the bed in a sweaty tangle. He positioned himself behind her, curling around her to keep her warm and safe with his body as the room went from dusky to full dark. Alex was quiet for a long time. Rebecca tried to think of something to say, but sleep took her before she could find the right words.

She awoke in the soft gray light of dawn, wondering if she could sneak out and leave for Atlanta without waking him. But she was already alone. There was a note on her suitcase in his careful block lettering. "Now you know how I feel. Maybe there are more choices than you think. Please stay. Love, Alex."

34

Under normal circumstances, the pomp and glamour of Suzanne and Dylan's public wedding in mid-October was the kind of thing that would have had Rebecca bragging for weeks to anyone who would listen. While the wedding was as lovely as she ever could have expected, Rebecca found she had little energy for bragging. She had already been facing the curious questions about her absence from her coworkers nearly every day since she'd returned to work a month before, and did not want to draw extra attention to herself.

The wedding was held at the Atlanta Country Club with nearly five hundred people in attendance, and at least as many paparazzi and onlookers outside the front gates. So far, no word of the first wedding had leaked to the press to dampen their fascination with this one. Suzanne, of course, looked strikingly beautiful in a custom mermaid-style bridal gown, with some kind of exotic orange flower tucked behind one ear. Dylan wore an expensive-looking tuxedo with a cummerbund of burnt orange, a nod to both his wife's tasteful headdress and his Tennessee roots. And of course, his ever-present cowboy boots.

The ceremony itself was a simple one: the two of them exchanged vows beneath a pretty gazebo overlooking the golf course at sunset, with the party of the season inside one of the club's biggest ballrooms. Between Dylan's four sisters and her own friends, Suzanne had simply chosen not to have bridesmaids at all, for which Marci and Rebecca were both immensely grateful. They had both offered to help Suzanne with the preparations, but given Rebecca's summer spent cleaning her mom's house, and Marci's ever-expanding midsection, neither was offended when Suzanne's devoted assistant Chad insisted on handling everything.

"He really did a lovely job," Marci said when they were seated around one of at least fifty resplendent round tables in the ballroom. There were gorgeous harvest baskets of gourds and fruit in the center of each table, with a small placard indicating that the basket would be donated to the

Atlanta Food Bank after the ceremony. "Don't tell Suze, but if I were getting married again, I'd have Chad do the planning instead of her."

"You will let me know if you decide to get married again?" Jake said behind her. He had been to the bar to get drinks for the three of them. "I would hope I'd be invited. I could give you away."

Marci made a face at him. "I'm not letting you off the hook that easy," she said. "You're stuck with me now."

Jake kissed her affectionately and rubbed her protruding belly. Rebecca watched them, for once without the accompanying misery their way-too-cute public displays had always brought her. She was still a little relieved, however, when Marci seemed to remember her presence as the only other person at the table so far. "Heard from Alex?"

Rebecca shook her head. "No. He won't return my calls since I left Alabama. I guess I missed my chance."

"Well, it was totally unfair of him to put you on the spot like that," Marci said. "He didn't really expect you to stay in that crappy little town. Ouch!" Jake had elbowed her and Marci went on. "I mean, it's a beautiful town, of course. It's just hard to picture you living there."

"Yes, it is," Rebecca said. "Can you imagine me being a forty-five-minute drive from the nearest mall? And even then, no Bloomingdale's."

As she heard the words in her own ears, they sounded hollow, even in jest. Marci shook her head as though the whole idea were ridiculous, but Jake avoided her eye. Rebecca went on, "Plus, he has a kid. Not just a kid, but a teenage girl. Can you imagine me as a stepmother?"

"Honestly?" Jake said, "I can. I think you'd be good at it. Of all people, you know how hard things can be at that age."

Rebecca stared at the black linen napkin on her plate.

"But she doesn't want to move to the middle of nowhere," Marci said. "And he didn't even have the courage to ask her to her face. Who puts their whole relationship on the line with a sticky note? He might as well have proposed to her via text message."

"He didn't propose," Rebecca said. "I don't even know if that's what he meant. It just said 'stay.' "

"See? The guy just asked her to stay," Jake said. "That could mean anything."

"Well, it freaked her out. Besides, how could she stay?" Marci said. "Her life is here: her apartment, her job, the Junior League, her friends *who are supposed to be supportive of her choices. . . .*" She said this last part through gritted teeth. Clearly they had talked about this before.

"Anyway, it doesn't matter," Rebecca said, cutting them off and sounding far more sure of herself than she felt. "I couldn't stay, I didn't want to stay, and now the Alex Chen chapter of my life is over. And I'm fine."

She stood and made her way to the edge of the dance floor, where Dylan and Suzanne were dancing to "Fire and Rain," sung by the actual, real James Taylor, who was actually, really in the room. She hoped she had outgrown her desire to be rich and famous, but she still had to admit it had its benefits. When Dylan and Suzanne glided past her, laughing at each other, however, she saw that their happiness had nothing to do with anything but being together. In spite of all her complaining about the wedding, Suzanne seemed to genuinely be enjoying her moment in the spotlight.

As the weeks had worn on, Rebecca was finding that her familiar routine made her listless, rather than comfortable. She was moody at work, and edgy with everyone. More than once she called Valerie over to deal with a difficult passenger, because she could feel the frustration mounting and knew her job would be at risk if she exploded.

Her luxury one-bedroom apartment overlooking the city felt more solitary than ever. Despite being surrounded once again by polished granite, stainless steel, and the hum of the busy city, Rebecca felt an odd yearning for her father's sparse bungalow in the woods with its cheap furniture and empty refrigerator. When Richard had called to let her know that her childhood home had been sold to a young music minister and his wife, Rebecca was surprised that her first thought had not been for the years spent in the white house with the green shutters. It had been for the last night spent in the crappy little rental. And Alex, unbuttoning her flannel shirt.

What Rebecca had told Jake and Marci was technically true: Alex was not returning her calls or texts. What she preferred not to say was that there was a strong possibility she had brought this on herself. The morning she left for Atlanta, and found Alex's note on her suitcase, she had panicked. Instead of waiting to talk to him, as a normal person might do, she had sent him a hurried text before pulling out of the driveway. "Thank you for last night. You're an amazing friend."

Even though she had intended this to be a noncommittal half step forward, the hours that clicked by that Saturday without a response from Alex made her realize her text may have sounded a bit dismissive. When she had not heard from him by midnight, she debated texting again to clarify what she meant. But what *had* she meant? What did she want from Alex? It seemed like too much to work out at midnight, and too late for a follow-up text.

So she had waited. Sunday morning had turned into Sunday afternoon. As she unpacked, laundered, pressed, and prepped to resume work Monday morning, she checked her phone every ten minutes. She vacillated between being irritated with Alex for not bothering to get back to her and annoyed with herself for being romantically inept. And also, completely terrified. Either Alex would get in touch and they would move forward, or he would not and she might never see him again. Both ideas scared the hell out of her.

35

The week after Suzanne's wedding, Rebecca sat with Valerie at a Chili's in the St. Louis airport, pushing a salad around her plate.

"Val, do you know anything about Southern Air?"

"A little. Why?"

"I was just curious if you knew anyone who worked for them."

"A few. They seem like a good airline, but they don't do much from Atlanta. Most of their crews are based in Birmingham."

"I know. I was considering a change of scenery."

"To Birmingham? Why?"

Rebecca shrugged.

"For that guy? What's his name? Alan?"

"Alex. And, no. Not for him. At least not entirely. I just feel I need to try something different for a while."

"He lives in Birmingham?"

"Not exactly. He lives a half hour away."

It was more like forty minutes, she knew, but why quibble?

"Be careful, kid. Give up too much at the front end of a relationship, and a man will walk all over you."

"I don't even know if there is still a relationship there to give anything up for," Rebecca said. "He hasn't called me in weeks."

"So you're thinking of changing jobs and moving cities to get closer to a guy who you're not even dating? I know I said you needed to make yourself more available, but this is a little extreme, don't you think?"

Rebecca laughed. "Well, not just that. I think I've needed a change for a while. I feel like I need a fresh start."

Her mentor stared at her. "This doesn't sound like you, kid."

"I know. But, maybe that's a good thing."

Valerie took a bite of her hamburger and chewed thoughtfully. "Well, what the hell do I know anyway? I've been married six times."

"*Six?* I thought it was more like four."

"Well, I guess you weren't *technically* wrong. Two were to the same man so that could count as one, and one of them wouldn't be legally recognized in most countries anyway."

"You are going to have to tell me that story sometime."

"Our break is way too short for that, doll. Maybe if we get put on the route to Indonesia we'll have enough time to kill in the air that I could cover it. Before you move to Birmingham, that is."

"I didn't say I was moving there. I said I was thinking about it."

"Fair enough."

They finished their meal in silence, and Valerie excused herself to the ladies' room before preboarding started back to Atlanta in fifteen minutes. Rebecca saw that she had missed a call from her dad earlier in the day and dialed him back.

"Hey, Rebecca," he said. He sounded tired. She realized he had not called her Rockstar in a while.

"Hi, Daddy. What's up?"

"I just wanted to let you know that I put a check in the mail for you today."

"A check?"

"Yeah, I thought about it, and with me and Sonia getting married, we both decided to try to wrap things up financially, you know. . . ."

She did not know. "Sure?"

"With all the work you did on the house, when your mother and I sold it last month, we decided you should get my half. It's not much, but I think you should have it. Neither of us needs it, and I would feel better knowing you had some money of your own. You shouldn't have to rely on anyone."

"Oh. I don't know what to say. Thanks, Dad."

He's passing on the fatherly stuff he doesn't want hanging over him, she thought. *This is money he never had to spend on a wedding.*

"The other thing," he went on, "I wanted to let you know that Cory's record will probably be broken next Friday night."

"What?"

"Yeah, they've got this kid, Holden Murray, who's really good. The coach called to ask if I could be at the game next week, because they're thinking he'll break the record then unless he gets injured or something. It's also homecoming."

How appropriate, she thought. "You're going?"

"Yes. They're going to give Cory some kind of posthumous award. I wondered if you would like to accept it with me?"

"Sure," she said. "I'll check the schedule. Do you think any of Cory's teammates will be there?"

"I'm sure Roger Simon will, and John Boozer is still in town."

"What about Alex Chen?" She tried to sound casual.

"Not sure. I haven't talked to him since he moved," her dad said.

"Moved?"

"Yeah. He finally got a job he'd been waiting on for over a year with the Birmingham PD. It's better pay, and he's closer to his daughter in Leeds. I thought you guys had sorta become friends. You haven't talked to him?"

"Not recently," she said. Her dad didn't need to know the details, she decided.

"Well, yeah. He sold the Pickney Place a couple of weeks ago to a big family with a bunch of kids. Let me know if you can be there Friday."

"Okay, Dad." She started to hang up, and then thought of something. "Hey, did you call Mom?"

"Yeah, honey. I did. I don't think she can make it. I'm sorry."

"No, that's fine. Probably for the best."

When they hung up, she went to the terminal by the nearest gate to pull up her flight schedule and verified that she was off the following Friday and Saturday. She glanced at the clock and saw she had just enough time to call her friends before pre-boarding began.

Late that night, when she finally dragged her wheeled carry-on bag down the hall to her apartment, Rebecca was surprised to find a large package outside her door. She had not ordered anything recently, and her heart jumped as she thought immediately of Alex. Could it be a peace offering in their silent standoff?

It had been nearly five weeks since she left Alabama with a text message. What had begun as uncertainty on her part had now hardened into prideful stubbornness. By the time she'd been able to admit to herself — at least somewhat — that she'd screwed up her goodbye and desperately wanted to talk to Alex, he refused to answer or return her calls. His continued silence intensified her sense that a simple apology and explanation was not going to cut it.

But this could be something, she thought, as she carried the package through her door. This could be the gesture that he intended to end their stalemate. It was about two feet wide and almost as tall, just three inches thick. As she went to the kitchen drawer for scissors, she wondered what he could have sent. She found the edge of a canvas and pulled it out, bringing with it scores of little foam packing peanuts. Rebecca tried hard not to notice the mess they were making on her kitchen floor.

It took only a few seconds to realize that the package was not from Alex, but Rebecca's eyes filled with tears anyway. The painting was on a sixteen-by-twenty-inch canvas, and she recognized the image immediately. She had come across this photograph while cleaning her mother's house.

Rebecca had been about five years old, she guessed. Her hair was still streaked honey blond, before it had become a true uniform brown a couple of years later. Sunlight glinted off her hair and she was surrounded by the greenery of the backyard.

In the original photograph, which was presumably snapped by her father, you could see that she and Cory had been playing with a garden hose. Cory seemed to be chasing her with the hose; his seven-year-old boy face was beaming with mischief in the nearby background. But Rebecca had run, squealing or laughing or both, into her mother's arms. The shutter had clicked just as she reached sanctuary, and caught both of them in profile. Rebecca's face wore the uninhibited joy only a child can experience, and her mother's expression was a subtler version of the same emotion.

Lorena had painted a masterful close-up of this section only, just their two faces, so that it was hard to tell if the two figures were actually touching in the space beyond the canvas. Rebecca tried to envision the original but could not remember whether their arms were linked, or if they were still reaching for each other. The portrait was unsigned, but on the back frame, her mother had painted a tiny inscription. "You are my sunshine. Always. Love, Mom."

Even though it was nearly 10 P.M., Rebecca decided the neighbors would forgive her eventually. And if they didn't, she was never here anyway. She left her suitcase in the middle of the floor and went to find her hammer and level to hang the first piece of custom artwork she had ever owned.

36

It happened within the first two minutes of the game. Holden Murray caught the snap, took a few unobstructed steps backward, and threw a pass forty-seven yards downfield to break Cory Williamson's record by thirteen yards. Jake squeezed Rebecca's hand on one side, and Suzanne — fresh from her honeymoon and disgustingly tan — on the other. Marci sat on the other side of Jake and covered her eyes when he threw the pass, as though it were a scene in a horror movie she could not bear to watch.

When the pass was caught, the crowd went wild, filling the stadium with a cacophony of sound for several minutes before the officials on the field could restore order. Holden Murray accepted high fives and chest bumps from his teammates, but otherwise seemed more interested in huddling for the next play than basking in his achievement. Without ever having met him, Rebecca liked him for this.

At halftime, there was a short ceremony on the field commemorating Cory Williamson as the holder of the record for nineteen years. Rebecca and her father stood on the field to accept a plaque from the principal and the athletic director, the latter of whom was also the head football coach. Behind them gathered about ten members from the 1996–97 varsity football team, most of whom were now showing signs of expansion around the middle. But they could still get into their old jerseys, and they stood at attention behind the folding chairs that had been brought to the field for Rebecca and Richard. They included Roger Simon, John Boozer, Will Caterman, and, she noticed at a glance, Alex Chen.

The principal made a short speech about Cory, with information apparently gathered from news clippings and old yearbooks. The athletic director unveiled a shadow box with one of Cory's jerseys framed within, officially retiring number 22. He shook their hands quickly and thanked them for being there, and then hurried off the field to rejoin his team in the locker room.

A smattering of applause followed the presentation, but most of the crowd seemed distracted by the imminent appearance of the homecoming court, who were waiting for their entrance in shiny convertibles at the other end of the field. Rebecca turned to say hello to Alex, but found him engrossed in conversation with Will Caterman and John Boozer about some amazing play that had occurred two decades before. Roger noticed her, however, and gave her a perfunctory hug and invited her to join "the whole gang" at Dickie's after the game. Then they were politely ushered to the sidelines and back into the bleachers.

There was no one Rebecca recognized among the faculty and staff present, except the band director Mr. Wallace, who had been at the beginning of his career when she played oboe as a freshman. For the most part, these people did not know her and did not remember Cory. Her dad waved stoically and shook hands with one or two friends who greeted him; a few older people wiped away tears or squeezed Rebecca's arm as they made their way back to their seats.

She tried to catch Alex's eye before he disappeared into the crowd, but he was gone too quickly. And whether intentionally or not, he never seemed to put himself where she might be in his line of sight.

When she regained her seat, Suzanne said,

"That was just lovely, honey."

"Suze is just excited because those girls over there asked for her autograph," Marci said.

"You're kidding."

"Nope," Suzanne said, barely holding back her delighted grin. "They recognized me from the wedding pictures in *Country Today*."

"Good thing they didn't recognize you from the incident at the museum," Jake said. "I guess those pictures may not have made it out here."

Suzanne glared at him. "Don't hate me because I'm married to a handsome, famous superstar."

All three of them groaned and Marci threw popcorn at Suzanne. It caught in her platinum hair and stuck to her sweater. It was beginning to get chilly now that the sun had set, Rebecca noticed.

"Are you guys ready to go?"

"Back to your dad and Sonia's?" Jake asked.

"Well, yes, or there's one other place we could go. Anybody want Buffalo wings?"

Dickie's was more crowded than Rebecca had ever seen it. On top of it being Friday night in a small town, it seemed that more than just the class of 1997 had gotten the memo about the after-game party. Since Oreville High was running away with the game and it was getting cooler out, large numbers had already defected from the stadium to seek warmth and beer.

The four of them got settled at the only remaining booth, and sat enjoying the ambience while they waited for Kevin to appear. When he did, he called Rebecca by name, earning her an impressed eyebrow-raise from Jake. They ordered a large platter of wings, a pitcher of beer, and a Sprite with lime for Marci, who had agreed to be the designated driver with the caveat that she would be the final judge of when it was time to go home.

She saw Alex right after their food was delivered to the table. He was standing near the bar with the other guys in green jerseys, and they were lifting a round of some kind of purple shot in a noisy toast. His skin looked ruddy from the wind, his eyes shining. Rebecca's heart surged, feeling as though she was seeing him clearly for the first time.

"Would you guys excuse me for a moment?" she asked, but did not wait for an answer before sliding out of her seat to approach him.

"Is that him?" she heard Marci ask Jake as she walked away.

For a few minutes, she had trouble reaching him in the crowd; once she did, she had to tap his shoulder a couple of times before he turned.

"Hi, Alex."

"Hello." The coldness in his voice should not have been surprising, but it stung nonetheless.

"I'm so glad to see you."

"Yeah?"

"I'm here with friends from home," she said, gesturing at the table. "You remember Jake, probably."

Marci and Suzanne waved fervently, grinning ridiculously, while Jake gave a more sedate nod. Alex lifted his beer toward them in a perfunctory salute, neither friendly nor hostile.

She searched for what to say next. "I heard you got a job in Birmingham. Congratulations."

"Thanks."

"Alex." She touched his arm and felt the muscles tense, and then pull away. "I am so sorry. Your note — I misunderstood. Or maybe I didn't, I don't know. But I was scared, and I left, and I knew you were mad, and then by the time I found the courage to call, it seemed too late, and you didn't call back. I didn't think I had anything to offer, and —"

"You know what?" he said. "I'm just going to save us both some time here. You were right. It just wasn't meant to be. I don't know why I was fighting so hard to make something from nothing." His neck was flushed and splotchy with anger.

"It wasn't nothing. You were right."

He ignored her. "And just because I'm taking some engineering classes now doesn't change who I am. I want to be with someone who loves me for *me:* cop, lawyer, engineer, trash man."

"I know, and I would. I mean, I . . . I do."

Alex stopped short. He gave her an appraising look and swallowed hard. In a voice so low it was almost menacing, he said, "Today was nice, for Cory, and your family. It was good for the community. Let's not tarnish the day by saying things we'll regret. You wanted me to leave you alone and I have. Take care of yourself, Rebecca."

With that, he turned and rejoined the conversation with the team. Feeling foolish facing the back of Alex's jersey, Rebecca turned and made her way back to the booth with all the dignity she could muster. Her friends were kind enough to continue an ongoing conversation about football and the South, and to behave as though they had not seen the interaction. When she ordered tequila shots a moment later, they were kind enough to pretend that was normal, too.

When she looked up a few minutes later, the football group had dispersed somewhat. There were green jerseys in different parts of the room now, and some new people had joined the group at the bar. A petite woman with a bright-red manicure now stood next to Alex, and he had his arm slung around her shoulders. Her hair was no longer streaked with blond, but when she turned to laugh at something he'd said, Rebecca recognized Tanya Boozer.

"That's it," she said.

"That's what?" Suzanne asked.

"I might need your help, girls. There's something I have to do."

They looked at one another doubtfully, but stood to follow Rebecca's lead anyway. For Marci, this took an extra moment of sliding her belly out of the wooden booth. There was a little more stumble in Rebecca's step than she expected as she headed for the stage, but she recovered her balance by grasping Marci's hand.

"Easy," Marci muttered. "I'm six months pregnant, not exactly a pillar of stability."

No spotlight shone on the stage that night, unlike the first time she had wandered into this place. Then, it had been nearly empty, and Rebecca could scarcely have thought of anything more horrifying than the prospect of taking the stage. Tonight it was full to capacity, which did little to decrease her terror. When she located the microphone and tried to talk into it, nothing happened. Suzanne flagged down the waitress with the long curly hair, who responded to a twenty-dollar tip with a slight smile and at least minimal helpfulness getting the microphone plugged in.

By the time it was working properly and Rebecca was standing on the plywood stage, looking out into the crowd, Suzanne and Marci had climbed up behind her. She hadn't even had to ask. She scanned the crowd and saw Jake at their table, smiling and shaking his head.

"Hello," she said into the microphone. "Hello? Can you hear me?" A few heads turned in her direction, but most ignored her. She found herself tempted to begin her airline safety speech and tell everyone where the emergency exits were located. There was only one person she really needed to hear her, however, and he was not looking up yet. She tried to think what to say.

"Sing!" yelled a man at a table near the front.

"Oh, no," she said, finding her voice. "I just have something I wanted to say to someone. Alex? Alex Chen?"

The deputy looked up at the mention of his name and shook his head. Tanya gave her a scornful look and put a possessive hand on Alex's chest.

"Sing!" the man down front repeated. "Sing or get off the stage! It's the rule."

"Trust me, sir, no one wants that. I *really* can't sing," Rebecca said. "I'm sorry. Alex, I just wanted to apologize and —"

"Sing! Sing! Sing!" the chant rose from several patrons near the man in the front, and this drew even more attention to her. She looked back at Suzanne and Marci for help, but they were chanting too, all smiles.

Alex was now covering his face with a bar menu. *Dear God.* There was nothing for it. She reached for the only song she could remember in that moment.

She started barely above a whisper, feeling ridiculous. "Baby put your hair up, or wear it down, or . . ."

Suzanne whispered, "Shave your head!"

"Shave your head." Her voice trembled.

Alex had lowered the menu and she could see the guys around him ribbing him. "Hey,

Alex! When you gonna let your hair down, sweetie?"

There was no going back now. She sang, "We can go out . . . fishing, to a ball game, or just . . ." Rebecca blushed, but finished the line anyway. "Rock the bed."

A glance behind her told her Suzanne and Marci were dancing, swaying from side to side, which was particularly funny with Marci's awkward belly.

Alex was watching her now, smiling a little but still shaking his head. "You can't sing," he mouthed. She laughed and kept on.

She made herself hold eye contact with him. She could feel her unsteady voice wavering even more. "Honey I don't care, what you do, or what you wear."

He lifted his hands, cupping them around his ears. "Louder!" he mouthed.

Her voice was painful even to her own ears but she got louder anyway. The crowd cheered. "You don't have to be perfect . . . but you're perfect for me."

To her astonishment, applause broke out, with some added cheering by the guys at the table down front. *Just roll with it,* she thought. *It can't get worse.*

"Thank you, thank you very much. That song goes out to my good friend, Alex Chen. Do y'all know Alex?"

Another cheer and whooping noises from around the bar. Alex lifted his beer bottle to her and took a long drink. She felt exposed on the stage, and worried that maybe that was all she would get from him. "Keep singing, sweetheart!" one of the men down front called out.

Rebecca spoke the next words in a tuneless sort of melody. "I'm here tonight because I screwed up, to see if I can get a second chance. Well, it's more like a fifth chance."

"Fifth chance!" Suzanne and Marci sang behind her, backup-singer style. She grinned at them and went on.

"But even if he won't give me that chance, I couldn't leave tonight without telling Alex I love him."

"Love him, oooooooh."

"I love you, Alex, even if you can't love me back anymore." She was no longer singing, just talking to him across the room, across the crowd, as though he were the only other person in the bar. His face was still, lips pressed together. He didn't move, but he didn't drop her gaze.

Rebecca turned back to the crowd in front of her. "That's the first time I've said that to anybody, especially into a microphone in a crowded bar, so y'all be gentle with me.

420

And maybe he will, too."

One by one, the faces turned toward Alex, who replaced his beer on the bar, and was disentangling himself from an annoyed Tanya Boozer. The same men who had been chanting for Rebecca to sing were now calling his name. "Alex, Alex, Alex . . ."

He crossed slowly to her, making his way gently through the crowd, leaving her twisting uncomfortably at the microphone. He patted shoulders as he went. He even nudged aside a woman who had just come back from the bathroom and was blocking his path while trying to figure out what the fuss was about. It may not have taken more than a minute for him to make his way over from the bar, but it seemed to take hours.

When he was a couple of feet from the stage, she held out her hand. "You always assume," he said softly, taking the microphone from her other hand and turning it off with his thumb, "that I'm going to take your hand."

"You don't have to, you know," she said, trying and failing to sound as though her whole life did not ride on his response.

"In this case, I think I do." He took her hand and pulled her to him, kissing her deeply and hoisting her off the stage. She slid down his body, slowly, surrounded by a bar that had erupted in cheers.

"Sorry if I embarrassed you with my bad singing," she said.

"Well, it's not an airport gate," he said. "But it will do."

He gave her another long kiss to the whooping approval of the crowd. One of the guys in green jerseys Rebecca didn't recognize walked past them, clapping Alex on the shoulder as he went. Alex nodded to the guy, but kept his arms around her. Someone turned the karaoke system off and put on music, and they swayed a little as others began slow dancing around them.

"I applied for a job with Southern Air," she said, a little sheepish.

"In Birmingham?"

"Yep. I need a change."

"Just need a change, huh?" He was smiling. *He knows the truth. He wants to hear me say it.*

"Actually, I must have hit my head on something, because I realized that I needed *you*."

He laughed. "When it comes to women, head injuries always work in my favor. I should warn you, though, the old house I just bought in Birmingham might be haunted, too."

"I think I can handle that," she said. "Just

promise me we can get someone else to clean it."

"Promise." He put his forehead against hers.

To one side, Rebecca saw Jake and Marci dancing nearby, and wondered if Marci would write about all this in her next blog. She would have to start reading more consistently to keep up with everyone, now that she was moving back to Alabama.

"So, this is *my* happy ending," she said, almost to herself.

"Nope," Alex said, pulling her closer. "This is the beginning."

EPILOGUE

GUEST POST BY JAKE STILLWELL (AKA SUBHUB HIMSELF)

Blog: The Care and Feeding of a Suburban Husband
{Entry #199: (Untitled)}

Wednesday, November 2, 2016

This week in Oreville, Alabama, they are changing signs all over the town. If you drive in on any of the highways that run through this pretty little town, you'll see them adding a name and number to some of the signs, while others are being replaced entirely. That's because Friday night, a long-held state high school record for passing yards in a single season was broken, when Holden Murray threw a simple forty-seven-yard pass for a season total of 4,140 (and counting). I know this because I was there and saw it happen.

Wait, you're saying, this isn't a sports blog. Hang with me.

The reason this matters, to me at least, is that the record for passing yards by a high school football player in Alabama was previously held by Cory Williamson, also from Oreville High. He was the older brother, mentor, and hero of one of our best friends, Rebecca. I would never have known about Oreville, Alabama, if it weren't for her. If my family hadn't been visiting her this past weekend, we would have missed a tiny moment of sports history. When we saw Holden Murray throw that pass, we all sucked in a breath, and yes, I'll admit it, said a little prayer.

Shortly after he broke that passing record nineteen years ago, Cory Williamson was killed in a car accident. He was coming home from a party in a nearby town, at which he'd had a couple of beers, and lost control of his car, running off the road into a farm fence. He was alone, and no one else was injured. Cory left behind a younger sister who adored him, and two loving parents who would never be the same. He also left countless friends and admirers, all over the county, who washed this little part of the world in their grief when they lost him. Cory Williamson had a scholarship to Auburn University when he died, and some say he was NFL material. Had he lived, he might be enjoying life as a retired player today, working as a sports announcer or owning a successful car dealership, or he might have chosen a different path entirely. We will never know.

What we do know is that Cory threw for 4,126 yards in the fall of 1996, and that his football portrait from senior year shows a smile of carefree, youthful energy and warmth. Even today, his family and friends cannot grasp the depth of his loss, and so we talk about it in terms we can understand. Of an all-American kid who worked hard and was loyal to his teammates, and the lost potential of the years he never got to know. Now that his record has been broken, and now that his high school has graduated a class that was not yet born when Cory died, his memory may begin to fade, at least in some parts of the town and the state. But never in the hearts of those who loved him.

Documenting athletes and their stories is central to my life and career. Still, it's always interesting to me that when someone dies, people seem to cling to that part of their identity. Maybe that's why I'm drawn to sports so much — it's a way of being in the world, the same way my wife puts her words into the world on this blog, the way together we are raising our expanding family and hoping that they will be a force for good in the world. Sports are something to *do.*

My wife often asks me why I love sports so much, since they are in large part lost on her. (Which, I'll say, is lucky for you, because she spends that time writing instead.) For me, however, it's more than just the score at the end of a game. More than the yards on the field, the strategies, the stats, and even the celebrations.

What I love about sports is the spirit that each individual player brings with him (or her), the histories they carry in their hearts, the people who love them watching from the stands. They play because they have something to prove — to their teammates and coaches, to their families, to themselves. Leaving everything you have on the field in the form of blood, sweat, and tears is just one way of saying "I was here. I did something. I matter."

More than any sport, though, what gives our life meaning are the people we have something to prove to. Our friends, our family, and even ourselves. Friendships are made strong through shared hardship, shared triumphs. Marriage, too. Sometimes you have to know what it feels like to let someone down, so you also know the victory of regaining their trust. Sometimes you have to know the tears of loss to appreciate the joy of winning. Sometimes the people who need love the most are the ones who seem to push it away. And in my case, sometimes your whole life hinges on something scrawled on a napkin.

Life isn't perfect. Love isn't perfect. People are taken from us too soon, lives unravel, families crumble. Even when we stay together, we take each other for granted, and the love that should lift us up to be better people sometimes leaves us room to become selfish, righteous, or controlling instead.

So how does love survive? How do any of us make meaning of it all? There are thousands of answers — none of them right, none of them wrong.

For me, it's about choosing teammates — friends, family, and most importantly my wife — who will not only forgive my imperfections but make me a better person in the process. I pledge them my loyalty, flawed as it is.

And then, win or lose, you just get back out there. Leave it all on the field — in love, in life, in work. Pick something that matters to you and commit your whole heart to it. Because none of us know how long we are given to play the game.

ACKNOWLEDGMENTS

Writing this series has been one of the most fun and challenging experiences of my life. So please let me say thank you to some incredible people. . . . Nicole Sohl and the rest of St. Martin's Press/Macmillan Entertainment, and Beth Phelan and Jenny Bent of The Bent Agency. I'd also like to thank those who've supported me in the writing of this book by giving me feedback, validation, and sometimes wine: Carla Birnbaum, Sarah Cutler, Jenna Denisar, Kristal Goelz, Marla Kaplan, Nan Merrow, Anna Needle, Stephanie Needle, Ross Newberry, Betsy Rainwater, Brenda Turetsky, Ryan Van Meter, and Rob Wade, as well as George Weinstein and the rest of the Atlanta Writers Club Roswell critique group. As always I'm indebted to Faith Williams at Atwater Group for being my punctuation safety net.

There has to be a separate paragraph for my family, especially my husband Sam

Turetsky and our children, for all the sacrifices they have endured so that I could spend time writing. Living with a writer is a special kind of domestic torture. I am so grateful to you for putting up with me.

I am also incredibly grateful to those of you who have taken time from your busy lives to read this book, and particularly those of you who chose to follow Marci, Suzanne, and Rebecca on their adventures from start to finish. Many of you have made an effort to review my books — including bloggers and readers — and I value your honesty and encouragement. Many readers have even taken the time to get in touch and tell me personally that you've enjoyed the books — I can't tell you how much that means to me. Cheers to all of you!

ABOUT THE AUTHOR

Manda (M. J.) Pullen is the author of complex, funny contemporary romances, including *The Marriage Pact* and *Regrets Only.* She was raised in the suburbs of Atlanta by a physicist and a flower child, who taught her that life is tragic and funny and real love is anything but simple. After traveling around Europe and living in cities like Austin and Portland, she returned to Atlanta, where she lives with her husband and two sons.

www.mjpullen.com
www.facebook.com/MJPullenBooks
Twitter: @MJPullen